Detours

BLUE FEATHER BOOKS, LTD.

This book is dedicated to Joseph Anthony Grillo. Thank you, Joey, for teaching me to see the beauty in life's detours.

Detours

A BLUE FEATHER BOOK

by
Jane Vollbrecht

NOTE: If you purchased this book without a cover, you should be aware that it is stolen property. It was reported as "unsold and destroyed" to the publisher, and neither the author nor the publisher has received any payment for this "stripped book."

This is a work of fiction. All characters, locales and events are either products of the author's imagination or are used fictitiously.

DETOURS

Copyright © 2009 by Jane Vollbrecht

All rights reserved. No part of this book may be reproduced in any manner whatsoever without written permission from the publisher, save for brief quotations used in critical articles or reviews.

Cover design by Ann Phillips

A Blue Feather Book
Published by Blue Feather Books, Ltd.

www.bluefeatherbooks.com

ISBN: 978-0-9822858-1-7

First edition: July, 2009

Printed in the United States of America and in the United Kingdom.

Acknowledgements

To my wonderful friends, Jane and Jerry, thank you for sharing your son with me and letting me be part of his life. Your candor in answering all my questions about caring for a child with special needs showed me time and again that, like our boy Joey, the two of you are truly special people.

To Lori L. Lake, a great big uff da, yah that was a heckuva deal, you betcha (that's Minnesota speak) for coming out of editorial retirement to work on this manuscript with me. I'm fortunate to have in you a supportive friend, creative colleague, and literary giant all rolled up in one. Thank you for all you did to improve the book, despite my carping and occasionally obstreperous obsequiousness.

Nann Dunne—you continue to amaze me. You not only found every typographical error and grammatical misstep, you saw deep into the forest of the storyline and identified each tree that needed pruning as well as those that needed to be chopped out altogether. Your line-by-line edit of this book leaves me eternally in your debt.

Ann Phillips, you created the perfect cover. Thank you for your patience and for giving my book the benefit of your creative talents.

To Kathleen, the woman who shares my home and my life, thank you for all the help with the animals that own us so that I could have the precious extra minutes I needed to chase these words across the page. The fur kids might not understand and acknowledge your commitment to the cause, but I do.

My sister Kathy and my brothers Paul and Tony—you've had to contend with some serious detours of your own of late. Nonetheless, you make time to cheer your kid sister on. I'm grateful to you for all your support through the years.

And lastly, to the human dynamo and kayaker extraordinaire, Emily Reed, I offer my most sincere, heartfelt gratitude. You are my mentor, my business partner, my publisher, and my dear friend. A few words here cannot begin to capture all of the ways I am enriched by your presence in my life. Thank you for making me part of the Blue Feather family. It's an honor to be in your company.

"Life is what happens while you're busy making other plans."

—John Lennon

Chapter 1

Ellis slapped the steering wheel. "I forgot how crowded the roads are the Saturday after Thanksgiving. I should have allowed myself more time to get there."

Traffic had been stopped for several minutes. She left her Toyota Tundra and made her way up the roadway on foot. Twenty vehicles ahead, she looked knowingly at a rainbow-colored cat decal affixed to the rear window of a forest green Xterra and she stopped beside the driver's door. A lanky woman with a cell phone against her ear leaned against the front bumper and hood. Looking past her, Ellis could see the long line of stopped vehicles snaked around the next curve in LaVista Road.

The woman snapped the phone shut and sashayed the few paces back to where Ellis stood. Ellis yanked off her Atlanta Braves baseball cap and pulled her hair back from her forehead. "What happened up there? Did Santa flip his sleigh?"

The woman shook her head. "Nothing quite that dramatic. I called a friend who lives about a half mile up the road. She said the driver of a beer truck misjudged the corner at Oak Grove. He rolled his gooseneck trailer and dumped half his load of Budweiser all over the roadway. The police called in a couple of tow trucks and a crane to get the rig back on its wheels. She said they've got everything blocked off in both directions down there."

"Lovely." Ellis twisted her wristwatch and checked the time. "I'm already an hour behind schedule." She kicked the pavement beside the left front tire of the Xterra in frustration. "I'm supposed to be trimming holly bushes at a house on Ponderosa Lane."

"If you've got Ben Cartwright's number, you can use my phone to call and explain." With a grin, she extended the phone toward Ellis.

"It's not quite that simple to reach my modern-day *Bonanza* guy. If I could solve this with a phone call, I'd use my own cell and take care of it." Ellis tugged her phone off the clip on her belt, then tucked it back in its holder. "The owner is at the spa this morning having an exfoliation and heaven only knows what else. He told me he would be—and this is his word—incommunicado—until at least two this afternoon."

"But he's in a hurry for you to get to his house?"

"He's hosting a huge party tonight to—his words, again—inaugurate the most festive season of the year, and he wanted me to do a buff and polish on all the shrubs out front." Ellis flung an imaginary boa around her shoulder. "Why is it that every gay man figures every other gay man takes notes about how the front yard looks on their way in from the curb?"

"Umm... because they do?"

"Yeah, I guess you're probably right." Ellis tugged at her cap again. "I've pretty much closed up shop for the season, but Fredrick is such a loyal customer, I agreed to do this as a favor for him."

"I'm sure he'll appreciate it."

Ellis glanced at her watch once more. "How long have you been sitting here?"

"Ten, fifteen minutes, maybe. Good thing Atlanta has mild weather in November. This would be a real pain in the butt if we were stuck someplace cold." She looked up and down the road at the assortment of drivers who had exited their vehicles and were making conversation with one another. "At least drivers here know how to make a gabfest out of a traffic tie-up."

She made a sweeping motion toward the edge of the road. "Pull up a curb and sit awhile. It doesn't look like we'll be going anywhere anytime soon."

Ellis was about to decline the invitation. If she went back to her truck, maybe she could convince the cars that had her boxed in to jockey enough that she could maneuver out of the traffic jam and find some other way to get to the landscaping job on Ponderosa Lane. Before she could speak, the woman continued.

"By the way, my name's Mary... well, people call me Mary, but my full name is MaryChris." She pocketed her phone and offered her hand. "MaryChris. My last name's Moss."

Ellis accepted the handshake. "Nice to meet you, MaryChris Moss."

"It's a little early, but Merry Christmas to you, too."

Ellis groaned. "I can't believe I fell for that."

"I wish I were joking. Swear to the goddesses, that's my real name."

"Right, and I'm Rhonda Korner."

"No, really. My dad was king of the punsters. I was born on December twenty-fifth, and he couldn't resist." Mary reached into her hip pocket and unfolded a small stack of bills. She extracted her driver's license and handed it to Ellis. "See?"

Ellis gave the license a cursory examination. "I'll be darned." She passed it back to Mary.

"So now you know my name, my address, and my birthday. All I know about you is you trim bushes and like the Braves." Mary pointed at the baseball cap on Ellis's head and flashed a captivating smile.

"Even though you didn't bite when I told you I'm Rhonda Korner, I'm tempted to tell you my name is Terry Dactul or maybe Sarah Bellum, but if you ask for proof, you'd know I was lying," Ellis said.

"I'd have thought Lon Moore or Wendy Boughbreaks would be better choices, given your line of work." Mary eased herself into a casual pose, leaning on the fender.

"Sorry to say that my parents weren't very creative with my name, not that it would have been an easy thing for them to do."

"So what's your name?"

"Most of my friends call me Ellis."

"Alice?"

"No, Ellis."

"Okay. Got it. Ellis. Is that your first name or your last name?"

Ellis laughed lightly. "Neither, but you'd think it might be, wouldn't you?"

"It's not?"

"No."

"So what's your name?"

"You don't really want to know."

"Of course I do. I asked, didn't I? It can't be that bad."

"Okay, but remember, you asked for it." Ellis made a show of taking in a really deep breath. "Gretchen Alina VanStantvoordt."

"What?" Mary cocked her head.

Ellis repeated her name and then spelled it. "It's Dutch. Or Flemish. At a minimum, it's a mouthful. That's why everyone calls me Ellis."

"I'm sure there must be a story behind that."

"Yep. The professor in one of my environmental science classes at UGA said my ancestors should have had the immigration people at Ellis Island give them an easier name when they got off the boat."

"Kind of a cruel thing for him to say."

"I thought so, too, but then I found out his given name was Wolfgang Schlenvogt, even though he changed it to Rolf Glenn. He was trying to be cute and establish some common ground with me."

"So he started calling you Ellis?"

"No, my friend Judith was in that class with me, and she thought it was ever so funny to call me Ellis. She and I hung out, and the next thing I knew, everywhere I went, I was Ellis. It stuck with me all through college, and I kinda got used to it, so I kept using it. A lot of my clients only know me by the one name—sort of like Cher or Kobe or Houdini."

"Does that mean I'm in the company of a celebrity?" Mary feigned a curtsy.

"About the only thing I have in common with celebrities is figuring out using a fake name can make life easier."

"Got it," Mary said. "Like Marilyn Monroe had more appeal than Norma Jean Baker."

"Right. Samuel Clemens wouldn't have sold nearly as many books as Mark Twain did."

Mary shifted so that her weight was on her other foot. "And it's true even in the corporate world. Google wasn't always Google."

"No?"

"Nope. It started out as BackRub."

"You're kidding."

"Uh-uh. I saw it on one of the trivia sites I browse." Mary opened the driver's side door. "Might as well be comfortable while we compare little-known facts." She gestured to the passenger door. "Climb in." She eased into the leather bucket, Ellis complied, and soon they were lost in conversation.

Half an hour later, Ellis glanced out the windshield and noticed a car coming up the road. "Looks like the gridlock at Oak Grove is breaking free. I'd better get back to my truck. Thanks for making this the only Atlanta traffic jam I've ever enjoyed." Ellis offered her hand to Mary.

"It's been fun talking to you. I hope you get your bush trimming done so that the earth isn't thrown off its axis when a group of gay men simultaneously recoil in horror at misshapen holly shrubs." Mary took Ellis's hand as she spoke.

Ellis grasped Mary's extended hand briefly and then got out of the vehicle. She walked around to the driver's side and leaned down so that she was eye to eye with Mary. "Right. I'd hate to be responsible for a catastrophe of that magnitude. Well, see you at the next overturned beer truck."

"That's a date, Gretchen Alina VanStantvoordt."

Ellis smiled, pleased at how easily Mary used her full name. "In case I don't get the chance to say it closer to the real date, Merry Christmas, MaryChris Moss."

"Thanks. Same to you. Take care of yourself."

"I will. You, too."

Vehicles several car lengths ahead of the SUV moved slowly forward. Ellis picked her way along the edge of the street. She was about to sprint down the now-creeping line of cars toward her truck, but reversed direction and ran to catch up with Mary's Xterra.

She half-shouted into the open window. "Hey, any chance you might want to go to a movie or something sometime?"

"I'm in the book. Call me."

Ellis flashed an "okay" sign. She thumped her fist lightly on the edge of the rear door of Mary's SUV. "Deal. I will. Soon." She turned and jogged down the uneven berm of the roadway.

The impatient drivers who'd been trapped in the queue were eager to make up for lost time. Horns honked farther down the string, and she was sure it was because her unoccupied truck was blocking the way. She picked up her pace and, in her haste, failed to notice a gap in the pavement. Her right foot hit the hole at the wrong angle, and the next thing she knew, she was a crumpled heap of humanity.

"Crap!" she yelled as she felt the pain tear through her ankle. "I don't need this." She grabbed her right calf. "Shit. How freakin' clumsy can I be?" She shrunk herself into a ball and rolled onto the narrow strip of dead weeds. She was grateful that she'd at least had the good fortune to fall in a stretch of road where she had a small oasis to huddle on rather than in one of the places where ancient pines crowded the heavily-traveled two-lane route in the northeast Atlanta neighborhood.

"Would it kill one of you to stop and see if I'm okay?" she shouted. "Your compassionate pre-Christmas spirit is astounding." She shook her fist at a couple of the cars zipping by. Ellis might have uttered more commentary, but the sound of screeching tires and the unmistakable crunch of bumper on taillights filled the air. "At least I don't have to worry about being run over," she said sarcastically as the procession of cars once again came to a total halt. "Serves you right, assholes."

Ellis pulled herself to her knees and tried to stand. A white-hot jolt shot through her lower leg and forced her back to a kneeling position. She gingerly eased onto her butt. Waves of nausea washed over her, and she wondered if she was going to pass out. She took half dozen slow, steady breaths and talked herself into a calmer state.

"Marvelous. How the hell am I going to get those bushes trimmed? Broken ankles and landscaping careers don't mix well." She reached down and gently probed her swelling foot.

"Do you really think it's broken, Ellis?"

Ellis did a double-take. "Mary? What are you doing here? You should be all the way to Clairmont Road by now."

"Yeah, but I took one last look in my rearview as you were trotting along the road, and I saw you fall."

"Now you know why I'm a landscaper and not a ballerina." Ellis tried to laugh, but the pain was growing by the moment, and the sound died in her throat.

"Can you walk?"

"I don't think so. When I tried to stand on it, I almost fainted."

"We'd better get you to an emergency room." Mary knelt beside her.

Ellis made a face. "That'll only cost a month's wages, and since I won't be working much again until the spring, make that a month's wages I don't have."

"Maybe so, but replacement body parts are hard to come by." Mary rubbed Ellis's forearm reassuringly.

"I guess you're right. Besides, I'd hate to be a one-legged gardener in an ass-kicking contest." Ellis tried again to put a laugh with her words, but once more, the throbbing discomfort stymied her.

"How much farther to your truck?"

"Just around the next bend."

Mary got to her feet. "Give me your keys, and I'll go get it."

"Wouldn't it be easier to take yours?"

Mary took a look in the opposite direction up the road. "Ordinarily, but it recently had the grillwork of a Crown Victoria planted firmly in its backside."

"It was your SUV I heard get creamed?"

"I told you, I saw you in my rearview. When I knew you'd taken a tumble, I guess I forgot what I was doing and slammed on my brakes."

"And you got rear-ended?"

Ellis caught the sheepish look on Mary's face. Mary flipped her hand dismissively. "You know how unforgiving the laws of physics are. Two solid objects can't occupy the same place at the same time."

"You need to get back to your car and exchange insurance information with the guy who hit you."

"I've already parked it on the driveway pull-off in front of where it happened. I got the other driver's business card and gave him my name and number. I can deal with the car later."

"No, really, Mary, you should call the police and file an accident report." Ellis pushed against Mary's legs with both hands.

Mary looked intently at Ellis. "Nope. In the game of life, people trump possessions every time."

Ellis wondered at the sensation that ripped through her and hoped it wasn't an indication that she was going to fall into unconsciousness. Mary's smile reassured her. "Okay, you win."

"Now, give me your keys and let's get you patched up."

Ellis fished her keys out of her vest pocket and handed them to Mary. "Here. It's a burgundy Toyota Tundra."

"Good color choice. First we'll get your ankle fixed, and then we'll get you some ballerina lessons. Your pink tutu will be a perfect complement to it."

* * *

"At least it's not broken. I've heard that a lot of people need surgery to fix a broken ankle." Mary perched on the edge of the gurney in DeKalb General Hospital's emergency room.

"Forgive me if I don't leap up and down in euphoria." Ellis gestured toward her foot and ankle encased in a Velcro-closure bootie. "I need to wear this soft cast and use crutches while the sprain heals."

"True, but that beats having plates and screws put in." Mary patted Ellis's good leg sympathetically and let her hand linger lightly on Ellis's thigh. "Is the shot the doctor gave you for pain starting to work?"

"Must be. I feel like I've got anvils on my eyelids."

"As soon as the nurse comes back with your discharge papers and the prescription for your meds, I'll get you out of here so you can lie down and sleep for a while."

Ellis tried to stifle a yawn. "She'd better hurry. I'm sinking fast." She chanced a glance. "I'm sorry you had to waste your whole day." She wrapped her fingers around the back of Mary's hand as it rested on her leg. "And I really hate that your first impression of me is that I'm a total klutz."

"Actually, my first impression of you was that you're a nice-looking woman with a good sense of humor and a quick comeback. I thought those Rhonda Korner and Sarah Bellum cracks were pretty funny." She squeezed Ellis's hand before withdrawing her own. "So your first impression was okay. And my second impression of you was that you were willing to ask me for a date, and that always boosts someone's stock with me."

Despite her deepening drug-induced stupor, Ellis caught the tinge of a blush creeping up Mary's neck. "So it wasn't until the third impression that you figured out I'm a stumblebum, huh?"

Mary tugged at the edge of the sheet on the gurney and looked anywhere except at Ellis when she said. "I prefer to think of it as a case of you falling for me."

Before Ellis could respond, the ER nurse bustled into the enclosure, carrying a sheaf of papers and pushing a wheelchair with a pair of crutches braced between the footplate and the back of the chair.

"Okay, let's go over your home care instructions." She handed Ellis a list of dos and don'ts for her badly sprained ankle. "Biggest thing is to keep it elevated as much as possible for the first forty-eight hours. You need to ice it several times a day, but no more than twenty minutes at a time. The soft cast will keep it immobilized and provide compression. Only take the cast off when you ice it and when you bathe." The nurse pointed to the last item on the list. "See this? It says, 'REST, REST, REST.' It's in capital letters and repeated three times for a reason. If you want this ankle to heal, stay off it."

"But—" Ellis said.

"No buts. I mean it. Today, tomorrow, Monday, you park yourself somewhere and let"—the nurse cast a look toward Mary—"your girlfriend wait on you. Rest, rest, rest."

She tapped her index finger on the sheet of paper she was holding and addressed Mary. "Make her take baths for the next week or ten days, but be sure she keeps that foot out of the tub. No heat of any kind on this ankle for the next two days. After the first forty-eight hours, you can alternate hot and cold. And I mean it, baths, not showers. It's too easy for her to lose her balance and slip in the shower."

She turned her attention back to Ellis. "Starting Tuesday, alternating hot and cold will increase the blood flow to the injury and help it heal, but for the first couple of days, only use ice. We want to get the swelling out of it." She looked quickly from one to the other. "Any questions?"

"What about the crutches?" Ellis asked. "How long do I have to use them?"

"At least for the first week. Doctor Thackeray said it's one of the worst sprains he's seen. You've got to keep your weight off that foot. Don't go hoppin' on your good foot, either. You'll end up with two sprained ankles, or worse." She helped Ellis to a standing position. "Let's be sure these are set right for you." She fiddled with the adjustment screws on the crutches and had Ellis take a couple of practice steps.

"Good. That should do. Next weekend, you can try to put a little bit of weight on it and see how it does. If it still hurts, keep using the crutches, understand?"

She handed Mary two prescription sheets. "One of these is for pain, the other for inflammation. Instructions for how she should take them will be on the bottles."

Mary jammed the papers in the back pocket of her jeans.

"Anything else I can do for you?" The nurse pulled a pen from the pocket of her smock.

"No, I don't think so," Ellis said, barely able to force her lax jaw to form the words.

"Then sign this release form, and I'll wheel you down to the door." She used one hand to hold the form in place on the supply table beside the gurney.

Ellis scribbled her signature on the bottom of the page. Without so much as a single grumble, she accepted Mary's help getting into the waiting wheelchair. The nurse placed the upper part of the crutches in Ellis's hands and guided the tips onto the footplate between Ellis's feet. She led them down the hall and through the lobby.

*   *   *

Mary left the nurse standing behind the almost-dozing Ellis while she hurried to get Ellis's truck from the emergency room parking lot. She pulled under the canopy and went around the cab to help maneuver Ellis from the chair into the passenger seat, then stowed the crutches on the floor of the backseat.

"Good luck to both of you," the nurse said as she leaned over Ellis and fastened her seatbelt. She lifted Ellis's arm and moved it inside the cab of the truck. It flopped loosely onto Ellis's lap. "That shot turned her into Raggedy Ann. Looks like she'll be your Sleeping Beauty for the rest of the day." She closed the door and waved at Mary through the rolled-up window. Mary waved back and pulled away from the curb.

"I live up in Tucker, just the other side of North Lake Mall," Ellis said.

Because Ellis's voice was so soft and her words were so garbled, Mary had to strain to understand what she said.

"I'm taking you to my place, Ellis. You're in no condition to be left alone."

"Won't be alone. Sam's there." The words were so slurred it sounded more like, "Woan bee lone. Sam's hare..."

"Who?" Mary tried mightily to keep any trace of emotion out of her voice.

"Sam. She's the best. And she's got the prettiest brown eyes. I'm so lucky to have her." With a goofy grin on her face, Ellis turned to face Mary. "You'll like Sam. She gives good kisses."

Mary laughed derisively. "I should have known this was too good to be true."

"Whaddya mean?"

"I thought you were unattached. When we were getting out of that traffic mess earlier, and you came back to my car to ask me out..."

"Sam won't mind. She wants me to go out. She likes to have the apartment to herself. Watches *Animal Planet* and eats cookies in bed."

Even though she felt like she needed an interpreter to decipher Ellis's mutterings, each comment from Ellis was pushing Mary closer to an eruption. The nerve. Acting as if there was nothing wrong in the least with asking one woman for a date while living with another one.

"I see." Mary's tone was icy. "How long have you and Sam been together?"

"I picked her up about six months ago." Ellis's head lolled back against the headrest. She yanked it forward. "It took about four months for me to convince her it was okay for me to go out and leave her at home alone."

"I see," Mary said again, the temperature in her words dropping well below freezing.

"'Course, as soon as I get home, she makes me take her for a walk," Ellis said. "If I don't, she pees right there on the floor—

sometimes right on my shoes." The matter-of-fact delivery of this observation sent Mary into peals of laughter.

She caught her breath and asked, "So Sam's your dog, I take it?"

"What else? My grandma?"

If Ellis was joking, it wasn't evident in the least, and her deadpan reply elicited more chuckles from Mary.

"I'll say this for you, Ms. VanStantvoordt, you're an enigma."

"Nope. I'm a Gemini." With that, Ellis gave in to the effects of the painkiller and dropped off to sleep, her head resting against the passenger window.

Mary reached for the button to turn on the radio, then decided some quiet time to think might be a better option.

She made her way through the heavy Saturday afternoon traffic. Worries about Ellis's foot had kept her from thinking of much else for the past several hours. She rounded the corner off North Druid Hills Road onto Willivee Lane and then made a right onto Wilson Woods Drive in the Laurel Hills subdivision. As the Toyota bounced over a speed bump, Ellis stirred in the passenger seat.

She reached over and rubbed the back of Mary's upper arm. More asleep than awake she said, "Sorry I'm so much trouble, Becky. You know I love you best, right?"

Before Mary could react to the comment, Ellis dropped back under the veil of the Darvocet.

Mary gave Ellis a skeptical look. First Sam, and now Becky, she thought. She couldn't wait to see who else was behind this Dutch door.

Chapter 2

Ellis edged closer to the realm of consciousness. As best she could tell, little green men wearing dirty boots were marching in her mouth. Her right foot felt like it was encased in cement, and she doubted she could lift it an inch, even if she wanted to. The dull, aching agitation in her head was on the verge of causing a spin cycle in her stomach. Worst of all was the eerie feeling that she was being watched—watched very carefully by several pairs of eyes.

She could tell she was lying on a sofa, but she knew it wasn't the one in her apartment. Cautiously, she raised her eyelids just enough that she could squint through her lashes. A long-haired gray and white cat lounged on the sofa back. Its tail could double as a plume in d'Artagnan's cap in a production of *The Three Musketeers.* The constant fwip-fwip, fwip-fwip of the tail, first on the front side of the sofa and then to the rear, brought to mind a demented conductor waving a fuzzy baton at a silent orchestra playing syncopated tunes. The cat was staring relentlessly at Ellis, and it wasn't a look of enchantment or welcome.

Ellis rolled her head slightly to the left. Instantly, a familiar wet nose poked the side of her face. "Hey, Sam," she whispered through gummy lips. "How'd you get here?" She rubbed the dog's ears with her left hand and was rewarded with a sloppy slurp as Sam dragged her tongue across her face. "Nice one, Sam." Ellis used her right hand to swipe some of the dog slobber from her nose and cheek.

Once Sam knew Ellis was awake, there was no point for Ellis to pretend otherwise. She opened her eyes wide, blinked several times, and looked at the unfamiliar ceiling as she tried to coax her mind into remembering what happened in her life the last time she was upright. Her first attempt at moving her right leg brought everything back in a snap. The yelp that escaped her sent the cat flying off the back of the sofa and out of the room, with Sam scampering after her.

Ellis put two fingers in her mouth and gave a sharp whistle. Sam hustled back to the sofa. "Down and stay, Sam." Sam dropped onto her belly and put her head on her paws. Ellis reached down and patted the dog's head. "Good girl. I've got trouble enough without you tearing up some stranger's house." She stroked Sam's head while she did a mental recap of what she could recall of her day. Her reverie was interrupted by a soft voice.

"I guess you're awake. Are you all right?"

Ellis lifted her head from the pillow to look at the person speaking. The person turned out to be a young girl, sitting on an ottoman on the other side of the room.

"Yeah, I'm all right, except my foot hurts like a son-of-a-bi…" Ellis caught herself mid-word. "It hurts a lot." She propped her arm on the back of the sofa and braced her hand on the sofa's arm. She half-pulled, half-pushed herself into a sitting position. As she eased her leg off the edge of the sofa, her ankle throbbed mercilessly, and she lowered herself back against the pillow on the end of the couch.

The youngster edged across the room and stood where Ellis could see her. "I'm supposed to tell you to have some cheese and crackers and then to take one of each of these pills." She held two pharmacy bottles out toward Ellis. "And I'm supposed to tell you that if you have to go to the bathroom, you have to use your crutches to get there." She pointed to the crutches standing against the glider rocker behind the ottoman she'd recently vacated.

Ellis looked at the girl. Something about the girl seemed somehow out of place. Damn, Ellis thought, she looks so familiar, but I don't know any ten-year-olds, or nine-year-olds… or eleven-year olds, for that matter.

"Okay, I guess that makes sense, but who told you to tell me that?" Ellis continued to wrack her brain to figure out where she could have encountered this girl before.

"She did." The girl pointed to the far side of the room.

Ellis hiked herself up enough to look over the back of the sofa. Mary stood in an arched doorway.

"Guilty as charged," Mary said as she glided into the room. She wore a blue chenille bathrobe, and her hair was wrapped in a bright pink towel. "I wanted to grab a quick shower, so I left Natalie on guard, in case you woke up while I was in the bathroom." She covered the rest of the distance to the sofa and stood beside the girl.

Ellis collapsed back on the couch, leg throbbing. She wasn't sure of the mechanics of her arrival at what must be Mary's house, but she now knew why Natalie looked so familiar—she was a miniature Mary Moss. The honey blonde hair, the lean, angular build, the eyes that were blue, except when they were shaded and looked gray-green, the soft, feminine face. Precious little doubt what the connection was between these two beauties who stood side by side in front of her.

Mary bent down and gave Sam a couple of quick pats on her rump. "Nice dog you've got, by the way." Sam responded with an appreciative groan as Mary rubbed the ridge down the middle of the dog's back.

"Thanks. Now, would you like to tell me how my dog got to your house?"

Mary straightened up and undid the towel, and her hair fell free. "Well, I'll give you a clue. It wasn't by cab." She rubbed the moisture out of her long, blonde hair. "So, I guess you've met my daughter." Mary stopped drying her hair and cupped Natalie's shoulder.

"Indirectly. She passed along instructions about what I'm supposed to do."

"And have you followed those orders?"

Natalie resumed her seat on the ottoman.

"Not yet," Ellis said.

"How are you feeling?"

"I've had better days."

"I bet." Mary wadded the towel into a ball. "Here, honey, take this to my bathroom and hang it up for me, will you?" Natalie took the towel and ambled out of the room. Mary called after her. "And bring my hairbrush when you come back, okay?"

"Cute kid," Ellis said.

"I think so, but I have to. It's in my motherhood contract." Mary used her fingers to pull self-consciously at the tangles in her hair. "I wasn't hiding her from you. I would have told you about her when we took in that movie you offered."

"No biggie." Ellis hoped her cavalier tone hid the lie. "Besides, it might be awhile before I can make good on that invitation." She made a face and trained her gaze on her foot.

"That reminds me, you're due for your meds." Mary swept a glance around the room. "What did Natalie do with your bottles of pills?"

"I think I saw her put them in her pocket when you first came into the room."

"I'll be right back." Mary set off for the back part of the house.

Once again, Ellis reached down and found Sam's soft head to caress. She thought that if her damn foot didn't hurt so bad, she could fall asleep. The next thing she was aware of was Mary shaking her gently by the shoulder.

"Wake up, sleepyhead. No telling what that foot will feel like if we don't get these drugs into you."

Ellis roused herself. "Sorry, guess I nodded off." She noted that Mary was now wearing sweatpants with a T-shirt under a flannel shirt. "Must be the drugs."

Mary grabbed the ottoman and pulled it nearer the sofa. "Sleep is probably the best thing for you, but you need to eat." She sat down and stretched her legs—halfway across the room, in Ellis's estimation. "Plus, we've got to get some ice on that ankle, and you're already about two hours past when you should have had another painkiller."

"What time is it, anyway?" Ellis looked toward the window and saw lights on in the house across the street.

"Almost seven-thirty."

"Wow. How long have I been asleep?"

"Only about ten minutes since the last time I saw you."

"I meant altogether."

"We got back here just after two, so you've had a good five hours of sack time."

"I don't even remember leaving the hospital."

"I can believe it. You snoozed in the truck almost the whole way home." Mary rose from the ottoman. "Are you hungry? How about a grilled cheese sandwich and tomato soup?"

"Now that you mention it, I'm starving. Soup and a sandwich sound fantastic." Ellis stretched, but stopped when her ankle protested the pull on the muscle. "You're right. I need a pain pill."

"Maybe you should eat something first. I'll bet you haven't had anything since breakfast."

"Which I didn't eat. I was going to get something on my way to my first landscaping job—oh, crap." Ellis slapped herself in the forehead with the heel of her palm. "Fredrick is going to kill me. He'll be so pissed that I didn't get those bushes trimmed for his party tonight."

Mary shook her head slowly from side to side. "All taken care of, so don't give it another thought."

"What?" Ellis's eyes flew open wide.

"I'll tell you about it while we eat." Mary started for the kitchen. "What do you want to drink?"

"Probably nothing until I make a trip to the bathroom."

Mary grabbed the crutches from beside the glider rocker. "Here, let me help you." She held a hand out to Ellis, pulled her to a standing position, and helped her get the crutches under her arms. "Down this hall," Mary said as she led the way. She stood aside as Ellis hobbled into the bathroom.

Ellis shinnied past the vanity and positioned herself in front of the commode.

"Yell if you need help," Mary said as she pulled the door closed.

"Uh, Mary… I can't get my pants unzipped while I'm holding these crutches. And if I sit down, then I can't get the zipper undone."

Mary stepped back into the bathroom. "Here you go." She deftly unbuttoned Ellis's jeans and pulled the zipper down. "Might as well help you get these out of the way." She tugged gently on the Levi's and eased them past Ellis's androgynous hips. Ellis stood stock still, balanced on her crutches.

"Should I do your underwear, too?"

Ellis laughed self-consciously. "Oh, why not? What little dignity I had left is lying in a heap on the side of LaVista Road."

"Hey, I'm a mother. Trust me, when you're lying in the delivery room with your feet in the stirrups and everyone from your OB-GYN to the guy who stocks the vending machines in the hospital break room drops by to check how much you've dilated, you lose your very last shred of modesty." She carefully grabbed the elastic of Ellis's panties and moved them low enough that Ellis could sit freely on the toilet.

Mary turned so that her back was to Ellis.

Ellis dropped onto the seat and dropped her crutches on the floor. The gush of urine splashing into the bowl echoed off the walls. "I feel like I should burst into a chorus of 'Old Man River,' or something." An awkward moment passed. "Gawd, this is embarrassing."

"Normal biological function," Mary said. "Everybody does it. While you finish up here, why don't I get you something else to wear? We can take that boot off and ice your ankle while you eat. You'd be lots more comfortable in some sweats."

Mary exited the bathroom, closing the door behind her and leaving Ellis to reflect on the cavalcade of horrors that the day had brought. How many more humiliations would be laid on her before day's end? Hearing Mary returning interrupted the embarrassing litany of possibilities parading through her mind.

"Ready?" Mary asked from the other side of the door.

"Sure, if you are."

Mary reentered the room. "I made an executive decision and cut the right leg of this pair of sweatpants off halfway below the knee. That way, your leg will stay warm, but you won't have to deal with the elastic pinching off your circulation from pushing it up high enough to clear your cast." She handed the pants to Ellis.

Ellis turned the sweats over in her hands. "Hey, these are mine."

"Well, yeah," Mary said. "I wasn't going to hack the leg off *my* pants."

"Where did you get these?"

"Same place I got your dog."

Ellis frowned. "That reminds me, where *is* my dog?"

"In Natalie's room with her. The last time I checked, they were watching *Little House on the Prairie* on TV Land."

Ellis stared at Mary. "You've got some serious explaining to do, Ms. Moss."

"Surely you can't object to your dog seeing a wholesome program like *Little House*. Besides, I thought you were a big Michael Landon fan, given our discussions about the Ponderosa earlier today."

"Yuk, yuk, yuk." Ellis made a show of holding her sides, as though she were laughing hard. "What I meant is my dog is here, my clothes are here, and when your child isn't keeping watch over me, she's entertaining my dog. I'm wondering if I've been abducted."

Mary offered a nefarious chortle. "So, my little pretty, you've seen through my ruse." She rubbed her hands together. "When I return you to your planet, you will remember nothing of your time here on this moss-covered orb." She cackled like the Wicked Witch of the West in *The Wizard of Oz*.

"Moss-covered. I get it. You're a laugh riot." Ellis tried to hide her smile, but failed. "I hate to sound coy, but how about helping me camouflage my half-naked state?" She leaned over and retrieved her crutches. "Whooo. I think I'd better eat soon. I'm feeling a little woozy."

Mary stooped down and undid the Velcro bands on the cast and gently removed it. "How appropriate. Quite a rainbow of colors you've got going here."

18

Ellis looked down at the bruises shining on her ankle. "I'm just a slave to queer fashion."

Mary eased the jeans from around Ellis's ankles and then held the sweatpants so Ellis could slip her feet into the leg holes. "Stand up and I'll pull these up for you."

After they got Ellis decked out in her sweatpants, they made their way back to the living room, Ellis gimping along on her crutches and Mary carrying the soft cast.

"Sit on the sofa and use the ottoman for your foot." Mary set the cast aside and moved the hassock into place. She propped Ellis's swollen foot up on some pillows, then covered it with a light blanket. "I'll be right back with ice, eats, and something to take your pills with."

Ellis let her head flop onto the back of the sofa. She was so light-headed she wondered if she was really sitting in Mary Moss's living room, or if she was having some kind of psychedelic mind trip.

Mary came back with her arms loaded. "Eat this." She handed Ellis a peeled banana. "You need to boost your blood sugar." She set a plastic container filled with raisins, a zip-top baggie with orange segments, and a bottle of water beside Ellis on the sofa. "And these, too. I'll bring your soup and sandwich in a minute." From under her arm, she took an ice pack wrapped in a towel and rolled it back and forth between her hands.

Ellis devoured the banana and started on the orange. She saw the worried look on Mary's face. "I'm okay. Really."

"And I'm Empress of all the Russians." Mary looked on while Ellis ate her fruit. "That's better," Mary said. "You're getting some color back in your face. You were looking kind of gray for a minute there."

"I'm feeling lots better." Ellis grabbed a handful of raisins. "Better, that is, if you discount the gang war going on in my right foot."

"Now that you've got something in your stomach to cushion it, go ahead and take your meds." Mary fished two pills out of the patch pocket on her shirt and dropped them into Ellis's hand. Ellis chased them down with three huge gulps from the bottle of water.

"I don't know how I'm going to repay you for everything you've done for me today, Mary." Ellis tipped the bottle toward Mary in a mock toast. "Cheers."

"I'm sure we'll think of something." She placed the bag of ice carefully on Ellis's ankle. "At a minimum, you'll owe me a reciprocal home-cooked gourmet meal."

"I'm sure the Kraft cheese and Campbell soup people would be pleased to hear their products described that way." Ellis shifted her leg on the ottoman. "Not that I've seen anything approximating a bowl of soup and a cheese sandwich, mind you."

Mary lightly cuffed Ellis's good knee. "Pushy broad."

Ellis saw the twinkle in Mary's eyes as she departed for the kitchen.

"Better a pushy broad than a soup tease," Ellis called out as she helped herself to more raisins.

* * *

Ellis used the last bite of crust from her grilled cheese sandwich to sop the final bit of soup from her bowl. "Exquisite. My compliments to the chef." She smacked her lips loudly.

"Good thing Natalie's still in her room. We've been working on her table manners. I can see you're not going to be a good influence." From her spot on the far end of the sofa, Mary reached the length of it and pulled Ellis's plate and bowl closer and stacked them with her own.

Ellis wiped her mouth with a napkin. "Speaking of... shouldn't she have had something to eat, too?"

"She ate hours ago. Right after she fed and walked the dog, in fact."

Ellis turned to look at Mary. "Your daughter walked my dog?"

"It's not exactly rocket science. Most any nine-year-old can do it." Mary pointed to the crutches resting between them against the front edge of the sofa. "Somehow, I don't think it would be a pretty picture to see you out there on those and trying to keep Sam in check when she catches sight of a squirrel."

"Natalie's only nine? I'd have guessed her to be older. She's so tall."

"Takes after her mother. And she's just barely nine. Her birthday was the tenth of this month." Mary stretched, her arms extended over her head and her legs flexed out full length. "Time to let your foot thaw out and get your cast back on." Leaning over, she lifted the towel and ice pack from Ellis's ankle. Mary helped Ellis get the cast back in place and fasten the hooks and loops. "How are you feeling?" she asked as she plumped the pillow and wedged it under Ellis's lower leg.

"Good." Ellis smiled broadly. "I'm fed, I apparently have a dedicated nurse, my dog has a full-time caretaker, and the drugs have beaten the screaming match in my ankle down to a dull roar. Who could ask for more?"

"Don't express that thought in front of Natalie. She's got a long list she'd happily recite for you."

As if on cue, Natalie came up the hallway and into the living room and stood behind the sofa. "For one thing, I'd ask for a little sister. I've been telling Mom I want one for years, but I still haven't gotten her."

Mary reached out and tugged affectionately on Natalie's hair. "Aren't you supposed to be reading your library book?"

"Uh-huh, I was, but I think Sammy wants to go outside, so I came to ask you if I should take her for a walk again."

"It's dark out, sweetie. Just put her in the backyard." Mary gave Ellis a quick look. "It's fenced. She'll be fine."

Natalie raced down the hall, calling as she went. "C'mon, Sam. We're going out back."

Ellis applauded twice very quietly. "Nice sidestep on the baby sister issue."

"Thanks. One of the great things about talking to a nine-year-old is that conversation topics can change in half a sentence."

"So I noticed." Ellis mustered her courage. "So what about Natalie's father?"

"Nathan?"

"If you say so…"

Mary pressed her hand against Ellis's forearm. "Wait a sec. Big ears coming into range."

Natalie, with Sam in tow on her leash, clomped back into the room. Sam took one look at Ellis on their way to the kitchen, offered a single "woof," and trotted to the back door with Natalie.

"Don't forget to turn the lights on out there, Nat."

"Oh, Mom." Natalie flipped the switch and exited to the yard.

"It would appear I've been replaced," Ellis said with a sigh. "Fickle dog."

"Look at it from Sam's perspective. If you had a choice between a whirling dervish who'll chase you around the yard for twenty minutes or a cripple on a crutch who'll keep telling you to hurry up and do your business, which would you pick?"

"Point, set, and match, to Natalie Moss."

"Natalie Kimbrough."

"She doesn't have your last name?"

"No, she goes by her dad's name. My ex-husband."

"Nathan?"

"Nathan." Mary rose, dragged the glider rocker halfway across the room, and placed it at a right angle to the sofa so they could talk more comfortably. "Nathan Kimbrough, who, by the way, trimmed those bushes for you at Fredrick's house this afternoon."

"Sheesh. I forgot all about that. I must be losing my mind." Ellis rubbed both temples.

Mary sat in the glider. "Or under the influence of strong drugs and recovering from a nasty fall."

"Still, you'd think I could remember that I'm a landscaper." Ellis rapped the crown of her head. "Hello? Anybody home?"

"Don't be so hard on yourself. Even if you'd remembered, you couldn't have done anything about it today."

Ellis raised her injured leg from the ottoman. "Blinding glimpse of the obvious. So your ex did the trimming. Wow. How'd you talk him into it?"

"Have you forgotten? I reign here on the moss-covered orb. All lesser beings, such as men, heed my every command."

Ellis swiveled so that she could stretch out on the sofa. "Do you mind if I lie down? I'm getting a cramp in my back."

"Go ahead. Here, I'll stuff these pillows under your foot to keep it elevated."

Ellis scooted up to brace her back against the arm of the sofa. "Is there anyone else in your family I'll need to put on the payroll? So far I've got nurse Mary, Natalie the dog sitter, and Nathan the emergency shrub tender."

Mary reclaimed her seat. "Swiffer would probably like honorable mention as bedside sentry."

"Swiffer?"

"Natalie's cat. Big gray and white fluffy creature. Looks kind of like a giant furniture duster. She was really giving you the hairy eyeball when I helped you in from your truck this afternoon."

"Come to think of it, she was on the back of the sofa when I first woke up earlier. I haven't seen her since she and Sam tore out of here like they had firecrackers up their butts. Probably a good thing I took Sam to obedience school, or we'd be looking for the both of them in the next county."

"Nah, Swiffer would have put Sam in her place with one quick left hook. I have to say, though, Swiffer and Sam were pretty funny when they met this afternoon." Mary laughed at the recollection.

"Which reminds me once again—there's a whole chunk of this day that's still a total mystery to me. Any chance you'd fill me in on what I missed?"

"For a fee." Mary offered another of her mock-evil laughs.

"Like I have a choice. Name your price."

"Geez, you're easy." Mary smiled warmly. "I like that."

"As I said, what are my options? I can't dash out the door, claim my dog, climb in my truck, and cruise on home. And let's not forget, you've already seen me in my birthday suit." Ellis gazed into Mary's eyes.

"Just the bottom half." She looked away, avoiding Ellis's stare.

"And to think you accused *me* of being a pushy broad."

"Maybe we're a matched set." Mary stole a glance at Ellis.

"Maybe. Now, tell me what happened this afternoon."

"We left the hospital and came here. I got you situated on the sofa, which was a little like hauling a sack of potatoes around, but I managed."

Mary smiled again, and the light in her eyes made Ellis's heart catch in her chest.

"Okay, so I'm doing my tuber impersonation on this very sofa, and then?"

"Natalie was spending the day with Nathan, but I called him and explained about your accident and your fate-of-the-free-world shaggy shrub situation. He brought Natalie home, and then he went to Fredrick's house."

"I want to hear more about Nathan, but first I need to ask how he knew what house to go to."

"When I was driving you to the hospital, I saw your appointment book and your address book in the console of your truck. One of the first things you told me this morning when we were stuck in the traffic backup was that the house you were trying to get to was on Ponderosa Lane. The appointment book said, 'Fredrick. Holly bushes. A.M.' I thumbed through your address book until I found a Fredrick Nyegard on Ponderosa." Mary twirled her right hand in the air and then made a seated, half-bow from the waist. "Voilá."

Ellis whistled a two-note appreciation. "Does the CIA know about you? That was pretty clever."

"Flatterer."

"Merely the truth." Ellis tipped her head in Mary's direction. "So tell me the rest of it."

"You'd given me your wallet to hold when they took you for x-rays at the emergency room. I knew you were too banged up to manage for yourself, and I didn't know if you had anyone you could stay with, so I decided the easiest thing would be to bring you here, at least for tonight."

Ellis tried to interrupt, but Mary kept talking.

"It was a simple matter to check your driver's license for your address. I already had your keys, so when Nathan got back here after doing the bushes, I had him stay to keep an eye on Natalie and an ear out for you while I dropped off your prescriptions and ran to your place to get Sam and her dog food and pick up some clothes and your toothbrush."

"But how did you know I had a dog named Sam?"

"You told me."

"I did? When?"

"When you were talking in your sleep on the drive from the hospital."

Ellis hesitated before replying. "Uh-oh," she said quietly.

"Pardon?"

Ellis squirmed. "I've been told that I sometimes say some stupid things when I talk in my sleep."

"Is that so? Told by whom?" Mary leaned forward in her seat.

"Never mind. That's a topic for another time." Ellis reached down and massaged her right leg just above the knee.

"I'll remember that and hold you to it. Does your upper leg hurt?"

"A little. I don't suppose bouncing it along LaVista Road did it any favors."

"You're right about that. My Xterra would probably say the same thing."

Ellis slapped herself lightly on the cheek. "That's something else I forgot all about—your SUV got hit because of me."

"Not exactly. It got hit because I was trying to do two things at once, one of which was looking backwards and the other of which was driving forwards."

"How bad is the damage?"

"Not too bad, as best I could tell, but I only got a quick look while the other driver and I were exchanging information. His Crown Vic looked a lot worse than my lichen wagon."

"Your lichen wagon?"

"Yeah, the old Moss mobile."

"Inherited your dad's penchant for puns, I see. Good thing you picked a green vehicle."

"Wouldn't have mattered. I'd have come up with an appropriate name no matter what color it was."

"I believe it." Ellis grinned wryly. "Sorry about the wreck. I'll be glad to take a look at it in the morning to see if I can tell if the frame is bent."

"It's still on the pull-off at the house on LaVista where I parked it after the accident."

"We need to go get it." Ellis reached for her crutches.

"Right. You can drive left-footed while you drape your cast over the center console. And then in the morning, you can hang upside down one-handed from the roof rack to check the frame. That should work out nicely."

"Oh yeah. I keep forgetting I'm damaged goods."

"Damaged goods is an overstatement. You're just temporarily incapacitated, Gretchen."

"I bet I haven't heard anyone call me by my real name in six months, and now that's twice today you've called me Gretchen." Ellis cleared her throat dramatically. "Since we're on the subject of names, about Nathan..." She looked sternly at Mary. "Even though I may not always act like it, I *am* more than nine years old, and I'm not going to let you get away with the quick-switch ploy you pulled on your daughter to change the subject."

"I haven't done any fancy footwork to avoid telling you about Nathan. I've simply been answering other questions as you asked them. What do you want to know?"

Before Ellis could speak, the back door flew open and Natalie and Sam bounded into the kitchen.

Natalie shouted, "Can we get a dog, Mom? Sam's lots better at bringing stuff back than Swiffer is." Sam raced to the sofa and flopped her head on Ellis's chest. Natalie was a pace or two behind the dog.

"Go close the door, Natalie, and turn off the outside lights."

"All right." Natalie did as her mother directed, then returned to the living room. "Can Sam sleep in my room tonight?"

"Sam probably should sleep with Ellis tonight."

"How come?"

"Because it's their first night here, and we don't want Sam to be afraid because she's in a strange house."

"Would she be afraid, Ellis?"

The same light that Ellis had noticed in Mary's eyes on more than one occasion danced in the bluest part of Natalie's eyes as she regarded Ellis, waiting for her reply. "I don't know. Sam has never slept anywhere other than at my apartment." Sam lifted her head from Ellis's chest, rocked back on her haunches, and sat on the floor between Ellis on one side and Natalie kneeling beside her on the other.

"Perfect." Natalie petted Sam as she spoke. "If she's never done it before, she won't know to be scared, so she can sleep with me."

Mary spoke in a low voice. "A word of advice, Ellis. You cannot win by reasoning. If you don't want the dog to sleep with her, it will be by enforced edict, not because you won the debate."

Ellis raised her hands, palms up. "I don't care if Sam sleeps in her room. Do you care?"

Mary looked heavenward. "If Natalie had her way, she'd have a dog, a bunny, a pony, a turtle, a gerbil, an ant farm, an emu, and an elephant sleep in her room every night."

"And don't forget Swiffer," Natalie said as she wrapped her arms around the dog's neck and hugged her. "Oh, and my baby sister."

"It's about your bedtime, missy." Mary rose from her seat. "Remember your manners and say good night to Ellis."

"G'night, Ellis. I'm sorry you hurt your foot, but I'm glad you and your dog came to live with us." To Ellis's surprise, Natalie edged around Sam, leaned forward, and gave her a quick hug. "Sleep tight, don't let the bed bugs bite. If you see some on the wall, take your shoe and squish 'em all."

"Natalie, really," Mary said. "Is that a nice thing to say to company?" She waved her hand toward the hallway. "Go on. Get into your PJs and brush your teeth. I'll be in to smell your breath in a few minutes."

"Maybe I'll just moosh some toothpaste around in my mouth. You won't know for sure if I brushed or not."

"When all your teeth are lying in a pile beside your pillow, I'll know, and then you'll be sorry." Mary swatted Natalie's rump. "No stalling. Move it."

Natalie left the living room, and Sam hastened along behind her. Mary waited until she heard the hallway bathroom door close before speaking. She extended her arm so that she could rub the back of Ellis's wrist with her index finger. "Thanks for being a good sport about letting the dog sleep with her."

"When Natalie finds out what a bed hog Sam is, she'll regret asking." Ellis grimaced as pain twanged in her ankle. "And as lousy as this foot feels, I'm glad I won't have to try to find a way to bend my body around her tonight. Sam's only about thirty-five pounds, but when she gets in the bed, she miraculously triples her size and takes up everything except my pillow and a postage stamp's worth of space."

"Should be quite a contest, then. Nat's the same way. I swear she grows four extra legs and three more arms when she falls asleep. She sprawls out like a mutant octopus."

"Maybe we should put a video camera in there with them tonight. Might be good for a few laughs."

"Better not," Mary said as she shook her head. "Either the ASPCA or the welfare board would have us up on charges." Mary rolled her shoulders, then rocked back and forth in the glider a time or two. "Excuse me while I go reenact Sherman's siege of Atlanta and try to convince my kid that going to bed is not the single worst punishment inflicted on a living entity."

"Sure." Ellis winced in pain. "How long 'til I can have my next happy pill, Mommy?"

"You're only supposed to have a pain pill every four hours, but the instructions on the bottle said you could take a second one sooner if you need it, as long as you don't have more than six in a twenty-four-hour period." Mary got up. "I'll bring you another one after I get Natalie settled in."

"Good deal. If I knew any military secrets, I'd tell 'em if it meant I could get something to make this foot quit yelling."

* * *

"Your dog is an amazing creature," Mary said as she breezed through the living room and into the kitchen. She was back in a moment and handed a bottle of water and a pill to Ellis, who was propped in the corner of the sofa. "Here. I promised you a boost to take the edge off your pain." Mary dropped into the glider, still sitting at a right angle to the sofa.

"Thanks." Ellis swallowed the pill with a quick slug from the bottle. "My dog is amazing because?"

"Because it usually takes me anywhere from thirty minutes to an hour to get Natalie into bed. Tonight, by the time I got to her room, she was under the covers. Well, under the covers except for the arm she's got wrapped around Sam's neck."

"Sounds like a Rockwell painting."

"It is, and when you add in the fact that Swiffer is on the end of the bed, tucked up into her usual impersonation of a meatloaf, they could be a fund-raising poster for the Humane Society."

"Sam and Swiffer are both on the bed?"

"Like it's the most normal thing in the world."

"No growling? No hissing?"

"Not that I heard. They didn't even really act out when they first laid eyes on each other this afternoon."

"Ah, yes, a chapter in that untold saga you've been promising to share with me."

"Not really all that much to tell."

"Humor me. I've got a royal boo-boo." Ellis made a pathetic whimpering sound and momentarily raised her foot. "See? It has its very own pillow throne."

"Yes, Your Highness." Mary bent forward and pretended to adjust an imaginary crown on Ellis's head. "I was a little worried that Sam wouldn't like some stranger coming into her territory, so I picked up some puppy treats at the drugstore where I got your prescriptions filled."

"Bribery is always a good approach."

"It works with nine-year-old daughters. I figured it might work on other semi-domesticated things, too." Mary hooked her foot on the rung of the footrest and pulled it closer to her chair. "If you didn't already know it, as a watchdog, Sam would make a good Wal-Mart greeter."

Ellis laughed appreciatively. "Yeah, I have to agree with you. She's a lover, not a fighter."

"So anyway, I grabbed a bunch of stuff at your place and then lured Sam out of your apartment with doggie biscuits. She loves to ride in the truck, doesn't she?"

"Uh-huh. I'm hoping I can take her with me on some of my landscaping jobs this spring and summer. I hate leaving her in the apartment all day."

"You said you'd only had her about six months, right?"

"When did I say that?"

"More of that talking-in-your-sleep conversation we had on the drive home from the emergency room."

Ellis squirmed on the sofa. "Finish telling me about Sam and Swiffer, and then you'd better tell me what other stuff I blabbed to you."

"Guilty conscience?" Mary asked as she tilted her head and raised an eyebrow.

"Not really. I just want a chance to set the record straight in case I said something I shouldn't have."

"Okay, that will be the next topic on our discussion agenda." Mary settled against the back of the chair. "So I loaded Sam up in the backseat of your truck and tooled on back here. She had her leash on and had long since figured out I had a pocket full of cookies she could get if she played her cards right. We came in the house through the kitchen door." Mary flipped her hand in the general direction of the kitchen. "Of course, I could see the living room from there. Nathan was sitting in this chair, but it was in its regular place. Natalie was on the footrest, with Swiffer on the floor between them."

"Did the cat freak out when she saw Sam?"

"You don't know Swiffer. She's quite sure she's the reason the sun comes up each morning and likewise sure any other living thing was put on the planet to bow to her wishes. She puffed herself out to twice her usual size—which is going some when you consider how fluffy she is to begin with—and fixed a stare on Sam that should have ignited Sam's fur."

"So what was Sam doing?"

"She was mashed up against my legs as though I was her last and best hope of salvation."

"And then?"

"Swiffer marched through the living room, out to the kitchen, and right up to Sam, who had hidden behind my legs and was busily trying to compact herself into the size of a teacup poodle."

"And I slept right though the fight on this very sofa?" Ellis patted the cushion as she spoke.

"What fight? Swiffer did a nose-to-tip-of-tail inspection of Sam and decided she wasn't worth her trouble. She sauntered back to Natalie and flopped on the floor."

"And Sam?"

"It took her a minute or two, but she realized she'd been snubbed by a feline. She came out from behind me and inched toward the living room. I still had a grip on her leash, so I could rescue her if I had to. We came in here, and I let the two of them size each other up."

"Which resulted in what?"

"I'd swear they came up with some interspecies silent dialogue that pretty much translated to Swiffer saying, 'As long as you know

I'm the boss, I will tolerate your intrusion into my realm,' and Sam replying, 'Who cares? I got to ride in the truck, and she's got a pocket of snacks she's going to give me.'"

"Maybe we could rent them out to the UN."

"It might be too soon to declare harmonious coexistence. They've only been under the same roof for seven hours."

"Yeah, but you told me they're already sleeping together." Ellis grinned devilishly. "Typical lesbians."

Mary sat mute as a boulder in her chair. The long lull in the conversation made Ellis regret the remark. When it became evident that Mary wasn't going to speak, Ellis laughed loudly, which only deepened the prevailing discomfort.

With effort, Ellis drew herself into a sitting position so that she could pivot on the sofa and face Mary. "I'm sorry. It was meant to be a joke. I didn't mean anything by it."

Mary smiled contritely. "I know that." She looked away. "It's just that I'm not—"

Before Mary could finish her sentence, a shout came from down the hall. "Mom, Swiffer just hacked out a giant hairball. Come clean it up. It's gross!"

Mary pushed against the arms of the glider and got to her feet. "We'll return to our regularly scheduled programming, but first this annoying interruption by the rest of the house's inhabitants."

"Let me save you the embarrassment of finishing what you were about to say." Ellis grabbed the sofa as she lay against the arm and pulled her leg up onto the cushion. "I wasn't expecting you to sleep with me," she said quietly.

"Oh, that wasn't what I was going to say," Mary said as she took a few quick steps toward the back of the house. "I was going to tell you I'm not yet a full-fledged, card-carrying lesbian."

* * *

"Is the hairball emergency over?" Ellis asked as she awoke. Mary stood at the end of the sofa with a blanket in her hands.

"Long since. You were asleep when I got back, so I just let you be. I was afraid you might be chilled, so I brought you this extra blanket."

"I'm a hell of a houseguest, aren't I?" Ellis rubbed her face. "I hog the sofa, make wild assumptions on facts not in evidence, crack inappropriate jokes that insult my hostess, and then fall asleep before I even offer a decent apology for being such an insensitive smart mouth."

"I can see where what you thought about me seemed like a reasonable assumption on your part, but you're right about facts not in evidence. We know next to nothing about each other." Mary spread the blanket on the end of the sofa. "I hope you won't take it the wrong way, though, when I tell you I'd like to know more about you."

"Unless you're going to use whatever you learn to blackmail me, what wrong way would there be?"

"It's too late to get into that tonight. How about let's sleep on it and start fresh in the morning?"

"Good idea. I need to make another trip to the bathroom, and if you'll tell me where my toothbrush is, I'll get the first layer of fur off my teeth."

"Your things are in my room. Come on." She helped Ellis stand and get her crutches in place, then ushered her down the hall.

"Wouldn't it be easier for me to use this bathroom?" Ellis asked as they passed the room she'd used late that afternoon.

"Not when you're sleeping in my room. It's got an attached bath."

"Whoa, Nellie. I've already disrupted your entire life. I'm not taking your bed on top of everything else you've done for me. The sofa is fine."

"Spending the whole night on that sofa will cripple you for life. It was okay for your naps, but you need a good night's rest. Besides, if you need something, I'll be right beside you, so all you'll have to do is ask."

Mary opened the door to her bedroom. Ellis followed on her crutches. "I... but... you... I..."

"You're the one who thought I was going to say I wouldn't sleep with you. I've known since I brought you home from the ER that we'd be in the same bed tonight. It's really the only smart way to do this." Mary pointed to the queen-sized bed. "You'll sleep on that side so you're close to the bathroom. I'll be your able-bodied assistant and sleep on this side, and I'll try not to do anything stupid."

"Okay, now I'm officially confused." Ellis swayed slightly on her crutches. "Why are you worried about doing something stupid?"

"Because for the first time in my life, I'm going to share a bed with a really attractive woman." Mary hesitated before continuing.

"It's something I've wanted to do for about twenty-five years, and I haven't a clue how I'll behave."

"These drugs are really corroding my brain. I could have sworn you told me you're not a lesbian." Ellis steadied herself against a chest of drawers.

"What I meant is I've never... umm... been intimate with another woman. At least not anywhere except in my dreams." Mary moved to the bathroom and flipped on the light. "And lucky me. My first chance is with a woman who couldn't run away even if she wanted to."

Chapter 3

Mary watched Ellis's eyelids flutter open. "G'morning. How'd you sleep?" Mary was propped up on her side, her elbow cocked, head resting on the palm of her hand.

Ellis arched her back and turned her head on the pillow. "I feel like my body was beaten with a lead pipe and my brain was doped to the near edge of total oblivion."

"I'm not surprised to hear you say that. You moaned and groaned half the night."

"I don't remember even rolling over."

"I don't think you did. You were out like a light as soon as you hit the mattress, but I could tell your ankle was making it hard for you to get comfortable."

"I don't remember a thing. As the DuPont Company used to say, 'Better living through chemistry,' I guess. Those pain pills must be potent."

"Do you remember my giving you a pill around three this morning?"

Ellis considered the question. "No, I thought it was part of a dream I was having." She wrinkled her nose. "Not unlike much of the past twenty-four hours, now that I stop to think about it." She raised her head and shook it. "Refresh my fog-bound memory. Didn't you tell me I'd be the first woman you ever slept with?"

"Uh-huh. In both the Webster's dictionary definition of the word and in its more disreputable vernacular usage."

"Since we're both still fully clothed, I have to believe it was something of a disappointment."

Mary suspected Ellis's light tone was mere camouflage and laughed from deep in her gut. "Talk about years of wasted fantasies." She used her free hand to run her fingers along Ellis's jawline. "But the holding hands part was really sweet."

"Say what?"

"Right after you had your pill, when I got back into bed, you reached over and took my hand and held it the rest of the night." Mary withdrew her fingertips from Ellis's face. "I suppose it might have been to keep me from groping you, but I'll never know for sure."

"Let the record show, I'd never stop you from groping me."

"My conscience would never let me take advantage of a woman with a bum leg."

"My leg will heal."

"Not soon enough." Mary gathered her courage, hoping she didn't falter on her first attempt at kissing a woman. Her lips were within an inch of Ellis's.

The bedroom door flew open. Mary and Ellis jerked away from one another like matching magnetic poles.

"Hi, Mom. Sam and I have already been outside. I'm hungry, and so is she. When's breakfast?"

"Natalie, I've told you a thousand times to knock before you come charging in here."

"Why? I've seen you in your undies a million times. I've even seen you out of your undies a million times. And this time, you've got all your clothes on." Natalie giggled, but stopped when her mother's irritated gaze apparently registered.

"Sorry, Mom." Natalie retreated a couple of steps. "I'll give Sam a scoop of dog food from her bag and get some cereal for me."

Mary jumped out of bed and hugged Natalie before she could leave the room. "I didn't mean to sound so cross. You just surprised me, that's all." She squeezed her daughter again. "Don't get them mixed up and put your cereal in Sam's bowl."

"Yuk. That would mean I'd have dog food with milk in mine." Natalie broke free from the hug. "You're so weird sometimes."

"Love you, too, Nat."

"I'm not going to say it back."

"You don't have to. You said I was weird. That's the same as 'I love you.'"

"Oh, Mom. You are so weird."

"And I still love you, too."

Natalie raced out of the bedroom with Sam on her heels.

Mary closed and locked the door, then sat on the edge of the bed. "Welcome to my idyllic, romantic world."

Ellis smiled wanly. "What can I say?"

"For one thing, please tell me I didn't just blow my only chance to kiss you."

"Do you see me wearing a catcher's mask?" Ellis opened her arms expansively. Mary eased onto the bed and folded into Ellis's embrace, careful to avoid bumping her injured ankle.

She rested her forehead against Ellis's chest. "I don't know how to do this."

"You must. I'm betting Natalie didn't get here by osmosis."

Mary relaxed, but then tensed again as she felt Ellis's hand caress her back. "No, she got here because her father is a very persuasive man."

Ellis wrapped both arms tightly around Mary. "I can't wait to hear that story."

"As soon as I remember how to breathe so that I can put three sentences together, I'll tell you." Mary gulped a breath. "Am I supposed to feel like every square inch of my skin is dancing the Macarena?"

"I don't think anyone ever wrote a how-to book for this." Ellis moved Mary's long hair so that it was all falling to one side of her head.

"Damn. I really need some pointers."

"Go with your instincts, and you'll be fine." Ellis kissed the top of Mary's head. "I like the way it feels to be close to you." Her voice was little more than a whisper. She ran her index finger over the top of Mary's ear. "Yesterday at the hospital when I was asking you about your first impressions of me, you said something that was so true."

"What?" Mary moved a little higher up Ellis's torso.

"You don't know how right you were when you said you thought I'd fallen for you." Ellis placed a soft kiss on Mary's cheek. "I just wish I hadn't torn up my ankle in the process."

"As I recall, I said 'hoped you'd fallen,' not 'thought,' but this isn't the time to split hairs over semantics. I'm sorry you're in pain, but from my perspective, it's turned out pretty well." Mary exhaled loudly. "Heaven only knows how long it would have taken to get you into my bed if it weren't for that detour on LaVista Road." Mary lifted herself enough that she could look into Ellis's eyes.

"In the immortal words of Mary Chapin Carpenter, shut up and kiss me." Ellis cradled Mary's face in her hands and pulled her close.

Their lips touched, lightly, then with more force.

The knock at the door all but lifted Mary off the bed.

Natalie's muffled voice came from the other side. "Mom, we're out of milk!"

* * *

"Hi, I'm Nathan Kimbrough. I'm here to pick up Natalie." Nathan had let himself in through the kitchen door. He strolled into the living room and extended his hand to Ellis who was, once again, propped in the corner of the sofa with an ice bag on her foot.

"Nice to meet you," Ellis said as she told him her name. "Thanks for taking care of those shrubs for me yesterday."

Nathan sat in the glider that was in its new spot near the sofa. "Glad to do it. Mary told me you're going to be laid up for a while."

"About three weeks, according to the doctor. Good thing it's my slow time of year."

"Not that there's ever a good time for a sprained ankle."

"Right." Ellis couldn't help but wonder what the nice-looking man chatting with her would think if he knew she had kissed his ex-wife a few hours earlier. Ellis sized him up. She guessed him to be only slightly taller than Mary. His short, light brown hair had a few flecks of gray at the temples, and his eyes were—like Mary's—a nice shade of blue, but they lacked the expressive highlights that made Mary's eyes so intriguing. He was handsome enough, pleasant enough, and obviously good-hearted, since he had done a mercy trimming of Fredrick's hollies the day before. While accepting his firm handshake, she had noticed that his hands were rough and calloused—a workman's hands. She wondered what he did for a living.

"I'm a linesman for Georgia Power," Nathan said, as though he'd read Ellis's mind. "I've had a lot of practice trimming trees. Those bushes on Ponderosa were kid's play compared to the pines I'm usually dealing with in my cherry picker."

"I bet. Thanks again for doing that." Ellis cast a glance down the hallway, then realized Nathan had seen her do so.

"I told Mary I'd be here at twelve-thirty." He looked at the LED readout of the time on the DVD player. It said twelve-forty. "I'll never know what takes Mary so long to put a couple of things in a backpack so that Nat can spend the night with me. You'd think she was going on a month-long trip instead of spending one night at my apartment." Nathan rubbed his hands together nervously, then jammed them in the pockets of his pants.

Since Ellis knew precious little about how or why Mary did anything—with the possible exception of kiss delightfully—she was at a loss for a reply. Two more silent minutes rolled slowly by. Finally, Natalie roared up the hallway and into the living room.

"Hi, Daddy. Can we eat at McDonald's tonight?" She wrapped her arms around Nathan's neck and perched on his lap, which was no easy task, given her long body.

"We haven't even had lunch yet. What's the rush for picking where we eat tonight?"

"No rush. I was just asking."

Sam trotted into the room and went directly to Nathan and Natalie. "This is Sam," Natalie said.

"I know. I met him yesterday."

"Not him, Daddy. Her. Samantha."

"Oh. My mistake."

"I forgive you." Natalie slid off his lap and stood by the chair. "We should go."

"We can't until your mom brings us your backpack."

"Oh, right. I'll be out in the backyard with Sam."

Girl and dog sped toward the kitchen door.

Nathan raised his voice in hopes of being heard before Natalie was out of earshot. "Don't get dirty, or you can't go to the movies."

"It'll be dark in the theater. Nobody will know." Natalie and Sam dashed outside.

Nathan said, "She's always got an answer for everything."

Ellis heard his fatherly pride. "So it seems. It's hard to believe she's only nine."

"Nine, going on twenty-seven, most days." The look on Nathan's face left no doubt of his adoration for Natalie.

Again, Ellis was left with nothing to add.

At last, Mary joined them. "Sorry you had to wait, Nathan. I wanted to send Natalie's library book with her, and I couldn't find it. For reasons known only to her, she'd put it between the mattress and box spring." Mary handed a bulging backpack to her ex.

"Couldn't quite get her desk and bicycle in, huh?" Nathan stood and hefted the small rucksack.

"Better to have it and not need it than need it and not have it."

Nathan chuckled. "In case you don't recognize it, Ellis, that's the overprotective, worried mother's motto."

Ellis grinned. "Somebody should put it on T-shirts and sell them at Toys"R"Us."

Nathan looped his arm through the strap of the backpack. "Only if they're made with flame-retardant fabric and the proceeds go to Mary's latest charitable cause."

"I'm cautious, not overprotective, and there's nothing wrong with wanting to help people who are less fortunate." Mary placed both hands on Nathan's back and gave him a little push. "Get the yard ape and hit the road, bubba."

"On my way. We'll have to hustle if we're going to make the next showing of *The Santa Clause 51* at the buck and a bucket theater at North DeKalb Mall." Nathan started toward the kitchen.

"It's only *The Santa Clause 3,*" Mary said as she left the room.

Ellis listened in on their conversation, hoping to get a better understanding of their relationship.

"Give 'em another year or two," Nathan said. "The sequel will be out before this one's on DVD. They know a moneymaker when they see it. This is at least the fifth time I've taken Nat to see it. Good thing the tickets only cost a dollar. The popcorn is making a pauper of me."

Mary followed Nathan to the door. "Enjoy it while you can. Prom dresses and college will be here soon enough."

He gripped the doorknob, and the door gave a creak as he opened it. "I'll have her back by dinnertime tomorrow night, okay?"

"Sounds good to me."

Nathan opened the door and summoned Natalie from the far corner of the backyard where she and Sam were playing tug-of-war with a stick.

"Behave yourself at Dad's," Mary said.

"I always do."

"Right. And I'm Miss America." Mary blew a kiss to her daughter. "Love you."

"You're weird."

Ellis heard the tires on the driveway and saw Mary wave from the doorway; a car horn honked in response.

* * *

"Sweet freedom," Mary said as she and Sam rejoined Ellis in the living room. Sam stretched out full length on the floor beside the sofa and fell instantly asleep. Mary repositioned the chair before sitting down. "I don't know how I'd survive if Nathan didn't take her as often as he does."

"And I don't know what I'd have done if you hadn't rescued me and my dog yesterday. Thanks for everything." Ellis shoved the sleeves of her sweatshirt up, then tugged them back into place. "Nathan seems like a good guy."

Mary rocked back and held the chair in place while she spoke. "He is. Sometimes I wish we could have made our marriage work." She rocked forward.

"How long have you been divorced?"

"It'll be five years in March."

"So Natalie was just a little shaver, not that she's exactly ready for Social Security now."

"Right, but I'm pretty sure there's no such thing as a perfect age to tell a child that her parents aren't going to be together anymore."

"What happened between you two? It looked to me like you and Nathan get along all right."

"Odd as it may sound, nothing happened between Nathan and me." Mary grinned dourly. "And if you were to ask him, Nathan would tell you that was about ninety-nine percent of the problem."

"Nothing happened? Care to elaborate?"

"Oh, we took walks, went to movies and concerts and plays, worked together in the yard, gave each other nice presents on our birthdays, almost never fought, shared chores around the house, took turns caring for and playing with Natalie. We looked like the perfect family."

"But?"

Mary chewed on the corner of her lower lip. "But I'd rather have eaten razor blades than go to bed with my husband."

"Oh."

Mary watched Ellis's face as the impact of her confession set in and wondered if Ellis would ask for more information.

"So Natalie…?"

Mary rubbed her jaw. "I don't want to say she was a mistake. She wasn't. I always wanted kids, and I think I got a great one—I won't even pretend to be humble when it comes to how I feel about her—and I wouldn't trade her for anything in the world, but I'm an old-fashioned girl. I think kids do better in a family than as an appendage to a single person."

"Half the kids in this country come from broken homes."

"Statistics only apply to other people's children, not mine."

"So why didn't you stay with Nathan?"

Mary frowned. "Lord knows I wanted to. For that matter, Lord knows Nathan wanted me to stay, too, but he wanted a whole wife." Mary made a sound between a laugh and a snort. "Let me rephrase that, and forgive me if this sounds crude. Nathan wanted a wife with a hole, and try as I might, I couldn't convince myself that having sex with him was something I could do—at least not anywhere near as often as he wanted me to."

"I see."

"On our honeymoon, I kept telling myself I only hated it so much because I was so new at it. I was sure if I got a little practice at it, I'd figure out what made all the dames on the nighttime soap operas fall in the sack with every guy who'd crook his finger at them."

Ellis squinted at Mary. "Let me get this straight. You were a virgin on your wedding night, and you got pregnant on your honeymoon?"

"Right on all three counts. Straight, virgin, honeymoon." Mary ticked off each word on her fingers as she spoke it. "So right off the bat, I told Nathan 'no sex while I'm pregnant.'"

"How did he take that?"

"Not well, but there wasn't much he could do about it." Mary held her arms in an X across her chest. "The store was closed."

"And after Natalie arrived?"

"That kid's head was the size of a watermelon. It took months for my episiotomy to heal. Then she had colic for her first year. We were exhausted. It was all we could do to even make the bed, let alone think about making love."

Ellis murmured sympathetically. "But the incision healed, the baby outgrew her colic, you caught up on your sleep."

"And the gods answered my prayers."

"How so?"

"Nathan went to work for Georgia Power as a linesman. Right from the start, he was put on a schedule that had him working four days—and I mean on call twenty-four/seven for those four days—then off for three days. We'd go for days at a time without even seeing each other because he was at work. And if there was a wind storm or an ice storm, he might be gone for a week or more cleaning up downed trees. He could almost always have as much overtime as he was willing to put in."

"But what about the days he wasn't working?"

"On his off days, he was so weary, he'd sleep eighteen hours a day. Any energy he did have went to playing with Natalie." Mary wrapped her arms around herself and purred the next words. "Pure heaven." She smiled ruefully. "For a woman who wanted to avoid having to dodge sexual advances, that is."

"Since you're divorced now, it obviously didn't work forever."

"No, after about three years of having sex maybe twice a year, Nathan started making noises about having an affair."

"Him or you?"

"Both, actually. He accused me of having a lover and threatened to find one for himself if things didn't change."

"I can't believe I'm asking you this, but we seem to have gone from zero to sixty in five seconds as far as telling each other everything, so here goes. Were you having an affair?"

"Does it count if I pretended?"

Ellis laughed knowingly. "You and Jimmy Carter—lusting in your hearts."

"Remember, he confessed to lusting after *women* in his heart. He and I were peas in a pod in that regard."

"Another nosy question—if you knew you were attracted to women, why did you marry Nathan in the first place?"

"One word. Mother."

"You wanted to be a mother?"

"Well, yes, that's true, I did, but what I meant was I did it to shut my mother up."

"Kind of an emotionally costly way to put a gag on someone, isn't it?"

"If you only knew the half of it. Someday when you're plagued with insomnia, I'll show you my wedding album."

"It would probably just make me jealous."

"You wanted a big wedding, too?" Mary couldn't keep the surprise out of her voice.

"Hardly," Ellis said with a scoff. "I'd be jealous of Nathan."

Mary found herself too tongue-tied to respond, so she looked at Ellis and hoped the expression on her face wasn't too stupefied.

Ellis's voice dropped as she spoke. "Sorry. I guess I stepped way over the line again."

"Why would you say that, Ellis? I'm flattered."

Apparently it was Ellis's turn to be at a loss for words. Mary waited, hoping that when Ellis did speak, it wouldn't shatter her heart.

"Look, Mary, this whole situation is just so... so... I don't even know how to describe it. I mean, I've known you for all of about twenty-eight hours now, but look at us. You have to help me get to and from the bathroom. You keep track of when I need to ice my ankle and have my meds. You make meals for me and wait on me hand and foot. You and your family have done everything from do my job to feed my dog." Ellis took a deep breath. "I'm used to being a lot more independent, and I'm not real sure how I feel about anyone doing so much for me, but that's not the worst of what makes this whole thing so strange." She mashed her thumb against her lips for a moment before continuing. "We slept in the same bed last night, and this morning, unless I miss my guess, we were on the verge of doing some heavy-duty kissing. All that is more than I can wrap my brain around, and I haven't even gotten to the real kicker yet."

"And what would that be?"

"Please don't think I'm complaining, okay, but you and I sit in this living room and talk to each other like we've been best friends our whole lives. It's like we're some old married couple shuffling around in our bathrobes and slippers—except, of course, I can't shuffle, thanks to the number I did on my leg. I've been wedged in this spot on your sofa for so long it probably has an indelible imprint of my butt on it."

"If what you just said isn't a complaint, what is it?"

For dramatic effect, Ellis let her jaw hang limply open. She used the back of her hand to put her jaws back together. "Damned if I know. An observation, maybe. Or a question. Or a wish." She blew the air out of her lungs and her lips flapped noisily. "You tell me. How do you feel about it? About us?"

Mary rocked in the glider, a pensive mood overtaking her. "Confused. Scared. Excited. Overwhelmed. Nervous. Out of my element. In over my head. Lucky."

Ellis stopped her before she could go on. "Lucky?"

"Blessed, fortunate, privileged—if you like any of those words better."

"It's not the word, but the sentiment I'm not sure I understand."

"I told you last night I've been waiting a long time to find out what it feels like to lie next to a woman."

"You were serious when you told me I'm the first?"

"Beyond serious."

"And the lucky part?"

Mary spoke softly. "Oh, Ellis, you're the perfect combination of every woman I ever conjured in my head. You're so... gosh, I guess I'd say handsome. I love your curly hair and your rich, brown eyes. You're trim and toned, and you're so much fun to be with. You like animals, and you're good with my daughter. Most of all, and you said it yourself, we didn't have to work at getting to know each other. We just started talking, and right away, it was familiar and comfortable—like coming home."

"What have you been doing these past four-plus years? I mean, you and Nathan got divorced and you knew you liked women."

Mary shook her head sadly. "I had urges and inclinations, but I also had feet of clay. I joined every lesbian group I could find—reading groups, gardening groups, exercise groups, lesbian mothers' groups. I swear I've been to enough potluck dinners to last me the rest of my life."

Ellis spread her hands wide apart. "Surely in all of those adventures, you met some women you wanted to know better."

"You're right. I did. And she'd ask me out, or I'd buy a tanker truckload of courage and ask her out, and we'd go to a movie or have dinner or go to the nursery and pick out plants."

"Followed by?"

"Followed by my spending the next however long refusing to return her calls and dropping out of the group where I'd met her."

"Why?"

Mary made a sour face. "I'm thirty-nine years old. I've known since I was fourteen that I was a lesbian, but I was too chicken to do anything about it. At twenty-nine, after a lifetime of listening to my mother's badgering, even though I knew it was the wrong thing to do, I took the coward's way out and married sweet, patient Nathan Kimbrough who had been courting me since we were in grade school. What self-respecting lesbian would want to get hooked up with a total rookie like me? A rookie who holds what I presume isn't exactly a big drawing card in the form of one Natalie Christine Kimbrough."

"So, should I be whistling for my dog, asking for my truck keys, and dragging my sorry self back to my apartment?"

Mary detected a hard edge in Ellis's voice. "My turn to ask 'why?'"

"Because it sounds like I'm the next one in a long line of women you think you might want to get to know, but when it comes right down to it, you're still not sure."

Mary was relieved that the sharpness was gone from Ellis's words. "If that's what I wanted, I could have simply dumped you off at your place yesterday afternoon when you were discharged from the emergency room."

"Okay. So, where were you headed yesterday morning when the beer truck blocked the road?"

"To Charis Books, where I was supposed to be part of a discussion group on a book called *There Are No Accidents* by Robert Hopcke."

Ellis laughed out loud. "How ironic. Obviously, there are."

Mary wagged her finger like a schoolmarm. "Don't rush to conclusions, m'dear. The premise of the book is that there is synchronicity in all of life's events—that what we call coincidences are anything but." Mary looked expectantly at Ellis. At last, the bulb over Ellis's head illuminated.

"So the overturned beer truck screwing up traffic, me noticing the rainbow cat on your car window, our talking while we waited for the wreck to be cleared, my turning my ankle inside out, and your bringing me here to recuperate is all just a giant blob of happy coincidence?"

Mary smiled so broadly it almost hurt. "Yes and no. It feels like a series of coincidences, but it was no accident. It had to happen so that we could find each other." Mary let the thought hang in the air for a moment, then issued her characteristic pseudo-evil laugh. "And now you are my prisoner, and we will tell each other our darkest secrets."

"So which dark secret of mine do you want to know first?" Ellis shifted her still-aching leg to yet another position.

"We should start with the simple stuff. Who's your favorite singer?"

"I really like the Dixie Chicks, and I think it sucks that most of the radio stations stopped playing them because of what Natalie said about George Bush. But let's not talk politics. Who's your favorite singer?"

"Melissa Etheridge. Every time I hear *I Wanna Come Over*, I need a change of underwear."

Ellis chuckled. "Okay, I'll remember that and only play that song when I'm sure you've got extra unmentionables near at hand. Where did you grow up?"

"Clarkesville, up in the foothills. Gorgeous countryside, but the locals are pretty much locked in a time warp. Most of my family's still there. How about you? Where was home?"

"Savannah. It's one of those places where people often say they're glad to be from—far away from. Tell me more about your family."

"When I told you my name, I told you my dad, Joe, was quite a jokester. He died of a heart attack when I was thirty-four."

"I'd have liked to meet him. I'm sorry he's gone."

"Thanks. I miss him. He almost made it possible for me to tolerate spending time with my mother. I still don't know how Joe the joker and Anna, the straight-laced Baptist, ever hooked up and had children. If it weren't for her constant nagging about how I had to get married and at least give the appearance of—as she always put it—obeying God's will, it's anybody's guess where I'd be right now. Make no mistake, she's still a pillar of prayer at the Hill's Crossing Baptist Church in Clarkesville. My two sisters, Naomi and Gloria, are traipsing right behind her and dragging their kids with them in the bargain."

"When did you leave Clarkesville?"

"Right after high school. I figured it was my only chance to save my sanity. I had this dream of being a newspaperwoman, so I went to Georgia Southern University in Statesboro and got a degree in Journalism and Mass Communications."

"Did you achieve your dream?"

"I surrendered the sanity I so desperately wanted to save and went back to Habersham County and got a job as a reporter for the biweekly newspaper."

"Habersham County?"

"Clarkesville is the county seat." Mary wrapped her hands around her throat. "I could have gone to a thousand other places, but noooo, I went directly back into the jaws of hell."

"Where's Nathan in all of this?"

"Waiting for me in Clarkesville. We got married in February of 1997, and as soon as I knew I was pregnant, I convinced him we had to get out of that backwater town, or our parents would drive us crazy telling us how to raise the baby. He wasn't wild about the idea, but we moved to Norcross. Nathan tried to find work as a bricklayer, and I planned to get another newspaper job as soon as the baby was old enough to go to daycare. For the first year, Nathan worked pick-up construction jobs, but when Natalie came, he went to work at one of the big-box home improvement stores."

"How'd he like that?"

"The steady paycheck was great and the benefits were terrific, but Nathan's a country boy. He couldn't bear being cooped up all day, every day."

"Is that why he got the linesman job with the electric company?"

"Right. And it was exactly what we both needed, but for different reasons. He was thrilled to be back in the great outdoors, and I was spared some of the confrontations about our lack of a sex life."

"Did you go back to work?"

"I liked being a stay-at-home mom, but my brain was turning into cold oatmeal, so I looked for jobs I could do from home. I lucked up on some freelance gigs at various community newspapers around Atlanta. That was the best of both worlds. I could raise my kid, but I didn't have to let my cranium rust shut."

"Are you still writing for the newspapers?"

"No. I was doing some research for a story one day, and I met a man who publishes a bunch of regional magazines, including one exclusively about Georgia. I wrote a couple of pieces for him, and about a year later, he offered me a full-time position."

"You write for *Georgia Life?*"

"Yup, all the fascinating stuff from peanut crops to golf courses. I am your resident expert on Georgia political races, changing demographics in the state, and why our education system stinks. And I do it all from the comfort of my computer in my office right down the hall." She pointed toward the rear of the house. "Part-time mom, full-time writer, erstwhile lesbian-in-training." Mary checked the clock on the DVD. "But enough about me. You need an ice pack and a pill, and then I want to hear about the VanStantvoordts."

Mary went to the kitchen and filled an ice bag, grabbed Ellis's pills and a bottle of water, and then hurried back to the living room. "Okay, now it's your turn. Spill it." She handed Ellis the supplies.

"For starters, I don't think our fathers could possibly be any more different from one another. I don't think I ever saw my father smile, let alone heard him crack a joke. He was a professor of art history at Armstrong Atlantic State University in Savannah. I'm pretty sure the fact that I share my birth date with Paul Gauguin— June seventh—was what he liked best about me."

"Oh, come on. It couldn't have been that bad."

"I came along in 1969. He was already fifty-two when I was born, so I don't think my arrival was exactly good news in his life."

"Was your mom that old, too?"

"No, she was forty-one, but she wasn't in good health. I don't remember a time when she wasn't sick. When I think back on my childhood, all I picture is darkened rooms and hushed voices and everybody acting like something awful was about to happen."

"Are your parents still alive?"

"My mom died the summer after I graduated from high school. My dad told her it was too cold for her to sit outdoors at my commencement ceremony, but she went anyway. She got pneumonia. It was pretty awful."

"I'm really sorry, Ellis." Mary hugged herself as she spoke. "Losing a parent is so hard. I don't care if it is the natural order of things. We need better users' manuals for how to get through it. What about your dad?"

"He died in 2002, just a month short of his eighty-fifth birthday. He lived by himself right up to the end, still in the house I grew up in down in Savannah. And I guess I should confess, I hadn't been there since Christmas 1999."

"How come?"

"I always felt like an afterthought in his life. His only passion was for paintings by Rembrandt, Jan Steen, and Vermeer. When I still lived there, we often went for days on end with nothing more than cursory greetings as we passed each other at the breakfast table. Sometimes, he took me with him when he went to museums, but I think it was to make sure I wasn't tiring my mother rather than so he and I could have time together. He'd lose himself in the artwork, and I'd make up games in my head to pass the time."

"Were you an only child?"

"No, I've got a brother, Nicolas, and a sister, Anika. They're twins, thirteen years older than me. By the time I started grade school, they were grown and gone."

"Do you see them much?"

Ellis shook her head. "Almost never. We don't even write to each other. The last I knew, my brother was working for the Smithsonian Institution in Washington, D.C., and my sister and her husband were in Richmond, Virginia." She eyed Mary and spoke more slowly. "Dedrick and Helen, Nicolas and Anika. Those were the real VanStandvoordts. I was just a footnote to the family history."

"Kids never believe they were important to their parents in the ways they wanted to be. Just ask Natalie. And as you've heard, the Moss tribe isn't exactly the great American family, either. Maybe we'd better move on to another topic before we need to take a break and seek emergency psychotherapy." Mary grinned maniacally. "Did you go to college?"

"I had two goals. One was staying out of museums, and the other was never listening to another droning description about the allegorical view of nature as represented by everyday objects in centuries-old works of art. I went to UGA and got a degree in Agricultural and Environmental Sciences."

Twilight settled over the room. Mary switched on a couple of table lamps.

"So that explains your landscaping business."

"I guess. I'd shovel manure out of horse barns before I'd lock myself away behind a desk every day."

"You and Nathan both. Hmmm. I see a pattern in people I'm drawn to."

"What else should I know about him?"

"He's a good man… a good dad. I consider him to be my very best friend. I'd honestly be lost without him. When Natalie was two, he had a serious health scare. He had horrible pain in his testicles. I told him it was probably nothing more than three years' worth of sperm staging a riot and demanding to be turned loose."

"Did he have cancer?"

"We went from doctor to doctor trying to find out."

"Not fun, I'm sure."

"Not fun in the least. One urologist suggested that, in case it turned out to be testicular cancer, we should bank some of Nathan's sperm so we could have more kids. The treatments almost always cause sterility."

"Did you follow his advice?"

"We found a place in Atlanta that guaranteed they could keep the little swimmers alive for at least twelve years. Nathan did his part, and they bottled 'em up, but we restricted access to only the two of us."

"So it was cancer?"

"No, his real problem was referred pain from kidney stones. Once the stones were dissolved, his testicles stopped hurting."

"And your account at the sperm bank?"

"Still there, as far as I know, with Nathan's wigglers in suspended animation, hoping for the chance to prove their motility."

Sam lifted her head and woofed twice, the first sign of life she'd offered since claiming her snooze spot right after Natalie left with Nathan.

"Any chance you'd give my dog a potty break?" Ellis asked.

"Sure." Mary leaned down and patted Sam's rump. "I'll put her out back and then make a trip to the bathroom to have a potty break of my own."

"I'll use the hall bath and take a turn, too."

While Mary and Sam headed for the kitchen, Ellis made her way to the bathroom. She'd discovered how to stand on one crutch while pulling down her sweatpants and underwear with her free hand. She gripped the edge of the vanity and lowered herself onto the seat, reflecting on the long chat she and Mary had just shared.

Not much common ground, but I like her. We could maybe make this work. She caught sight of Natalie's pajamas hanging on the back of the bathroom door. *I wonder if Nathan has a girlfriend. And I wonder how she'd feel about raising a stepdaughter.*

Chapter 4

Around seven p.m., Mary excused herself to check her e-mails. Ellis used the time to watch *60 Minutes*. When she finished on the computer, Mary roamed around the living room picking up odds and ends Natalie had left there.

"Even though I love that Nathan and Natalie get along so well, and even though I always feel like it's the start of a vacation when he pulls out of the driveway with her, when it gets to this time of day, I miss my baby and wish she were here with me." Mary lifted the sweatshirt she'd just claimed from atop the bookcase and held it to her nose. "Yep, that's my girl. If I go blind, I'll still always know if it's really Natalie standing beside me." Mary tossed the sweatshirt over her shoulder. "Unless I lose my sense of smell, too."

"What makes this time of day so special?" Ellis asked from her seldom-changed, fully-reclined location on the sofa. Sam sat on the floor, her head resting on Ellis's shoulder.

"This is when I start getting her ready for bedtime. House rule is that Nat's in bed by nine, though it's anybody's guess when she'll actually stop talking and settle down to sleep. If I start around seven-thirty, by the time she's bathed, changed, and out of arguments, I can get her there by nine." Mary tried to decipher the look on Ellis's face. "You must think I'm some kind of nut case."

"Not at all. I don't pretend to understand what it feels like to have a child." She gave Sam's head a generous rub. "I know how warm and fuzzy it makes me feel when ol' Sam here acts like I'm the best thing in her life. That's probably as close as I'll ever get to knowing what a mother feels."

"You never wanted kids?" Mary asked. "The two-legged kind, I mean." She paused in her collection process long enough to give Sam a quick scratch behind her ears. "No disrespect intended, Sam."

Mary anticipated a quick answer and was surprised when Ellis seemed to contemplate her response. "Not of my own, no."

Mary dropped the armload of miscellany she'd rounded up onto the ottoman. "Did you want someone else's kids?"

Once again, Ellis seemed to take a long time to answer. "No, I wouldn't say that, either."

Mary sat down in the glider, the chair she'd spent most of the afternoon and early evening in as she and Ellis compared notes on their lives. "Then what would you say?" Mary was greeted with yet another uncomfortably elongated lull in the conversation.

"I'm afraid anything I say will come out all wrong." Ellis used her good foot to push against the far end of the sofa and sit up a little straighter. "We've had a good day together, and I don't want to ruin it."

"We talked about everything from our families to religion to sperm banks, and we got along fabulously well. Why would talking about kids ruin things?"

"It wouldn't. It's just that—"

The ringing of the portable phone on the end table interrupted Ellis's thought.

Mary checked the clock. "Twenty minutes to eight. That'll be Natalie. Nathan has probably told her it's time to start getting ready for bed, and calling me is one of her typical delay maneuvers." Mary lifted the phone. She said to Ellis, "I'll only be a minute or two," and pushed the talk button. She pointed to her chest and then to the hallway. She mouthed the word, "bedroom," then held her index finger across her lips and pointed to the TV.

Ellis nodded. She heard Mary's side of the conversation as she left the room. "Hi, honey. How was the movie? What did you eat for dinner tonight?" Sam jumped up from her place by the sofa and followed Mary.

Ellis fixed her eyes on the television screen. Maybe she could pick up the thread of the story Leslie Stahl was reporting, or at least get a chuckle out of Andy Rooney's witticisms.

And maybe she'd run for president or form a rock band or win a Nobel Prize in physics. She hit the "off" button on the remote control. The memories of one of her last conversations with her ex-lover, Becky Blumfeld, washed over her like the surge from behind a burst dam.

* * *

She and Becky had stood in the entryway to their jointly-owned house in the Candler Park neighborhood in east Atlanta. They'd been together almost ten years—ten great years, in Ellis's estimation. Ten great years minus one essential ingredient by Becky's reckoning.

"You know I don't want to lose you, Becky." Ellis fought the tangle of emotions inside her. Losing Becky would be worse than death. The argument had grown old from hundreds of repetitions, but the prospect of life without Becky made Ellis hope their differences could be resolved.

"I don't want to lose you, either, Ellis, but I told you right from the start that I wanted to have a family."

"We *are* a family. You, me, two cats, a dog. We live in a nice house. We're both doing jobs we love. We've got a few bucks in the bank. Your parents like me. My brother and sister ignore us—which is just fine." Ellis lifted Becky's chin with her fingertips. "What's wrong with the life we've got?"

"What we have is fine. But there's a huge missing piece, and without it, I'll never feel complete."

"You're stuck in a fairy-tale world." Ellis spun away and waved her hands in the air in exasperation. "Having a baby would complicate everything."

"I agree. It would affect every detail of our lives, but I see it as a blessing, not a complication. Yes, babies change everything, but in a good way."

"What's good about not being able to sleep late on the weekends or to take off and run to the beach for a couple of days? What's good about needing a babysitter every time we want to see a movie or go for a bike ride? Hell, we couldn't even make love when we wanted to if we had to worry about a baby's schedule." Ellis stomped a few paces away, then returned to Becky, who started to cry. Ellis reached out to hold her, but Becky pushed her hands away.

"Don't, Ellis. We've had this argument for years. You won't change your mind, and I can't change mine." Becky cried harder. "If you won't agree to let me be inseminated, then we just can't stay together."

Ellis tipped her head back and forced herself to wait before speaking. She lowered her head and looked Becky in the eye. "It's not like taking a wild notion to get a horse or raise sheep. A kid is forever. You can't take it back to the store if it turns out to be more work than you expected or if it gets sick a lot and costs piles of money."

"I know that. And no amount of money can replace what it would feel like to hold my own child in my arms and feel its heart beating against my chest. No movie or bicycle ride or walk by the ocean could ever be as entertaining as hearing my child call me 'Mom' and watching her take her first steps." Becky sucked in a shaky breath. "I was a hell of a lot of work for my parents, and I cost them a mountain of money, but I remember the look on my dad's face when I got my MBA at Emory. My mother has scrapbooks full of my report cards and track ribbons and programs from my piano recitals." Becky clenched her fists and glowered at Ellis. "I want my chance to be proud of my son or daughter. And I don't care if he's a C-student, finishes last in every race he ever runs, and can't pick out *Twinkle Twinkle* after six years of lessons."

Becky suddenly stopped crying and fixed a withering gaze on Ellis. "When we had our commitment ceremony, you promised to always believe in the future."

"And I meant it."

"What could be a bigger belief in the future than having a child?" Sparks fairly flew from Becky's eyes.

Ellis couldn't meet her gaze. She stared at the floor and spoke softly. "It was so different for me. My childhood was nothing like yours." She knew what was coming next, and even uttered the words with Becky as she said them.

"We're not your parents…"

Becky exploded. She thumped her fists on Ellis's chest. "Damn you, Ellis. Damn you to hell and beyond. You win. I'll spare you the horrible inconvenience of having a child. You can fatten up your bank account and keep your schedule free and clear for whatever spur-of-the-moment adventure might beckon. Take your precious freedom and get the hell out of my life. I won't tie you down with something so wretchedly confining as a child who'd have the unmitigated gall to think of you as a parent."

Ellis stood in stunned silence. Becky seemed to sink into herself. Her voice broke as she said, "I love you, Ellis. I've loved you as best I know how. The worst part is I know I'll love you for the rest of my life, but I can't do this anymore." She smiled, but it was without warmth or light. "I'm thirty-five, and I'm not willing to wait any longer to accomplish the one thing that I've known for thirty years I need to do."

Becky picked up an overnight bag and opened the door. "I'll be at my mom's. We'll talk in a couple of days. Be thinking about what we should do with the house and which of us should take the animals."

"Becky, please…"

Becky paused on the threshold. "It's no use, babe. The one thing that you could do to make me change my mind isn't even a possibility. If it had been, I know you'd have done it years ago."

With that, Becky was gone, and Ellis was left with what she thought she wanted, but somehow, freedom didn't feel at all like it ought to.

* * *

And now, here she was cheerfully established on the couch of a woman with a child, and she still had no reason to believe that being a parent was all that fulfilling. What she'd seen of Natalie only underscored what she'd envisioned: a lot of thankless work for a demanding, unreasonable, small person who gave back precious little for all the money and energy expended on her.

Mary returned to the living room, portable phone in hand. Ellis said, "So, motherhood duties completed for another day?"

"In your dreams. I had to promise to call her at five minutes to nine to say good night." Mary put the phone in its place. "You're due for one more round of ice and a pain pill. Do you want something to eat first?"

"No, in fact, I think I might skip the pain pill. I haven't had one since right before Nathan and Natalie left, and I'm doing fine. If I can, I'd like to get by without it. I probably should take the anti-inflammatory, though."

Mary took a step toward the kitchen.

"I've gotten good at getting around on my stick legs, you know." Ellis hefted one of her crutches. "I could get it myself."

"You could, but I'm going to grab a beer and some pretzel sticks anyway, so I might as well bring it to you."

"Any chance you've got two beers out there?"

"Yeah, I do, but I don't think you should have any alcohol until you've been off the Darvocet for twenty-four hours."

"What was it Nathan said about you being an overprotective mother?"

"Thank goodness Natalie was out of the room when he brought it up. She'd have gone on for an hour about what a pain in the ass I am."

Mary went to the kitchen and came back with a Coke for Ellis, a beer for herself, a bag of pretzels, and Ellis's pill. Ellis pulled the ottoman near enough that she could sit with her foot resting on it. Mary sat at the other end of the sofa.

"Don't let me forget to call Natalie, okay? As much as I ride her about remembering to keep her promises, the very last thing I need to do is give her ammunition by forgetting my own." Mary took a long drink from her bottle of Budweiser. "I'm so glad the beer truck that rolled yesterday wasn't the only one in town." She set the bottle on the end table and grabbed the pretzel bag. "Maybe Natalie wouldn't be such a nitnoy if she weren't an only child. She's so accustomed to being the absolute center of attention. It was bad enough when Nathan and I were still together, but we both made the classic mistake of trying to overcompensate after we divorced. She can be a total tyrant."

"Did you and Nathan want more kids?"

"Absolutely. And if I hadn't had to have intercourse to get them, we'd probably have had three or four." Mary passed the pretzels to Ellis. "And if that had happened, we wouldn't have split up, and you and I wouldn't be sharing this delicious bag of white flour and salt."

Ellis pulled a handful of sticks from the bag. "You make them sound so appetizing."

"It's a gift. Comes from all my years of working with words."

"Tell me more about the magazine you work for."

The hour flew by as Ellis and Mary picked up from where they'd left off in their earlier conversation of that afternoon. At eight-fifty-eight, Mary called Natalie, as promised, and then had to make a new promise to call again before Nathan took her to school the next morning.

Mary wiped her brow in mock exhaustion. "Now I think my motherhood duties are finally complete—for today, anyway."

Ellis nearly melted into a puddle from the seductive look Mary cast her way.

"My daughter is with my ex-husband. My cat and your dog are once again asleep on Natalie's bed." Mary peered around the room, then completed her thought. "It would appear that we're alone."

"Is that a good thing or a bad thing?" Ellis inched over as far toward Mary as she could get and still keep her right leg on the footstool.

"I'm inclined to say good, but remember, I'm new at this."

Ellis shoved the pretzel bag out of the way and left her hand palm up on the sofa cushion. Mary reached over and slid her palm over Ellis's, just barely making contact.

"Mmm. Nice." Ellis leaned her head against the back of the sofa. "Last night you were a soup tease, tonight you're a hand-hold tease."

"You're not exactly lily-white in that regard, you know." Mary laced her fingers with Ellis's.

"What do you mean?"

"Seems to me you owe me some information about a major character flaw and an explanation about someone named Becky."

Without thinking, Ellis yanked her hand free.

"How do you know about Becky?" she blurted.

Mary seemed taken aback. "The same way I knew about Sam. You mentioned them both when you were talking in your sleep yesterday on our way here after getting your ankle checked." Mary stretched and reclaimed Ellis's hand. "I guess calling that a character flaw was a little strong."

Ellis knew her laugh sounded tinny and nervous, but she couldn't manage one less forced. "Oh that. Yeah, I can be a real orator, when I'm not a snore-ator." Her palm felt moist, and she hoped Mary didn't notice. "Darn good thing I'm a sleep talker and not a sleepwalker. That could cause all sorts of trouble with my cast and crutches."

"If you don't want to tell me about Becky, you don't have to."

"Not much to tell." Another forced, fake laugh. "We used to be a couple, but now we're not."

"What went wrong?"

"Nothing. Everything." Ellis used her free hand to graze the back of Mary's hand with her knuckles. "We just had different goals for our lives. We figured out it was better if we each went our own way."

"Do you still keep in touch with her?" Ellis felt the tension in Mary's question.

"We don't have much in common these days. We don't go out of our way to avoid each other, but we don't talk on the phone every week, either."

"So she's in Atlanta?"

"Yep. Candler Park."

"What kind of work does she do?"

"She's the office administrator for a nonprofit research group."

"A real brain, huh?" Mary lifted their hands off the sofa, then let them plop back onto the cushion.

"That's a strange comment."

"Not when you realize I consider myself the dumbest woman on the planet."

"Get in line behind me."

"Oh, right, Little Miss Agricultural and Environmental Sciences. I bet there were plenty of biology and chemistry classes involved in getting that degree."

"So? What have I done with them? I mow lawns in the summer and eat mac and cheese all winter, wondering if the bank account will stretch far enough to get me back to the busy season so I can buy a hamburger once in a while, and then for a splurge, have fries and a Dairy Queen treat."

Mary furrowed her forehead. "It can't be all that bad. You've got a nice truck, and your apartment isn't exactly a dump. I've been there, remember?"

"The truck was part of the deal I made with Becky. We'd each gotten a new vehicle shortly before we split up. She kept the house and paid off my truck loan to pay me back for what I'd put into the mortgage there."

"How long had you two been together?"

"About ten years."

"And all you got out of that was your pickup truck?"

"No, she agreed to pay off whatever was on the credit cards we had, and I got a promissory note, too."

"Not that it's any of my business, but has she paid on the note?"

"I haven't asked her to."

"Why not?"

"I wanted to see if I could make it on my own."

"Can you?"

"Too soon to say. We've only been apart for a little more than a year."

Mary looked at Ellis out of the corner of her eye. "Have you dated anyone since you and Becky broke up?"

"Just one, but it's serious." Ellis gave Mary's hand a quick squeeze. "You've met her. Black, curly hair. Sweet brown eyes. Good kisser. Loves puppy cookies, squirrels, and nine-year-olds named Natalie."

"Sam, the bed hog?"

"That'd be the one. She's the only girl I've dated since Becky kicked me to the curb."

"At least Sam seems loyal and devoted."

"True enough."

"Despite her loyalty, I bet she's grateful she has a night's reprieve from my holy terror."

"Or she's pining away for her new best friend."

"Either way, she seems to have decided she likes it here."

"Can't say as though I blame her." Ellis sidled a bit nearer to Mary. "I could get used to it myself."

Mary released Ellis's hand and eased close enough to drape her arm around Ellis's shoulder. "Good. That's saves me the trouble of trying to convince you to move in."

Ellis stiffened.

"While your ankle heals, I mean," Mary said. "I didn't want to have to argue with you about you and Sam staying for the next few weeks 'til you're off the crutches and out of the cast. It was my fault you got hurt, after all."

"Your fault?"

"Uh-huh. You fell for me, so the least I can do is help you get back on your feet."

Chapter 5

"How can Christmas be less than a week away?" Mary poured ketchup on Natalie's hamburger and passed the plate to her. "Seems like the last thing I knew, it was the Saturday after Thanksgiving, and I was on my way to a book discussion at Charis Books."

Natalie ignored her lunch and instead continued her inspection of her Christmas gift from Ellis.

"This is so cool. I love it!" Natalie used her new, kid-version digital camera to snap three more pictures of the dog and cat sleeping in the sunny spot on the living room floor. "Sam and Swiffer look like they've been together forever." She held the camera so Ellis could see the image in the camera's playback viewer. "This is a great present."

"I'm glad you like it, toots." Ellis accepted Natalie's hug. "After you and your mom get back from visiting your relatives, I'll show you how to organize the pictures on your computer, but now, you'd better sit down and eat before your hamburger gets cold."

"Okay." Natalie paged back through the two dozen shots on the camera. "I wish you and Sam were coming with us."

"We've talked about that, Nat," Mary said as she sat at the table. "You know how Gramma Anna and Aunt Gloria and Aunt Naomi are about having strangers around for Christmas."

"They let Daddy come."

"That's different. Daddy's family."

"But Ellis is family. So is Sam. They've been with us lots more than Daddy lately." Natalie perched on the edge of her chair. "And Ellis sleeps in your room every night. You're gonna miss her while we're at Gramma Anna's."

Ellis didn't dare look at Mary. It had been three weeks and six days (not that she was counting) since Mary had brought Ellis and Sam to the house on Wilson Woods Drive. She had shared Mary's bed every night. Although she'd been surprised when Mary insisted on sleeping with her in case she needed help on her first night there, she was beyond delighted when Mary continued the practice on subsequent nights, even though it was apparent Ellis could readily get around on her crutches. They'd shared dozens—no, make that hundreds—of delicious kisses and some tantalizingly inviting touches, but that was as far as it had gone. They had talked at great length about their feelings for one another, but between Ellis's painful ankle (and her barely admitted hesitancy over becoming involved with a woman with a child) and Mary's shyness and lingering Baptist-induced horror over fulfilling her lifelong urges, frustration and inertia had thus far won out over desires and hormones.

Now, here it was the Friday before Christmas, and the next day, Mary and Natalie would be driving up to the foothills of the north Georgia mountains to spend the holiday with Mary's mother, sisters, brothers-in-law, nieces, nephews, and other assorted relatives. Nathan would be going up to his parents' house—just down the road from Mary's mother's house—in his own car on Saturday, too, and he and Mary had agreed to specific periods of time when Natalie would be with the Kimbrough family during the coming week.

Ellis would stay in the city, probably at Mary's house, so that Sam could use the yard, thus sparing Ellis the strain of walking her. Ellis's ankle was certainly much improved, but being able to let Sam roam in a fenced yard was far better than Ellis limping up and down stairs at her apartment building and trying to keep Sam on a leash. Besides, that way she could take care of Swiffer without having to drive between her apartment and Mary's house a couple of times a day.

Since Mary and Natalie would be away, it didn't make sense to put up a Christmas tree, so they'd moved the coatrack that usually stood in the front entryway to a spot in front of the picture window in the living room. For a face, atop the coat rack, they'd secured a round tin serving plate bearing one of the classic Coca-Cola Santas grinning cherubically. Ellis had rigged a small spotlight that illuminated their skinny Santa from the floor up, making the scrawny figure look even more bony and garish. When they were done decorating it, it looked suspiciously like an anorexic Saint Nick with homosexual tendencies, given the number of rainbow-themed items affixed to the threadbare Santa suit bagging off the spindly post. Natalie had dubbed him "Jolly Old Saint Stickalus," and the three of them spent time over the past week adding more adornments to the hopelessly overdone substitute for a tree.

Mary, Ellis, and Natalie had just shared their version of Christmas Eve, albeit in the middle of the day on December twenty-second. Ellis gave Natalie the digital camera, her first, which she mastered in far less time than it had taken Ellis to read the instruction booklet. Ellis gave Mary a gold ankle bracelet with a polished turquoise heart interwoven in the strand. Mary's gift to Ellis was a custom-made key chain with a clear Lucite fob containing a picture of Natalie, Sam, and Swiffer bundled together, sound asleep on Natalie's bed. Keys to Mary's house were attached to the chain.

Ellis refused to admit to herself how accurate Natalie's observation about her missing Mary was. No, she and Mary weren't exactly lovers, but the thought of spending the next many nights apart felt like being exiled to a distant galaxy. Being in Mary's house—Mary's bed—without her would make it even worse. She and Mary hadn't discussed the impending week's separation, other than to say they didn't want to talk about it.

Of course, they hadn't decided how much longer Ellis would stay at Mary's house, either. They had considered what they should say to Natalie about their relationship, which seemed to be a nonissue to the nine-year-old, and a good thing, too, since they weren't at all confident they could describe for Natalie (or anyone else) exactly what their relationship was. They'd pondered what they needed to tell Nathan—again something of a mystery. Telling him they slept in the same bed and kissed a lot didn't really seem like a definitive explanation.

"Did you even ask Gramma Anna if Ellis could come with us?"

Sam trotted into the kitchen. Natalie dropped to one knee and folded Sam's ears on top of her head, giving her a canine version of the original Aunt Jemima look.

"No," Mary said, "and I've warned you about going on and on about Ellis to Gramma."

"I'll have to tell Gramma where I got my new camera." Natalie picked it up from the sofa and swung it by its carrying string. "You always tell me not to lie."

"There's a difference between truthfully answering a question that's asked of you, and telling everybody everything you know just because you like the sound of your own voice."

"'Tis the season to be jolly," Natalie sang, "Fa la la la la, la la la la. Who wouldn't want to hear me?"

"Why don't you go to your room and make sure you've picked out the seven outfits you want to take to Gramma's? I don't want to have to discuss that with you tomorrow morning when it comes time to put them in your suitcase. And you can sing your heart out the whole time if you want to."

"Okay." Natalie headed for the hallway. "Can Sam come, too?"

"Sure," Ellis said.

Girl and dog, with the added bonus of a cat, vanished from the room. In a moment, Ellis and Mary heard the muffled sounds of Natalie singing.

"I guess you're a little worried about what she'll tell your mother," Ellis said.

"Rest assured, what little information Natalie doesn't volunteer, my mother will pump out of her."

"Does your mother know about your—uh—shall we say—inclinations?"

"The lesbian thing? Oh, please. My mother is on a daily crusade for me to reconcile with Nathan. I think it's the number one entry on her many prayer chains."

"So Natalie telling her that I've been sleeping with you for the past month isn't going to be cause for celebration."

"Good thing Baptists don't do exorcisms, otherwise I know what I'd have in my stocking Christmas morning."

"Or as your birthday present."

"No danger of that. I decreed years ago that we'd observe my birthday on June twenty-fifth. No way was I going to get short-changed every year just because I was born on Jesus's birthday."

"That was clever of you."

"I thought so, but I wish I was smart enough to figure out a way to make my mother understand that my sleeping with you isn't cause for her to call out the religious militia."

"Is it poor form for me to point out that we really haven't done anything?" Ellis asked.

Mary's voice quivered as she spoke. "Is it poor form for me to point out that what I feel when I'm lying in bed with you, even though we're doing absolutely nothing, is the most exciting thing I've ever done?"

"Yeah?" Ellis inched her chair a little closer.

"Oh, yeah."

Gawd. To Ellis, Mary's voice was like velvet brushing on satin. Ellis felt a hitch in her heartbeat. She savored the anticipation of Mary's lips on hers.

"Mom!" The shout from down the hall froze them both. "Where's my pink Bratz shirt? The one with the fuzzy stuff on Yasmin's skirt."

"Sorry, love," Mary said to Ellis. "Fashion emergency. I'll be back as fast as I can. Hold that thought." She plopped a quick kiss on Ellis's lips. "Where did you leave it, Nat?" Mary called as she departed. "It's not my job to keep track of your clothes."

* * *

Their good-bye on Saturday morning was drawn out and difficult. Mary's Xterra, long since repaired after it was rear-ended following Ellis's fall a month earlier, was loaded to capacity with clothes for Mary and Natalie and gifts for all of Natalie's cousins, aunts and uncles, grandparents, and for her Gramma Anna's cat.

"You'll call me when you get there, right?" Ellis asked for the fifth time as she leaned on the driver's door.

"Yes, I'll call you. I'll call you from the parking lot at the gas station just before the last turn to my mother's house. I won't be able to talk long, but at least you'll know we're less than half a mile from our destination."

"I'll miss you, Mar."

"I'll miss you more, El."

"Guess I'd better not kiss you out here on the street."

"Probably not. Never know when the neighbors are going to have their binoculars trained on my driveway."

"Wish I could."

"Wish so, too." Mary started the engine. "Thanks for taking care of Swiffer."

"Thanks for letting me hang out here with Sam while you're gone."

"Promise you'll be here when we get back."

"I promise. I'll be counting the minutes."

Mary grabbed the gear shift. "We'd better roll. If I'm not there within ten minutes of when I said I'd be, Mother will have the Highway Patrol out looking for us."

"Be safe, okay?"

"Not to worry. My little copilot over there"—Mary pointed her thumb at Natalie in the passenger seat—"will alert me to every conceivable road hazard."

Ellis leaned farther into the cab. "You take good care of your mom for me, okay, Natalie?"

"Got a quarter?" Natalie said, grinning.

"If you do it right, I'll give you a dollar."

Natalie held out her hand. "That's a deal. Pay me."

"Not until you bring her back safe and sound."

"Meanie."

"Just a smart businesswoman."

Natalie stretched across the console and her mother's torso, her hand still held out.

Ellis slapped her palm against Natalie's. "Have fun." She eased back and rested her forearms on the open window.

"I will. I hope Gramma Anna got me what I asked for."

Mary said, "Nat—"

"I know, I know. Christmas isn't about presents." Natalie fussed with readjusting her seatbelt and crossed her arms across her chest. "But I still hope she got what I told her I wanted."

"Really, we've got to go."

Ellis backed away from the car, and Mary shifted into reverse.

Ellis waved as Mary maneuvered down the short driveway. "Merry Christmas, MaryChris Moss." Ellis fought the lump in her throat as she spoke.

"Merry Christmas, Gretchen," Mary called out the car window. She hesitated. "I love you."

In all their many conversations, Ellis had never heard those words from Mary before. The SUV was on the street and pulling away before they registered with her, too late for her to say them back.

* * *

"How's everything going up there?" Ellis pressed the phone tight against her ear, hoping it would make her feel like Mary wasn't a hundred miles away.

"No wonder the suicide rate jumps during the holidays. Whoever said this is the most wonderful time of the year never spent the weekend before Christmas incarcerated at Anna Moss's house."

"How'd you get out?"

"Mother needed more pecans and cranberries for her special Christmas morning bread, and I raced out the door to get them before anyone else could beat me to it. I've just spent almost an hour in line at the Ingles Market to procure one of the last bags of cranberries in town."

"Poor baby. Sounds like hard time on the rock."

"Don't mess with me, VanStantvoordt. I know where you live and where you're staying. I can hurt you—and your dog, too."

"You really are in a bad mood."

"Merry freakin' Christmas."

"Want to tell me about it?"

"Yes, but I don't have time to right now."

"Can I get a preview, at least?"

"My big-mouthed daughter, aided and abetted by my well-intentioned but clueless ex-husband, has given my mother enough ammunition to do her version of the assault on the Alamo."

"And your role?"

"Davy Crockett, but instead of a coonskin cap, mine's made of live skunk, and instead of Betsy the trusted musket, I've got a Betsy-Wetsie doll."

"Sounds awful."

"It is, and there's still five more days to go before I can tunnel out and make my escape to freedom."

"How can I help?"

"Will you hold me when I get home?"

The wave of desire that welled in Ellis caught her off-guard. "You know I will."

"Then I'll keep that image in my mind and sneak some fortified eggnog over the next few days and do everything I can to avoid being trapped alone with my mother."

"I'm sorry if I've complicated your life, Mary."

"Don't you ever say that to me again. I mean it."

Ellis thought she detected tears in Mary's words. "Okay, I just meant—"

"I know what you meant, but you need to get clear on something right now. These three days away from you have showed me how much I want to be with you. I know I haven't done any of the things a real lover should do, but when I get back to Atlanta, I'm going to fix that."

Ellis nearly jammed the phone inside her ear canal. The spontaneous burst of warmth in her pelvic region made her weak in the knees.

"You'll help me learn how, won't you El?"

"Yes, sweetheart. We'll take as long as you need. I'll do whatever you need me to do."

"Right now I need you to let me get off this phone and slide back into the flames of hell, but when I get home on Saturday—"

"Come home Friday, Mary. Better yet, come home now."

"I wish I could, but I've got to do Christmas at Mother's tomorrow and then Nat goes with Nathan for two days at his parents'."

"So you come home tomorrow and let Nathan bring her back with him."

"It's not that simple. Nathan's not coming back to Atlanta right away. He says he's got things he needs to do up here, but I haven't a clue what that means. Besides, my mother would never understand why I'd rather be in Atlanta than here with her."

"Oh." The word hung like an icicle.

"I'm sorry, Ellis. Christmas is a super big deal to my mother. It won't always be like this. I swear."

"Okay. I was just wishing out loud."

"I can't wait to make your wishes come true."

Again, Ellis had to will herself to stay standing, and it had nothing to do with her old ankle injury.

"You still there, El?"

"Yes, but I'd rather be with you."

"Me, too. Soon, babe."

"Not soon enough."

"I gotta go. I probably won't be able to call you again until Wednesday."

"I understand. I hate it, but I understand."

"Thanks. I almost forgot to ask, is everything okay with Sam and Swiffer and your foot?"

"If you don't count missing you, the three of us are fine."

"Good." Mary sighed loudly. "Ellis, I—"

"Let me say it first this time. I love you, Mary. Come home."

"Love you, too. I'll be there as soon as I can. Bye for now."

Ellis cradled the phone against her chest and let Mary's words echo in her heart. At last she had her own MaryChris Moss miracle, and just in time for a Merry Christmas, too.

*   *   *

Ensconced on the sofa, Ellis read another of Mary's articles in the back issues of *Georgia Life* magazine. She'd come across a stack of them next to Mary's computer in the third bedroom and decided it was a perfect way to learn more about the woman she'd fallen in love with. It was only December twenty-sixth, so she still had three days to fill before Mary and Natalie's return from Clarkesville.

Ellis found Mary's writing style to be the perfect blend of crisp exposition and evocative metaphor. Even her articles about yawn-worthy topics like what peanut farmers do with the shells from their legumes proved to be entertaining as well as informative. (Kitty litter, wallboard, animal feed, paper, and fireplace logs. Who knew?)

Ellis set the magazine aside and glanced toward the picture window. Jolly Old Saint Stickalus still stood there in all his outlandish glory.

Christmas.

As best she could tell, it was more a marketing ploy than a holiday. Even when she was a child, her mother's infirmity meant that celebrations were low-key, almost nonexistent. Nicolas and Anika, her brother and sister who were more like strangers than family, were so much older than she, that she had no memories of her family gathered around a tree, anticipating an exuberant opening of gifts or of joyful dinners with friends and family. Then there were her college years—the years immediately following her mother's death—years when she stayed away from Savannah because it was easier to be alone than to face the unspoken accusation that she was responsible for her mother's demise. Ellis had, after all, pleaded with her mother to attend the high school's outdoor graduation ceremony. Nicolas and Anika never said so in as many words, but she knew they blamed her, and not only for their mother's early grave, but also for the even more pronounced reclusiveness of their father following her passing.

Maybe her family history was part of what made hooking up with Becky Blumfeld so appealing. Casting her lot in with a nonpracticing Jew alleviated the need to mess with all the typical Christmas trappings. And since she felt no warmth from (or for) her father and her siblings, all the better to steer clear of them altogether and not subject herself to the endless questions she had about why there was such a void between them.

The last time Ellis had seen Nicolas and Anika had been at their father's funeral, four years earlier. Neither her brother nor her sister had sent so much as a postcard in the intervening four years. Then again, she hadn't kept the postal service hopping with correspondence to them, either.

So what?

When she and Becky were still together, it didn't matter that she felt like an only child. She had a home, a family, a future.

That was enough.

Enough for Ellis, but not enough for Becky.

Why hadn't Becky been able to see that adding a baby to the mix would have ruined everything? Criminy, even having a nine-year-old around was a pain. How many perfectly wonderful kisses—kisses that might have led to all the things Ellis longed to do with Mary—had Natalie interrupted?

Natalie.

Try as she might, Ellis couldn't help but miss her. Not as much as she missed Mary. Not by a damned sight. But she missed watching the way Natalie interacted with Sam and Swiffer. Missed how she'd unexpectedly throw her arms around Ellis and give her a hug. Missed the quick-witted-bordering-on-cheeky remarks she'd make to her mother. Missed the special look that passed over Mary's face whenever Mary saw Ellis and Natalie hunkered together over a book or a computer game or Natalie's homework.

Maybe Becky hadn't been totally wrong in wanting a child, but why couldn't children be a part-time proposition? Couldn't they at least come with a remote control and a mute button—or better still, a pause button?

Swiffer was in her customary spot on the back of the sofa. Sam was on the floor at Ellis's feet. Ellis gave each of them an appreciative rub. Furry kids. Now, that made sense. You could love them. They loved you back, but they never got nose rings or tattoos. They didn't date unsavory characters who rode motorcycles and wore leather vests and thought selling coffee at the local dive was the pinnacle of employment aspirations. You didn't have to save for their college or wedding fund or figure out how to pay for their auto insurance.

Ellis still hadn't found an opportunity to sound out Mary about Nathan's love life. Maybe he was on the verge of remarrying. Sure, Mary would need an adjustment period if Nathan became the primary parent and she had Natalie alternate weekends or something, but with the right incentives…

Maybe right after the second time they made love, she'd find a way to work the subject into the conversation. And if she had her way, the second time they made love would be no later than the coming weekend.

* * *

Ellis recognized the caller ID and scooped up the phone on the second ring. "Hi, sweetheart. I'd hoped to hear from you yesterday."

"Sorry. I really thought I'd get a chance to call, but what was already the Christmas from hell took a hard left at You Can't Be Serious, and I'm still recovering."

"What happened? Nobody's sick, I hope."

"Just me, and I'm only sick at heart."

"Tell me what's going on."

"I don't know where to start."

"Sounds like bad news."

"It is, and it isn't."

"C'mon, Mary. Give me a clue what this is all about."

"It looks like I'll be moving."

"Moving where?"

"Somewhere up here."

Ellis wondered when she'd climbed on a roller coaster and how it was she hadn't noticed the precipitous drop. "Clarkesville?"

"Or the near vicinity."

"Why? I thought you hated it up there."

"Sort of. I hate the way my mom and my sisters think they can run my life, but I love the quiet and the green and the mountain views."

"That still doesn't tell me why you think you're moving to north Georgia."

"Nathan's transferring to the Cleveland office of Georgia Power."

"Cleveland, Ohio?"

"No, of course not. Cleveland, Georgia. Home of the original Cabbage Patch Kids."

"I guess I didn't know Georgia had a Cleveland."

"All two thousand residents would probably just as soon no one knew it existed."

"But it does."

"Yes, it does, and yesterday afternoon Nathan sealed the deal to start working right after the first of the year in that booming metropolis as one of the linesmen for the Georgia Power Office."

"That must have been what he needed to take care of instead of coming right back to Atlanta after Christmas."

"Right. I thought he might be trying to hook up with some friends or something. I never dreamed he was lining up a job here."

"That explains why Nathan would be moving, but why do you have to pack your tent?"

"It's a complicated story."

"Try me. I'll do my best to keep up." Ellis knew she sounded defensive and cynical, but she didn't really care.

"When Nathan and I divorced, we didn't change the title on the house. It's still in both our names."

"So?"

"So, Nathan wants to sell the house and take his share of the equity to buy something up here."

"Okay, but couldn't you convince him to transfer the title to you if you bought him out? I could come up with some money to help with that. I've got the promissory note from Becky I could use."

"Oh, he'd be fine with that, but neither of us wants Natalie to be so far away from her dad. It'd kill them both if they couldn't see each other a couple times a week."

Ellis fought the urge to shout, "Let him have her all the time." She waited what she thought was the right amount of time before speaking. "Couldn't he take over custody, and you have visitation rights?"

"You're kidding, right? We've got joint custody of Natalie, and I'm not about to give up my time with her. She's my daughter."

Ellis harnessed her emotions again. "Just a thought." She listened to Mary breathing on the far end of the line. "I'm still not sure why you have to move, though."

"Nathan hates living in Atlanta. We thought it was the right thing to do when we got married because the job market is so much better there and it gave us some space from meddlesome relatives, but his whole family still lives right around Clarkesville, and now that he can have a decent job up here, he wants to come home and live in the woods."

"And as I said, that's great for Nathan, but what about you?"

"I can do my job from anywhere. My managing editor doesn't care if I'm in Atlanta or Seattle, as long as I get my stories in on time. One of the stipulations in the divorce decree says both Nathan and I will make reasonable attempts to accommodate each other's needs to have time with Natalie."

"Clarkesville is only a couple of hours from Atlanta," Ellis said.

"But to a nine-year-old, two hours is an eternity. I don't want to chase up and down the road with her three times a week, and neither does Nathan. Even doing that once a week would make us all crazy in less than a month, not to mention what it would do to our bank accounts, thanks to what gas costs now."

"Don't you like living in Atlanta?"

"God's truth—I'm totally indifferent. I like being able to go to the women's bookstore, and it's nice to have some shopping malls close by, but for the most part, I'm still a hayseed who's happier with blue jeans and barbecue than with dress clothes and sushi."

Once more, Ellis let the rancor have full play in her voice. "Sounds like it's all decided and settled."

"Nathan and I talked about this for hours yesterday. It was a big shock to me. I won't pretend it wasn't, but I've watched Natalie having the time of her life with all her cousins, and I think it's going to be good for her to be part of a bigger family. You know how spoiled Nathan and I let her get by being the center of our worlds. This will help her understand that she's only one piece of the pie, not the only sweet on the menu."

Ellis felt sick to her stomach. She swallowed repeatedly to push the bile down. She almost called Mary a liar and a fool, but caught herself before the words fell out. "I hope it all works out for you."

"You're mad, aren't you?"

"Not in the least," Ellis lied. "You need to do what's best for you and your family."

"Ellis, we need to talk about this—about us."

"What's to talk about? You were doing fine before I fell into your life. You'll do fine without me in it at all."

"So just like that, it's over?"

"How can anything be over? Nothing ever got started."

"Ellis, please…"

Ellis hung up the phone.

* * *

"Damn it, Sam, when I whistle for you, you're supposed to come." Ellis stormed down the hall of Mary's house and smacked her dog's rear end. "I don't care if you think this kid's bed is your new clubhouse, we're going home." Sam cowered momentarily at Ellis's tone but leaped off the bed and followed Ellis back to the kitchen.

"What the hell was I thinking? I threw away ten years on a woman who decided having a child was more important than having a partner, and I damn near made the same mistake a second time." She grabbed the bag of dog food from its place in one of the lower cabinets and slammed it onto the kitchen table. The force burst the bag, and kibble scattered everywhere.

"Oh, fuck. Like I needed this." Ellis hunted for a broom and dustpan. She gave up and used her hands to sweep the spilled food into piles on the floor. Sam thought it must be some new game and wandered from pile to pile, eating a few morsels from each.

"Stop it, Sam! This is hard enough without you slobbering all over everything." From her squatting position, Ellis swung at Sam's butt, but missed. She lost her balance and landed hard on the floor. Bitter tears stung the back of her eyelids. "Goddamn it to hell and back." The tears spilled down her cheeks. "I hate you, Mary Moss. I hate you and your stupid kid and your fairy-tale life. I hate that I wasted a month of my life sharing your bed like some kind of perverted nun. I hate myself for thinking I was in love with you, and I hate you for making me think we were anything more than a side trip after an accident on LaVista Road."

Ellis dragged herself over to one of the kitchen chairs and used the seat to help her stand up. Her ankle was aching fiercely, and pain shot through it as she put her weight on it.

"You were just a detour, MaryChris Moss. A damned detour that I'm sorry I took. From now on, I'm traveling light and traveling alone."

She yanked a set of keys from her pocket. It was the key chain Mary had given her a few days before. The sight of the picture of Natalie sleeping with Sam and Swiffer was nearly more than she could bear. She flung the keys on the counter, then took a step toward the door. Swiffer whisked into the kitchen from wherever she'd been napping.

The sight of the cat brought Ellis up short. "Oh fine. I suppose I have to take care of you until the Mother of the Year gets back." Ellis reclaimed the key chain with Mary's house keys on it and crammed them in her pocket. "You've got food and water to hold you 'til morning." Swiffer wrapped herself around Ellis's legs. "Don't bother. I'm done with you, and I'm done with the woman and the kid you live with. Tell them I said 'Thanks for nothing.'"

Ellis clipped Sam's leash on her collar. Without so much as a single backward glance, she let herself out of the house and, she hoped, out of the pain that threatened to obliterate her heart.

* * *

"Open the door, Ellis. I know you're in there. Your truck is in the parking lot, and I can hear Sam woofing. I'm not going away until you talk to me." Mary leaned her forehead on the door to Ellis's apartment. "C'mon, Ellis. Please."

Mary heard footfalls coming toward the door. The deadbolt thunked, and the pushbutton lock in the handle popped free. She tried the doorknob. It turned, and she pushed the door open.

"Hi," she said softly as she stepped inside. "I was really disappointed that you weren't at the house when I got there last night."

"Why? It's not like we had plans or anything." Ellis slouched into an overstuffed recliner on the far side of the room. Sam slunk behind the chair and curled up in a ball. "Pull up a chair. Make yourself homely."

Mary went to Ellis and leaned down to kiss her.

Ellis turned her head, and Mary settled for giving Ellis a peck on the cheek.

"I thought we did have plans. You promised me you'd be there when I got back, and you told me you'd hold me when I got home."

"That was when I thought I was more than just another of your charitable causes." Ellis pulled the handle for the footrest and cranked back in her chair, nearly clipping Mary's kneecaps in the process. "Sorry," she said half-heartedly.

Mary put her heel on the extended footrest and shoved it back into place, jerking Ellis into an upright position. "Look, I know you're pissed at me, and I guess I don't blame you, but if you think I'm going to let you act like a petulant child, think again."

"No, you've already got one of those. I'd be redundant."

Mary's anger flared. "Knock it off. You're thirty-seven-years old, but you're behaving like a two-year-old who didn't get her nap."

"Thanks. I appreciate the comparison."

Mary spun away and took a few steps. She stopped, calmed herself, then turned and faced Ellis. "Okay, I know now I should have waited to tell you face-to-face about Nathan's transfer and the effect it has on Nat and me. I was too upset when I talked to you on the phone to think about how it would seem to you." She gulped some air. "But I'm here now, and I want you to tell me how you feel."

"Bullshit."

"You feel like bullshit?"

"No, what you're telling me is bullshit. You don't give a flip how I feel."

"If I didn't care about how you feel, why did I come back from Clarkesville early? Why have I tried to call you forty times in the past twenty-four hours? If you didn't matter to me, would I have stood outside your door for ten minutes begging you to let me in?" Mary watched Ellis's face in the dimly lit room.

Ellis said, "I guess this is only Friday, isn't it?"

"Uh-huh. I left Natalie with my mother and drove back last night. When you weren't at my house when I got there, I got so scared that I threw up."

"What did you tell your mother?"

"About throwing up?"

"No, about why you left Clarkesville. Didn't she want to know why you had to come back to Atlanta?"

"I told her my cat sitter had been called away on an emergency, and I had to make sure Swiffer was all right."

"And your mother bought that?"

"Who cares?" Mary slapped her thighs with her palms. "I needed to see you. You didn't answer the phone at my house. You didn't answer your cell. You weren't at the house when I got there. You didn't leave a note. I knew you were upset, and I needed to find you. If I hadn't been so tired and so sick, I'd have come over here last night, but I didn't think I'd make a very good impression, tossing my guts all over your apartment."

"I'm sorry you were sick." Mary was glad to hear a hint of genuine compassion in Ellis's words.

Mary knelt at eye level in front of Ellis. "From the minute I left my driveway last Saturday morning, you are the only happy thought I've had. I missed you so much I thought I'd shrivel up and die. I kicked myself all the way to Clarkesville for turning down your offer of a kiss in front of my house because I was afraid one of the neighbors might see us. When I saw my sisters with their husbands and Nathan's brothers with their wives, all I could picture was you next to me in my bed." She rubbed Ellis's upper leg. "I know we haven't talked about you and me—long-term you and me—and I sure as hell didn't think we'd have to talk about long-distance you and me."

"Me either."

"When I found out Nathan was moving to Clarkesville and he basically said I'd better think about moving, too, my brain went numb." Mary caressed Ellis's cheek. "One of the first things that flashed in my mind was, 'Oh, God, my mother will have a stroke when I tell her I'm living with a woman.'"

"But you're not living with a woman."

"Thanks to two unfortunate spills on LaVista Road, one by the beer truck and one with you hurting your ankle, I have been living with a woman for the past month, and I can tell you sure as your name is Gretchen Alina VanStantvoordt, it's what I was born to do."

Mary couldn't decipher the look on Ellis's face. She waited, hoping some of what she was trying to say was registering with Ellis. She stood and paced.

"I'm not much of a catch, Ellis. I don't know how to make love to you, and heaven knows if I'll ever learn. I've got a child. I've got an ex-husband who's still a big part of my life because of that child. Let's not even talk about my mother, who would make Jesus Christ himself consider becoming a Hindu if it would spare him her Baptist preaching." She stopped and rubbed her face with both hands, then clasped her hands together beneath her chin. "Can't we at least talk about trying to make this work?"

Ellis left her chair and crossed the room. "C'mere." She opened her arms and Mary rushed into them. "I was afraid I'd lost you. A month ago, I didn't even know who you were, and then just when I thought we were falling in love, you tell me you're moving away." She hugged Mary hard. "I'm sorry I'm such a big baby. I'm the one who's a lousy catch."

"To quote your earlier eloquent observation, 'Bullshit.'"

Ellis released her hold on Mary and they sat down on the sofa. "Have you had anything to eat?" Ellis asked.

"I had some crackers on the drive over here. My stomach and I still aren't on very good terms. Have you eaten?"

"I grabbed a chicken biscuit on my way back from your house this morning."

"My house?"

"I thought I needed to check on Swiffer, but when I saw your Xterra in the driveway, I came on back here."

"You could have come in, you know. You've got your own keys."

"I didn't feel like I was welcome."

"Oh, Ellis," Mary said, her voice cracking, "I can't believe how screwed up everything is. That'll teach me to think I've got things figured out."

"What do you mean?"

"I was sure Natalie and I would live in our house on Wilson Woods Drive until she went to college, and then I'd stay on there until I needed a wheelchair. I figured Nathan and I would stay friends, which is all we've ever really been, and he'd find someone new, while I withered away, lonely and alone in my bed. Eventually, my assorted unused parts would atrophy and rot, and then I wouldn't care anymore." She took Ellis's hand. "I spent the last five years running scared from every woman who acted like she might be interested in me. I was sure if I ever finally found one I didn't want to run from, she'd run screaming from me when she discovered what a lunatic I am."

Ellis dropped Mary's hand and put her arm around Mary's shoulder. "But then one Saturday on your way to a book discussion group, life threw up a roadblock."

"I always thought roadblocks were bad things. Now I understand that it's all in how you look at them." Mary leaned in against Ellis's body. "Nothing like a good roadblock to make you think about whether you're heading in the right direction and if the journey you're making has the right destination."

Ellis pulled Mary closer to her. "Where are we going, Mary?"

"I don't suppose I know for sure. I just hope wherever it is, we'll go there together."

Ellis put her fingertips under Mary's chin and lifted her head. The muted light in the room gave her eyes that gray-green hue that Ellis found so alluring.

"Maybe we should make a day trip first," Ellis said as she stood and helped Mary to her feet.

"Where to?"

"The bedroom."

"Do I need to pack?"

"No. In fact, you've got too much clothing with you as it is." Ellis tugged at the light jacket Mary was wearing and helped her shrug out of it. "It's a warm climate, so this sweater needs to go, too."

Piece by piece, Ellis removed all of Mary's clothing. Then Mary did the same for Ellis.

"I've seen you almost naked dozens of times," Mary said, her voice a coarse whisper. "Why do you look so different this time?"

"Maybe because we know we're doing it for real this time," Ellis answered. "Come with me." She offered Mary her hand.

Wordlessly, they made their way to Ellis's bedroom.

Ellis wrapped Mary in a tight embrace. Skin against skin… silky feeling against her hands and breasts… quiet gasps… hot breath in her ear and the flood of heat throughout her body. She reveled in the feelings, her body on fire. She kissed Mary over and over, unable to get enough of her. And Mary was insatiable as well. They made love all afternoon, stopping only because fatigue overtook them, and then Mary curled softly against Ellis's shoulder until she slipped into quiet slumber.

Ellis held Mary against her, tenderly, unable to sleep. How could she feel so blessed and so doomed simultaneously? Her tired limbs sent a message of satisfaction while her busy brain screamed dire warnings. Could they make this work? What would happen to them if Mary moved to Clarkesville? Would it ring the death-knell for their newly formed relationship? Troubled, she lay there for what seemed like hours until she finally fell into a fitful sleep.

She awoke to find their limbs entwined, much as she felt their lives now were and forevermore must be. Whatever else awaited them on the road ahead, they'd have to find their way home together.

Chapter 6

"I can't believe I agreed to do this." Ellis fidgeted in the passenger seat. "When we dropped Sam off at your house this morning, I should have been smart and stayed there with her."

"It'll be fine," Mary assured her. "We'll swing by Mother's and collect Natalie and all her loot from Christmas and be on our way back to Atlanta by noon."

"Unless your mother summons the Baptist brigade to disembowel me."

"We're not going to tell my mother what we've been doing for the past twenty-four hours."

Ellis temporarily forgot her discomfort as she remembered the ecstasy of the previous day. "Then just make real sure you stand at least ten feet away from me, or I make no promises about being able to keep my hands off you." Ellis sighed contentedly. "For a rookie, you make one helluva lover, Ms. Moss."

Mary changed lanes on Interstate 85. "You should talk. And here I thought I didn't like sex." Mary chortled. "Poor Nathan. All those years he presumed he was married to an ice maiden. Turns out, the maiden melts rather quickly. It's all in who's holding the torch."

"Don't you dare use the words ice, melt, or torch while we're at your mother's, either. Maybe I'd better stay in the car when we get there."

"Don't be silly. We'll be perfectly circumspect in our conduct. I'll introduce you as the new friend I met the day my Xterra got rear-ended. She knows the basics of that story. I'll tell her she forgot that I'd told her you stayed with me while your ankle healed."

"I thought Natalie had already spilled that can of worms."

"Yes and no. Nat never missed a chance to mention you to her grandmother, her cousins, her aunts." Mary laughed lightly. "Now that I think about it, she fell in love with you as quickly as I did. Anyway, your name was always on the tip of her tongue, and whenever Nathan came by, Natalie got him talking about you, too. Between them, they left little doubt that you'd been a very prominent fixture at our house lately."

"So everyone knows I've been staying with you?"

"Pretty much."

"And that's not cause for alarm?"

"I saw my sisters exchange a couple of raised eyebrows when Nat said something about how happy I've seemed since you've been living with us."

"How did you handle that?"

"I made some remark about your not having any friends who could help you out while your leg healed."

"Terrific. Now they think I'm an unlikable, colossal loser."

"Not at all. You're from the South. You know doing good works for the less fortunate is what fine southern women do." Mary fluffed up her pretend bouffant hairdo.

"So now I'm a pity case?"

"If it shuts my mother and sisters up, why not?"

They spent the next part of the drive to Clarkesville strategizing for what they should and shouldn't say in hopes of minimizing Mary's mother's and sisters' suspicions.

When Ellis got her first glimpse of the mountains, she veered from the topic. "You told me it was pretty up here. I had no idea. This is amazing."

"I didn't appreciate it when I lived here as a child, but now that I've been away from it for a while, I really think it's one of the most beautiful places on earth." Mary took her hand from the steering wheel and gave Ellis's leg a squeeze. "Welcome to my part of Georgia."

"How far is Athens from here?"

"I don't know. Maybe sixty or seventy miles."

"Sixty miles in distance, but light years in topography. I can't believe all these folds of mountains and valleys." Ellis drank in the view as they rolled closer to Clarkesville. "If I had known this was what it looked like over here, I wouldn't have spent all those boring weekends while I was in college looking at the flat, dreary landscape around UGA."

"It is nice, isn't it?"

"Rumor has it everything is twice as potent when you're in love," Ellis said. She looked around a bit more. "I'm really glad my first experience with this incredible scenery is with you."

"Me, too, El. If we have time, I want to drive you through the Sautee-Nacoochee Valley before we go back to Atlanta today. It's spectacular."

Ellis gazed appreciatively at Mary. "So are you."

"I'm glad you think so." Mary accepted Ellis's outstretched hand. "Sorry to say it's almost time to straighten up and fly right. We're only a little ways from Mother's place."

"You sure know how to ruin a moment." Ellis kissed the back of Mary's hand before relinquishing her hold.

Mary made the final turn into the yard of her childhood home. "I learned from the best. I only hope Mother isn't in the mood to give you a demonstration of how she's elevated ruining moments to an art form."

Two towering columns flanking the steps supported a wraparound front porch. The largish white house with its dark green trim struck Ellis as massive. The yard was manicured to a fare-thee-well. Half a dozen hundred-year-old oaks stood guard on either side of a front walkway that sloped gently toward the house.

Ellis asked, "Is it just my imagination, or do I hear the opening strains of the theme from *Gone with the Wind?*"

"It does have sort of an antebellum look, doesn't it?"

"If Olivia de Havilland comes skipping down those stairs, I'm outta here."

It wasn't Melanie Hamilton who appeared at the front door and hastened toward them. Rather, it was Anna Moss, Mary's mother, moving with what Ellis considered to be amazing speed, given her sixty-nine years and stout body.

"Oh, MaryChris," Anna gushed as Mary opened her car door, "Nathan told us about how y'all are moving back home. I just know once y'all are settled here in the hills, you'll find your way back together so little Natalie doesn't have to be torn between the two of you. Jesus answered my Christmas prayers."

"Hi, Mom," Mary said evenly. She got out of the car and hugged her mother. "We still have a lot of details to work out about the move, and even if I do come back up here to live, Nathan and I will each have our own place, and Natalie will still go back and forth between us."

"Oh, that'll only last for a little while. When we get you away from all those bad influences down in the city and you come to church with me again, you'll see God has a plan for putting you and Nathan right. Next year at this time, you'll be telling me my seventh grandbaby is on the way."

Ellis sat still as a yard ornament in the passenger seat. Mary leaned down and looked through her open door. "Come on, Ellis. I'll introduce you to my family."

Hesitantly, Ellis opened her door and exited the SUV. Mary's mother hurried around the front of the Xterra.

"You must be Ellis. Our little Natalie has told us so much about you. Welcome, welcome. I'm so sorry about your ankle. Does it still hurt? Have you had anything to eat? I've got biscuits and gravy left from breakfast, or I could make you a ham sandwich from our Christmas dinner leftovers. And there's pie. Apple, pumpkin, pecan. Maybe you don't like pie. I've got cookies. The grandchildren love them. I bet you will, too. Who can say no to a homemade chocolate chip cookie? And I've also got sugar cookies. Or would you—"

"Mom, slow down," Mary suggested as she joined them on the passenger side of the vehicle. "We had breakfast at home, and that was less than two hours ago, so we don't need lunch yet. Give us a chance to use the bathroom and say hi to Natalie, okay? And remember, we're just here to pick up Nat and our stuff, and then we're on our way."

Anna wrapped Mary in a motherly bear hug. "I am so excited about having you back where you belong. When Nathan told me, I dropped right to my knees to thank the Lord for bringing my MaryChris and sweet Natalie home to me. You know I fought your daddy tooth and claw when he said we should name you MaryChris. I thought it was mocking our savior, but now that I've got my own MaryChris Moss miracle, I see that Daddy was wise enough to know that God has a sense of humor." A tear slipped down her face. "Law, how I've missed that man these seven years he's been with Jesus, God rest his soul. I can just see him dancing in the streets of heaven, knowing his three angel daughters are going to be right here to help me in my last years before I'm called to join him in God's holy rest."

"Let's go inside, okay?" Mary trudged toward the front door. "Who's here besides Nat?"

"Just Kendall and Amber and Ashley." Anna ushered Ellis along behind Mary. "Did MaryChris tell you about her nephews and nieces, Ellis? My daughter Naomi and her husband Barry gave me grandsons, Matthew and Kendall. My other daughter, she's my baby, Gloria, she's just nineteen months younger than MaryChris. She and Adam have three girls, Amber, Ashley, and Erin. I thought they should have picked another A name to go with Amber and Ashley, but they liked Erin, so Erin it is. And of course, you know

Natalie. She is so mature for her age, don't you think? I always thought an only child would be slowed down by not having brothers or sisters, but it sure hasn't hurt Natalie."

Anna kept up a running discourse all the way up the walk, up the steps, and through the front door into the living room. Natalie and a young boy, who Ellis thought looked to be about Natalie's age, and a slightly older-looking girl were playing a board game in the middle of the living room floor. All three looked up as the adults entered the room.

Natalie launched herself toward Ellis. "Ellis! You came. I hoped Mom would bring you." Ellis returned Natalie's exuberant hug.

"Hi, toots. Who's winning?"

"Who knows? Gramma Anna won't let us play computer games at her house. She says it's the devil's handiwork and that we can't use computers in her house, so we're playing this lame stone-age game where you have to roll dice and move plastic thingies." She unwrapped her arms from around Ellis's neck, but kept a grip on Ellis's hand.

The boy, who Ellis guessed must be Kendall from what she'd extracted during Anna's ramblings, spoke up. "Natalie says she doesn't know who's winning because she's losing. I'm way ahead. I rolled a six and landed on her guy and said 'Sorry,' 'cuz that's what you're supposed to say when you hit a square where somebody else already is, and she had to go back and start over."

"So what?" Natalie shot back. "I could still catch up, but now I don't have to play anymore because my mom and Ellis are here, and we're going back to Atlanta, where I've got a dog and a cat. You and Amber and Ashley can stay here and play your dumb game."

"My mom says pets are too much work," Amber said to no one in particular.

Mary tapped Natalie on the shoulder. "Remember me? I'm your mother. Do I get a hug, or at least a hello?"

"I saw you day before yesterday. I haven't seen Ellis since forever." Natalie dropped Ellis's hand and hugged her mother. "Hi, Mom. You're weird."

"Thank you, sweetie. I think you're weird, too."

Natalie tugged on Ellis's sleeve. When Ellis stooped down, Natalie cupped her hand around Ellis's ear. "That's our code so we don't have to say 'I love you' in front of other people."

Ellis whispered in Natalie's ear, "Thanks for explaining that. I've heard you do that before."

"Ready to head for home, Nat?" Mary asked.

Anna took Mary's elbow. "Oh, no, honey. You can't bolt in here like a hound after a coon and chase off down the road without so much as a bite to eat. Naomi and Gloria and them will be here around noon. I've got some potpies all ready to go in the oven and Naomi is bringing a green salad. Gloria said she'd fix some cornbread and collards, so we'll be able to make a meal of it. You and Ellis sit right down, and I'll get you some tea. We need to talk about where you're going to live when you move home. I don't know why you and Natalie don't just take over the second floor of this house. Heaven knows I rattle around here like a June bug in a gymnasium. No reason in the world you two couldn't share this big old house with me. That's how it used to be, you know. All the generations under one roof."

When Anna stopped to draw a breath, Ellis wedged her foot in the conversational gap. "Could I use the restroom, please?"

"Where are my manners? Of course, child. Natalie, show Ellis where the bathroom is."

"Back here," Natalie said as she led the way out of the living room. She stole a look over her shoulder. "Don't worry," she said conspiratorially. "Me and Mom won't move in with Gramma Anna. Mom always says one day with Gramma is about twenty-three hours too many."

Ellis dawdled in the bathroom. Listening to Mary's mother was akin to being in a blender that was set to "auditory frappé." So much for their plans to head back to Atlanta right away. If the entire Moss family was assembling for lunch, it would be at least two o'clock before they could load up and make tracks. At a minimum, that translated to four more hours of enduring Anna's verbal wind sprints.

Her thoughts were interrupted by a knock on the door. "Almost done, Natalie. I'll be right there," Ellis said.

"It's me. Let me in."

Ellis unlocked the door, and Mary slipped through. "I came to massage your ears," she said, slipping her hands along either side of Ellis's head. "When my mom gets excited, she gets talkative."

"Gee, I never would have guessed." Ellis rested her head on Mary's shoulder while Mary gentle kneaded her earlobes. "Mmmm. That's nice."

"And I'll bet your lips are numb from having been denied use for so long." Mary kissed Ellis gently. "This should bring some feeling back."

"You'd better stop that. My lips aren't the only part of my body you're bringing feelings to."

"I know what you mean." She kissed Ellis quickly again. "Get out of here before I forget where we are, but wait for me outside the door. I have news that I think you'll want to hear."

Ellis stole a kiss, then left the bathroom to wait for Mary.

"So, what's your news?" Ellis asked as Mary joined her in the hall.

"I negotiated a reprieve. I told my mother I wanted to drive around a little to see if there are any houses for sale I might want to look at. You and I are going to sneak out the side door and get gone before the kids can beg us to ride along."

"You're a genius, MaryChris Moss."

"No, I'm a woman who needs to be alone with the woman she loves." She took Ellis by the hand. "Quick like a bunny, and watch my feet. Some of these floorboards squeak, so be sure to step over the ones I avoid. We don't want to tip off the little people with sonar hearing."

* * *

Mary parked the Xterra on a wide, flat spot beside a narrow side road to the north of Route 17, and they got out. The sun played off mountain ridges all around them. The dark pines shone green in the bright light. Brown leaves clung to gray branches.

Ellis drank it in. "You were right about this valley. I don't think I've ever been anywhere more serene."

"The Cherokee thought this was sacred land." Mary stood behind Ellis and put both hands on Ellis's shoulders. "It probably wasn't very serene, though, when they were forced to leave."

"Is this part of the Trail of Tears?"

"Uh-huh. Can you imagine being told you had to leave the place your ancestors had called home for centuries?"

"If I remember any of my Georgia history, the discovery of gold was behind it all, wasn't it?"

"Yep."

"A perfect example of the golden rule—he who has the gold, rules."

Mary stared into the cloudless blue sky. "Sometimes I wish I didn't know what happened before my family came to live here." Reluctantly, she took her hands from Ellis's shoulders.

"They've been here a long time?" Ellis asked.

"About a hundred and fifty years. Four generations' worth."

"Did they come for the gold?"

"Probably, but they stayed for the lumber. My great-great-grandfather claimed land here in the early 1830s. He started one of the big lumber mills that tore down half the forests. His sons worked the business and his sons' sons, and so on."

"Was your dad in the lumber business, too?"

"No, by then lumbering had tapered off. He owned a Dodge dealership over in Cornelia. My brother-in-law Adam runs it now."

"Runs it, or owns it?"

"Runs it. Technically, my mother owns it. It passed to her when Dad died. Of course, she doesn't know a Cummins diesel engine from Vin Diesel, so thank goodness Adam handles it. If you want to witness a real test of wills, be around sometime when Adam is trying to convince her that the dealership should be open on Sunday afternoons."

"It makes sense. That's one of the few times working people can shop as a couple."

"It makes sense to someone living now. My mother's stuck somewhere around 1950. Women belong at home in the kitchen and shouldn't worry their pretty little heads with things like horseless carriages and all such tomfoolery."

"Surely your mother drives?"

"Using a loose interpretation of that word, yes. If she could convince Naomi or Gloria to go to as many church events as she does, she probably wouldn't ever take her car out of the garage."

"Speaking of your sisters, don't we have to be back at your mother's for lunch soon?"

"Don't remind me. If I weren't concerned about how badly it would warp Natalie's brain, I'd leave her with my mother for the coming week, since she doesn't go back to school 'til the eighth of January. Then we could blow out of here for home right now." Mary looked quickly in both directions to be sure they were alone, then gave Ellis a quick kiss. "I like how it feels to be home with you."

"Me, too." Ellis slid her arms around Mary's waist. "Are you absolutely sure you're moving up here?"

"I don't see any way around it. Nathan is happier than I've seen him in years. He's hooking up with all his old buddies and making plans for camping trips and weekend fishing excursions. His family's so thrilled about Nathan moving to Clarkesville and Natalie being nearby all the time they've almost forgotten they're supposed to hate me for ending our marriage." She pulled free of Ellis's embrace.

"Mom drives us all insane, but she'd give both arms for any of her grandkids, and they all know it. Here's a prime example. She goes on and on about what an awful thing technology is, and yet she gave Nat an iPod for Christmas. You saw how Natalie was at my mother's house. It's the same thing when she's with Nathan's family. She needs to be part of something more than just her dad and me."

Ellis thought for a moment before answering. "With all the family she's got up here, maybe Natalie could spend weekends with them, which would leave your calendar a little more open for other activities." A smile spread across her face.

"Sure. Besides having sleepover nights with Nathan, she could stay at Mom's sometimes or with my sisters. She's got Kimbrough cousins she'll want to spend time with, too. You could come up every weekend."

"Probably not every weekend. I'll need to stay in the city to keep up with my landscaping jobs. This winter lull has given you a warped notion of what my usual schedule is like."

"I understand. Besides, I can't let Nat spend every weekend away from me. Somebody has to be the disciplinarian. It already takes me until Tuesday to get her back on track after she's been with her dad for two days. Imagine what it would be like if she had endless freedom from my iron-mom rules."

"Is there any reason you couldn't come to Atlanta sometimes? On weekends when you've made plans for Natalie to be with relatives, I mean."

"I don't see why not. I've had one day's jubilant experience with how comfortable your bed is." The expression on Mary's face left no question about the reference. "I could get used to more."

Ellis feared she might collapse from the swell of adrenaline prompted by remembering how it felt the previous afternoon to have Mary's body next to hers. "Sorry I was such a grizzly bear when you first told me you'd be moving up here."

"Forget about it. It hit me like a runaway locomotive, too." She inched her foot forward and gently kicked the toe of Ellis's shoe. "In a way, I was glad it upset you."

"What? Why?"

"At least I knew you cared enough about me to be upset at the prospect of my moving out of Atlanta."

"I'm not glad it took a sprained ankle and a crumpled bumper to bring it about," Ellis said, "but Sam and I have loved living at your house."

"Nat and I have loved having you there." Mary eased forward and put a foot on either side of Ellis's feet. "I was planning to try to talk you into moving in with us, but that wouldn't make much sense now, since we'll be packing up and heading north in a month or two."

Ellis accepted Mary's kiss, then opened the Xterra's hatch. Ellis sat down, propelling herself far enough into the cargo compartment that she could lean against the back side of the backseat. She drew her right ankle up to rub it. Mary followed her to the vehicle and sat with her legs hanging down to the ground. "Do you think it will be that soon?" Ellis asked.

"Nathan wants to list the house right away, maybe even next week."

"Wouldn't it be better to wait until spring and let Natalie finish the school year?"

"Yes and no. Nat knows these plans are in the works, and you can bet she'll badger us day and night about when we're moving. It will be a major distraction for all of us, so the sooner we get settled in our new place, the sooner she can get into a new routine."

"What about you, Mary?"

"What about me?"

"Are you looking forward to a new routine, too?"

"Yeah, there is a new routine I want in my life—a routine with you."

"But you'll be in Clarkesville, and I'll be in Tucker."

"You make it sound like it's Guam and Greenland."

"Might as well be." Ellis rubbed her ankle again.

"How bad does it hurt?" Mary wrapped her fingers around Ellis's ankle.

"Not too bad. Standing on the cold ground made it ache a little."

Mary gingerly probed the area beneath Ellis's sock. "Feels like it might be swollen, too. I wasn't thinking. I shouldn't have made you stand that long."

Ellis laced her fingers with Mary's. "Not your fault. I could have suggested we sit down sooner."

"If I had my way, we'd be lying down somewhere."

"We could fold the seat down and rock this old Moss mobile."

Mary scooted next to Ellis. "Don't tempt me." They exchanged a deep kiss. "On second thought, tempt me."

Ellis pulled Mary to her as tightly as she could in the cramped enclosure. As they were about to kiss again, Mary heard the sound of an approaching vehicle and hurriedly withdrew from Ellis's hug. A shiny Dodge crew cab truck crested the hill behind them.

"I don't believe this," Mary said as she boosted herself out of the Xterra. "That's Naomi and Barry."

"Who?"

"My sister and brother-in-law. Stay there."

The Dodge slowed and cruised to a stop at the edge of the road. Mary hurried to the passenger side. "Taking the scenic route to Mother's?" she asked her sister.

"Sort of," Naomi said. "She called a little while ago and asked me to bring her a gallon of milk. We didn't want to chase all the way into town, so we decided to swing by the convenience store at the gas station and pick one up. What are you doing clear over here?"

"My friend Ellis—the one with the bad ankle, remember? Nat told you all about her. She came up from Atlanta with me this morning. I was just showing her a little of the countryside, but her ankle flared up from walking too much, so she's got her leg up to get the swelling out of it."

Naomi waved to Ellis in the Xterra. Ellis waved back.

"Mother said you were out looking for a house to buy."

"As often happens, Mother misstated the case. I told her we were going to drive around to get an idea of where I might want to buy. Things have changed around here in the ten years I've been gone. I wanted to get a feel for areas that might be worth looking at."

"Whatever. The next area you better look at, sister dear, is the front yard of Mother's place. She told us lunch at noon sharp, and that's only ten minutes away."

"We'll be right behind you," Mary said. "By the way, where's Matt?"

"Since Kendall stayed at Mom's so that he could hang out with Amber and Ashley and Natalie, Matt stayed at Gloria and Adam's house last night. They're already at Mother's with all the kids."

"Okay then. Next stop, Anna Moss's house of too much lunch. See you there. Bring your own Pepto-Bismol."

Barry pulled the Dodge onto the road, and Mary plodded back to the SUV. Ellis exited the rear and closed the hatch.

"Did your brother-in-law even say hello?" Ellis went around to the passenger door while Mary got behind the wheel.

"No, but that's not unusual. If he's seen me anytime in the past week, he doesn't feel the need to waste words on silly things like greetings. Just don't mention anything sports-related to him, though, or he'll talk your ear off."

"Seems we nearly got caught with our pants down, if you'll pardon the expression," Ellis said as she latched her seatbelt.

"It wouldn't have helped our cause if they'd caught us in a lip lock. You're right about that."

"Maybe their showing up like that was an omen."

"What kind of omen?"

"An omen about how you and I aren't supposed to be together. The first car that came down the road was someone we wouldn't want to see us kissing."

"Oh, come on, Ellis. I'm related to half the people in a thirty-mile radius and know at least fifty percent of the other half. The odds of my knowing whoever was the first one to come over that hill were at least three to one."

"Does that mean we're going to have to hide our relationship from everybody?"

Mary was silent for a moment. "Until I've had a chance to explain it, I suppose so." A couple of quiet miles rolled by. "Clarkesville isn't as progressive as Atlanta."

"And no one will accuse Atlanta of being a bastion of forward thinking," Ellis said.

"I'm sorry we can't talk more about this right now," Mary said as she turned into her mother's driveway. "And the drive home won't be much better with Natalie in the backseat doing her impersonation of an information sponge."

"No problem," Ellis said as she undid her seatbelt. She couldn't help but think that maybe Guam and Greenland would be a better arrangement after all.

Chapter 7

Mary might as well have poured honey on Ellis and flung her in an ant hill as subjected her to lunch with her family. How could twelve people make that much noise? Natalie and her five cousins chattered nonstop through the entire meal. And why wouldn't they, with Anna, Naomi, and Gloria as role models? Ellis didn't remember ever being peppered with more questions in such a short span of time. The questions weren't overly nosey, and it wouldn't have mattered if they had been. Naomi would ask about some topic—say, Ellis's family or her line of work or movies she'd seen lately—but before Ellis got half a sentence out in reply, Anna or Gloria would pose a semi-related question, and then the three women would tear off on a tangent, oblivious to Ellis ever having been part of the exchange. A minute later, another question from one of the Moss women, another attempt by Ellis to respond, and another couple of laps around a new topic only vaguely connected to the original query.

By the time Anna hauled out the pies, cookies, cakes, and homemade candy, Ellis felt she'd been tossed in a cement mixer for an hour and then dumped out with a concrete block in her stomach.

By Ellis's estimation, the pot pies, cornbread, collards, and other side dishes had to have required at least four pounds of butter, never mind the cholesterol quotient of the final course. Ellis wasn't sure if it was the food or the surroundings that had her feeling as though she'd need an industrial strength antacid to soften the concrete block and an entire bottle of aspirin to soothe her head before the day was done.

It had been a long time since she'd thought about meals with her family or reflected on that time in her life when, on those rare occasions when her sister and brother came home from college, she and Anika and Nicolas would sit at the dining room table with their parents. Those hushed meals where, if anyone spoke at all, it was always only one person at a time and then in soft tones, usually about current world events or about ancient art. She had hated those meals with her family. They were so stifled, so stifling. Sitting at the huge table in Anna Moss's house, she was stunned to find herself craving that stultified circumstance. She ached for her mother's paper-thin voice and her father's measured monotone. She'd have welcomed the familiar raising of her hackles when her siblings talked down to her or tossed an easy question her way. She always assumed their including her wasn't because they cared to hear her opinions or make her feel included, but rather because it made her siblings look good to their parents.

"Ellis?" Ellis gave a start at hearing her name. "Ellis," Anna said again, "would you like ice cream or whipped cream on your pie?"

"I'm sorry," Ellis said as she returned from her backward time travel to the Savannah of her youth. "I'm full. Thanks, but no pie for me."

For the reaction it elicited from Mary's sisters, Ellis wondered if "no pie" were really code words for "I worship Satan." As soon as they recovered from the horror caused by such an unheard of refusal, they set about their crusade to convert her.

"Oh, Ellis, you've got to have at least a little piece," Gloria said. "The crusts are so light and flaky you almost have to hold it down on the plate with your fork."

Naomi added, "Women have been after Mama for years to get her pie recipes, but she won't tell anybody how she does it. I hope she'll leave them for us when she's gone, not that we want that to be anytime in the next thirty years." She lifted a slice of apple pie from the pan to a plate and passed it to her husband. "And even if we get the recipes, we'll never equal her technique. She knows just the right number of times to put a rolling pin to a ball of dough."

It's a pie, for God's sake. Stop acting as though she's perfected a new surgical procedure for curing brain disorders.

"I'm sure they're delicious," Ellis said, "but everything else was so good, I've already eaten more than I should have. I really can't."

Apparently, she was speaking a foreign language unintelligible to the Moss women. Gloria set a plate with a slab of pecan pie in front of Ellis. Twenty seconds later, Naomi put a second plate with a wedge of pumpkin pie next to it. "Skip the ice cream, if you want," Naomi said, "but you'll hate yourself if you miss out on Mother's pie."

Between the din of the conversation and the unfamiliarly heavy meal, Ellis felt in danger of tossing her cookies... er, pie... and then some. The crusted layer of pecans atop the gelatinous base of corn syrup and sugar seemed to stare up at her, daring her to put a forkful in her mouth and swallow it down without gagging. Anna hadn't spared the spices in her pumpkin pie. The aroma of the cinnamon, nutmeg, and cloves left Ellis feeling like she was trapped in the hold of a cargo ship on a forced voyage over rough seas from the East Indies. She scrambled to find an acceptable excuse that would let her bolt from the table and rush outside for some quiet and some fresh air.

"Mrs. Moss—" Ellis said, but before she could say another word, young Kendall pushed his chair back from the table.

"I don't feel so good," he said.

Naomi leaped to her feet. "Come on, son." She took him by the arm and started out of the room. "I knew you ate too many cookies this morning." She picked up the pace as the sounds of the first heave of his stomach escaped Kendall's lips. "Run, Kendall. I don't want you throwing up all over Gramma's hall."

Barry turned to his mother-in-law. "How many times do we have to tell you not to let the kids eat junk the whole time they're here?"

"Oh, Barry, don't start in on me. It's Christmas. They like my cookies. He didn't have any more than Natalie or Ashley had this morning."

"So what? I'll bet they ate a dozen each. He's not like the others, Anna. Sweets get to him. You know that. Now he'll be sick for a week." Barry's chair scraped on the hardwood floor as he shoved away from the table. He slapped his napkin down on the seat. "Matthew, go see if your mother needs anything."

"I don't want to go back there if Kendall's sick."

"You don't have to go into the bathroom. Just stand outside the door and ask your mother if he's all right."

"Do I have to?"

"Yes. Now go."

Matthew turned to Natalie, sitting beside him, and poked her in the arm. "You're so lucky to be an only child."

"I'm not an only child. I've got Swiffer and Sam and one day, Mom's going to give me a baby sister. You'll see." Natalie set her jaw and glared at Matthew as he left the table.

"That about ruined my appetite," Adam said as he moved his half-eaten pie away. "Maybe I'll run over to the dealership for a while." He turned to his wife. "You and the kids could catch a lift home from Naomi or Mary, couldn't you?"

"Sure. Go on before you're sick yourself." Gloria gave Adam a push. "Big strapping man can't handle a kid's upset stomach." She accepted Adam's quick kiss. "Who wants Daddy's pie?" she asked.

"Not me," Ashley said. "My tummy hurts."

Gloria put her hand on her daughter's forehead. "Uh-oh, she's feverish. I think we might have a flu bug about to make the rounds here."

Anna shoved her palms flat on the table to help herself rise from her chair. "Happens every Christmas. You'd think the Moss family was cursed." She smoothed her hair into place. "Take her upstairs and put her to bed, Gloria." Anna reached for the bowl of collards still in the middle of the table. "I'll clean up down here."

"No, if she's getting sick, Amber and Erin won't be far behind. We need to get home. Maybe I can catch Adam before he gets gone." She raced out of the room and was back in a moment. "He's halfway to Cornelia already. Mary…?"

"Sure, I'll run you and the kids to your place." She looked at Ellis, white as a ghost and equally as quiet. "Want to ride along, El?"

Ellis shook her head. "Uh, no. I'll stay here and help your mother."

"Okay. Nat, what about you?"

"I'm staying with Ellis."

"Fine." Mary scooped up Erin and braced her on her hip. She addressed her sister. "I'll grab the spare car seat from the laundry room and get her buckled in while you round up Amber and Ashley's stuff." Mary dragged her free hand over Ellis's shoulder on her way past. "I'll be back in twenty minutes, and then we can head home ourselves."

Twenty minutes. As far as Ellis was concerned, it might as well have been a life sentence. A sick child in the bathroom and a solo stint with Mary's mother. Could it get any better?

"Hey, Ellis," Natalie said as she slid from chair to chair around the table to get next to her. "Do you think maybe you and Sam could sleep in my bed instead of in Mom's room when we get home tonight?"

* * *

Ellis held the bowl of leftover salad. "Do you have a storage container big enough to hold this, or should I put plastic wrap on it and put it in the refrigerator?"

From the icy look on Anna Moss's face, Ellis wondered if there'd be any need for stowing the greens. If she kept it up, in a matter of moments, the entire kitchen would be a deep freeze.

"I'll take care of things here. Why don't you go outside and wait for MaryChris?"

"I'm happy to help, Mrs. Moss. After all, I was hungry and you fed me."

Anna smacked the pot she was holding on the kitchen countertop and wheeled around to face Ellis. "I will thank you not to use words from scripture in that mocking tone."

Ellis dropped back a step. "I wasn't mocking anything. I wanted to show my appreciation for the meal you served by helping clean up."

The menacing glint in Anna's eye only intensified. "If a man also lie with mankind, as he lieth with a woman, both of them have committed an abomination. They shall surely be put to death. Their blood shall be upon them." She squared her shoulders and scowled at Ellis. "Leviticus twenty, verse thirteen."

Ellis nearly dropped the bowl she was holding. She dared not speak for fear that both the wrong words and her partially digested lunch would fly out of her mouth.

Anna's fury picked up steam. "I heard what Natalie said to you about how you've been forcing your perverted attentions on my daughter by sleeping in her bed as a man does with a woman. I will not stand for it. And I'm warning you, if I find out you have so much as set foot in Natalie's bedroom, I'll have you arrested."

Ellis thought back to Natalie's actual words. Time for some quick footwork. "Mrs. Moss, you misunderstood what Natalie said. Your daughter is such a gracious hostess that she insisted I take her bed while I've been staying there. As I recall, what your granddaughter said was that she'd like me to spend the night in her room instead of in her mother's room. Who knows why she thought that would be a good idea? Maybe she's had so much fun spending nights with her cousins she doesn't want to sleep by herself tonight. Whatever conclusions you might have drawn from Natalie's comment, I want to set the record straight. Mary and I have not—to use your words—lain as man and woman in her bed."

Okay, so it was tomato/tomahto. No, they hadn't done *the* deed in Mary's bed… yet… they'd only done it in Ellis's bed. And under other circumstances, using the expression "setting the record straight" would have made her snort at the irony, but this was her first verbal skirmish with Anna, and she had precious little hope it would be her last.

Anna's furor ratcheted down a notch. "I see."

Ellis wedged her weapon in the chink in Anna's armor. "Mary, or MaryChris as you call her, is one of the most generous people I've ever met. She was the only person who stopped to see if I needed help when I fell and hurt my ankle back in November. She put all her plans for the day aside and took me to the emergency room, and when she found out I didn't have any family or friends to lean on, she went the extra mile and opened her home to me." Ellis forced herself to smile. She hoped it looked genuine and heartfelt. "She and Natalie have become two of my best friends. I don't know how I'd have gotten through the mess with my ankle without them."

"Well, yes, her father and I did try to raise her to be mindful of the needs of others."

"From my own experiences with her over the past month, I can definitely confirm that you and Joe succeeded on that count."

Anna's surprise registered on her face. "You know my husband's name?"

"Mary talks about him, about both of you, several times a day."

All right, so another serving, this time potato/potahto. So what if almost every comment Mary made about her mother was prefaced or appended with, "She makes me crazy"? She *did* talk about her a lot.

Anna fingered the hair at the nape of her neck. "That does my heart good. Sometimes I worry that she's forgotten all about me and the rest of her family."

Ellis smiled again. This one came a bit more naturally. "Absolutely not. You're never far from her mind."

"Well then, let's get this kitchen cleaned up. I'll get you something to put that salad in." Anna busied herself digging in a cabinet for a suitable plastic tub with a lid.

Lies, damned lies, and statistics. If she gave herself credit for the "several times a day" remark being a statistic, Ellis had used every one of them in the past few moments. I may have scraped by in the first round, Ellis thought, but the real confrontations are yet to come. Now, what the hell is taking Mary so long to get back so we can get out of here?

* * *

The drive back to Atlanta seemed to Ellis to be taking forever. Yet again, she looked over her shoulder at Natalie and repeated a question she'd asked more than once.

"You've already asked me a hundred times how I feel." Natalie scooted as far forward on the backseat as the shoulder belt would let her and tickled her fingers along the back of Ellis's head. "I feel with these, just like everybody else does." She laughed at her own joke. "Don't worry about me, Ellis. I won't holler for Huey on the way home."

"Holler for Huey?" Ellis asked.

"You know." Natalie leaned over and shouted "Huey," as though she were throwing up.

"Okay, got it. But are you sure your stomach isn't bothering you?"

"I just told you no."

"But if it does, you'll let me and your mom know, right?"

Mary said, "I'm guessing you haven't spent much time around sick children."

"No, not much time, sick or otherwise."

"You get used to it." Mary gave Ellis's thigh a reassuring pat.

Getting used to children—sick or well, getting used to Mary's family, getting used to having to drive two hours to see Mary. Too many adjustments. Too many impossibilities. She never should have given in to her hormones yesterday. Was it really only yesterday that they'd made up and made love for the first time? Ellis had the feeling she'd been trapped in a low-budget remake of *The Brady Bunch* movie for at least two years.

"I don't get sick much, do I, Mom?"

"No. You're like your dad that way. You picked the right parent to take after."

"I wonder if my baby sister will be that way, too."

"Nat, we've been through this a thousand times. You're not getting a baby sister."

"Maybe not right away, but I know I'm going to get one."

"Not unless you build one in science class."

"That's not how you get babies, Mom."

"It's the only way I'll get another one."

"But—"

"Enough, Nat." Mary looked in the rearview mirror and gave her daughter a stern stare. "Either pick a new topic or put your earphones on and listen to some music."

"Kendall has Matthew, and Amber and Ashley and Erin have each other. How come I have to be an only child?"

"I said that was enough." Mary looked briefly at Natalie. "I mean it." She returned her attention to the road.

Natalie fiddled with her iPod and grumbled something unintelligible.

Mary took her hand from the wheel and touched Ellis's cheek. "Next time we go to Clarkesville, I promise it won't be this much of a production. Christmas is always way over the top at Mother's, and this year was even worse because of Nathan's big announcement. It's not always the three-ring circus you saw today."

"Whatever you say."

"Are you okay, Ellis? You haven't said much since we left."

"I guess Adam and I react the same way to someone getting sick."

"I'm sorry. It never occurred to me Kendall's upchuck bothered you."

"Let's not talk about it, please."

"Sure. Now that Nat's lost in whatever track she's picked on her iPod, we can talk about anything you want to."

"I need to tell you about my conversation with your mother."

Mary gave a cautionary glance in the rearview toward Natalie. "Hmm. Maybe better save that topic for later."

"Then maybe we should listen to some music, too."

Mary regarded Ellis's profile. "Help yourself." She gestured to the in-dash CD player. "Discs are in the console."

The remainder of the trip was spent with old Melissa Etheridge tunes in lieu of conversation.

*   *   *

Shadows filled the backyard at Mary's house. Ellis leaned on the fence while Sam sniffed all her favorite places. Natalie and Mary busied themselves hauling everything from the loadbed of the Xterra into the house. Twilight gave way to darkness. Ellis opened the door to the kitchen and stepped inside.

"My mother sent tons of leftovers," Mary said as she crammed containers into the refrigerator. "What would you like for dinner, Ellis? Ham and scalloped potatoes? A sandwich?"

"I think I'll skip dinner." She patted her abdomen. "Lunch still lingers."

"I'm sure Nat will want something." Mary swung her head to shift her hair back from her face. "I'll go see how she's doing with unpacking."

Sam followed Mary out of the room. Ellis edged one of the chairs farther under the kitchen table. Her thumb stuck to a spot on the back. She looked at her thumb. Peanut butter and grape jelly. Disgusting. Ellis dampened a sponge from the sink and wiped the chair.

On her way to the living room, she kicked Natalie's sneakers over to the doormat. She grabbed the unzipped backpack to move it from the sofa, and a cascade of Natalie's treasures spilled onto the floor: two half-eaten candy bars, four pencils with broken leads, assorted bracelets and hair clips, one sock, a word puzzle book, a rubber-banded stack of two-inch square pictures of kids Ellis assumed were Natalie's classmates, a box of colored pencils, homework assignment sheets, a zip-top bag of raisins, her new digital camera, and three small spiral-bound notebooks.

Ellis stuffed things back into the pack. One of the notebooks fell open. The caption under the hand-drawn picture caught her eye. Uneven penciled letters, some in caps, some in lower case, spelled out "My old family." No one would mistake it for museum art, but Ellis found the drawing itself rather well done. A man stood off to the far left side, holding his arm at a right angle. Wiggly lines in front of his hand seemed to indicate he was waving good-bye to a tall, long-haired blonde woman and a nearly-as-tall female child on the opposite side of the picture.

Ellis turned the page. "My new family," it said. The picture there was of the same tall woman, but this time, she stood beside another woman, who was wearing a cast on one foot and leaning on a crutch. The girl child was there, too, with a black dog lying at her feet and a baby in a blanket in her arms.

Thoughts of Becky Blumfeld flooded Ellis's mind, threatening to sweep her out to the desolate sea she'd struggled to escape for the past year. She slapped the notebook shut and stuffed it in the backpack.

Mary's voice startled her. "Looks like Nat is coming down with whatever hit Kendall at lunch. I put her to bed in my room. We'll have to make do with the double bed in her room tonight."

Ellis looked at Mary standing in the arched doorway. Backlit by the hallway light, Mary was beautiful, like a golden maternal angel whose wingspan Ellis could never equal. Conflicting emotions tumbled through her—intense desire to stay coupled and become part of that new family she'd seen in Natalie's notebook argued with the need to flee and keep her freedom. "Maybe Sam and I should spend the night at my place."

"You don't need to leave just because Nat has a touch of the flu."

"It's not that. I'm not feeling a hundred percent myself. I don't want you to have to take care of me, too."

Mary crossed the room and came to a stop in front of Ellis. "I've had some practice. I'm pretty good at it." She put her arms around Ellis. "A little TLC might fix you right up." Ellis resisted fleetingly, then melted into Mary's embrace. Their lips met.

"Mom! I'm gonna be sick. Come hold my head." The urgency in Natalie's voice was unmistakable.

"I'll call you in the morning," Ellis said as she scanned the room, searching for Sam's leash. "Your kid needs you."

"Okay," Mary called over her shoulder as she hurried down the hall. "I'm coming, Nat. Get in the bathroom!"

At Ellis's whistle, Sam hustled into the living room as if she were as repelled by the child's barfing as Ellis was. "C'mon, pooch. We're going home." Just as she had done two days earlier, she let herself out of Mary Moss's house and wondered again why she'd ever been fool enough to think she had any hope of building a future there.

* * *

Her call to Mary the next morning lasted less than two minutes. Mary had succumbed to the intestinal virus, too, and was frequently paying her respects to the porcelain god. Ellis offered to come over and take care of Mary and Natalie and was flooded with relief when Mary insisted that she stay away.

Ellis and Sam spent New Year's Eve going for long walks—for as long as Ellis's not-quite-healed ankle would permit—and wallowing on the sofa at her apartment in front of the TV while football droned as background noise.

She phoned Mary again midafternoon on New Year's Day, but Ellis's hopes for an auspicious start to the year were dashed when she learned Mary and Natalie were still feeling the effects of the illness. After offering the appropriate get-well comments, Ellis snapped her cell phone shut and buried the twinge of guilt that poked at her for failing to ask if she could bring them anything.

A cold rain spit against the apartment windows. Ellis sat at her small desk in the corner of her living room and reviewed her ledgers for the past year. If she could line up a few more steady clients for the coming season, she'd have enough income flow to give her a comfort margin. Presuming Mary would make good on her stated intentions of moving up to the foothills, Ellis decided to focus on building up her client base. She wouldn't have anything else to do on weekends, anyway, so she might as well edge driveways, fertilize shrubs, and keep the monkey grass in check.

Ellis addressed New Year's greeting cards to her best customers. She slipped a couple of her business cards into each envelope and added a P.S. to her handwritten note: *If you're satisfied with the work I've done for you, please give my card to a neighbor or friend. My calendar has room for one or two new customers for the coming season. Wishing all the best to you and your family.*

Ellis looked up from sealing the last envelope. Gray clouds still hung in the air; raindrops meandered down the windowpane. Too bad she'd already cleaned the apartment. All her indoor chores were done, and spending time outdoors wasn't appealing. She tried to remember what she'd done to get through last winter, her first winter without Becky. The only image that came to mind was one that looked remarkably like the current one: Ellis alone in that very room, staring out the window and wondering how to get through the next minute, hour, day, the next eternity.

Once winter was over and she could be outdoors, it wouldn't be so bad. Working from the first drop of sunlight until the deepest part of dusk from early spring until late fall staved off the worst of the loneliness. Fall. *I prefer to think of it as a case of you falling for me.* That's what Mary had said in the emergency room that Saturday in November when Ellis got her cast. Ellis looked at the calendar beside her on the wall. How could it only be five weeks ago? Maybe she should call Mary again to see if she was feeling better. Maybe they could go out for a late New Year's celebration after all. She stuck her hand in her shirt pocket, but she didn't pull out her cell phone.

She looked over at Sam stretched out on the sofa, her feet twitching in hot pursuit of whatever quarry was in her canine dream.

Even though work had filled her days over the last year, coming home to an empty apartment proved more than Ellis could bear. In early May, she'd gone to the DeKalb County Animal Shelter and choked back tears as she went from cage to cage hoping to find a bandage for her bleeding soul. Puppies were out of the question because of her work schedule, but she didn't want someone's problem dog, either. In the next to last cage, she spied a young adult spayed female. The card outside the cage said her name was "Spade," and that she was housebroken, affectionate, and good with children. In the Reason for Surrendering box, the entry said "new baby in family; can't keep dog." Ellis had smirked at the paradox— she was good with children, but when the baby came along, the dog got the gate.

That makes two of us, Spade, she'd thought. *I got shoved out of my home because of a baby, too.* She took the dog home that afternoon and renamed her Sam.

Remembering that moment hit Ellis like a blast of arctic air. Damn. Why did Becky have to be so unyielding in her demands about having a child?

Ellis wandered over to the couch and buried her face in Sam's neck. "It's you and me, Sammy."

Sam stirred slightly, sighed contentedly, and settled in for the next installment of her snooze. Ellis eased onto the sofa beside the dog and gave in to the sorrow that never was more than a memory away.

Chapter 8

Ellis parked her truck in front of Mary's house. She stomped around to the passenger door and noticed Mary coming toward her down the driveway. "You sure didn't waste any time, did you?" Ellis jerked her thumb at the real estate agent's sign in the front yard.

"Nice to see you, too, and by the way, Happy New Year." Mary stopped in her tracks.

"Sorry. I was surprised to see that you've already got the house on the market. You didn't say anything about it when we talked on the phone last night." Ellis opened the door and grabbed the end of Sam's leash as she jumped off the seat. "I'll put Sam in the backyard and then maybe you can bring me up to speed."

"All right. I'll meet you inside."

Mary retreated up the front walk while Ellis took Sam through the side gate to the backyard. Ellis came through the kitchen door, draped the leash over the doorknob, and looked at Mary leaning against the counter.

"Finally feeling better?" Ellis asked. She crossed the room and gave Mary a soft kiss.

"Yeah. I can't remember the last time I was knocked out for three days by an upset stomach."

Ellis felt the reaction deep in her gut when Mary edged close enough to make contact with Ellis's hip as Ellis joined her in leaning against the counter. "How's Natalie?"

"Back to her old sassy self. She's with her dad, supposedly helping him pack. I told him he was a fool to have her underfoot, but I think he's worried he won't get much time with her in the coming weeks while we wait to see if there's any hope this house will sell."

"How soon is he moving?"

"This coming weekend, if you can believe it. He starts his new job—well, same job, really, just a new home office—next Monday.

Since he doesn't feel he can commit to buying something up there until this house sells, he found a month-to-month lease on an apartment right outside Clarkesville."

"Wow, that's quick."

"Other than his long-suffering patience in waiting for me to be a decent wife, Nathan's not known for letting moss grow on him."

"Because it's a new year, I'm going to pretend I didn't catch that lame pun." Ellis offered a crooked smile. "Just don't think you can get away with a lot of them."

"You know what? I didn't even realize what I said. To tell you the truth, I'm so overwhelmed right now I don't think you can hold me responsible for anything I say."

"Want to talk about it?" Ellis wasn't sure she was up to hearing all the items on Mary's list, but not knowing what was on her mind was even worse.

Mary took two quick steps to the kitchen table and dropped onto a chair. "What's to say? My house is up for sale. My child and I are moving back to a place where I swore I'd never live again. That means every single thing in this house"—she waved her hands frantically—"has to be boxed and toted out of here. I know that the couple of hours you spent with my family last Saturday made you want to run screaming for Alabama, if not someplace even farther away." She laughed lightly. "Half the time, that's what they make me want to do."

Ellis, still braced against the counter, said nothing.

"For all I know, you're here to tell me that the first time we made love a couple of days ago is the last time we'll make love." Mary grabbed the napkin holder and tidied the edges of the napkins in it.

Ellis pulled out the chair across from Mary. She reached over the table and grasped Mary's hand, stopping any further fumbling with the napkins. "We probably need to talk about us."

Mary lifted her head, but couldn't bring herself to look into Ellis's eyes. "Is there an us?"

"I'm not sure."

"Is it because I don't know what to do in bed?"

Ellis heard the tremor in Mary's voice as she spoke. "Don't be ridiculous. You're a wonderful lover."

"Might have been beginner's luck."

"The only way to know for sure is to try it again."

"I'm not the sort of person who just has sex with somebody."

Ellis was pleased that Mary finally met her gaze. She wouldn't let her look away. "Me, either, Mary."

"But you said you're not sure if we have a future."

"Because I'm not."

"Do you have feelings for me?"

"I think so."

"Ellis, either you do or you don't. Which is it?"

Sam barked at the back door. "Let me get her," Ellis said. "Otherwise, she won't give us a minute's peace."

"Of course. Your *kid* needs you."

Ellis recoiled at the harshness of Mary's words, recalling they were the very ones she had used when Mary needed to tend to Natalie a few days earlier.

Ellis let Sam in, then reclaimed her seat at the kitchen table as Sam ambled to the living room and flopped on the floor in front of the sofa. "Is there something you want to say to me, Mary?"

"Not so much want to, but I think I have to."

"So say it."

"I will, but first, I want to remind you I've been sick. I haven't gotten much sleep the past several nights. I'm on the verge of a huge change in my life, and less than a week ago, I had my first real lesbian experience. I'm not exactly at my mental and emotional best, so if this comes out all wrong, I need you to promise me I get to try again."

"Okay, that's fair."

Ellis strained for patience as Mary moved the salt and pepper shakers and used the spoon in the sugar bowl to scrape the crystals off the rim. Then she pulled a napkin from the holder and rubbed at an old milk ring on the tabletop. Ellis continued to wait while Mary looked out the window, looked back at Ellis, then sucked in a loud breath.

"I'm pissed that you didn't come by here the last couple of days. We were sick. It would've been nice to have someone feed Swiffer and clean out her litter box. You could have at least brought us some Cokes or offered to make soup and toast for us. Natalie kept asking why you were mad at us. What could I tell her? I didn't have a clue about why you were treating us like lepers."

"I'm sorry."

"Sorry about what?"

Ellis reflexively moved back an inch or two at Mary's resurfaced bitterness. She feared what Mary might say next, but dared not interrupt.

"Are you sorry that we're more trouble than we're worth?" Mary spoke each word deliberately. Ellis felt as though they were lying on the table between them, taunting her for her failure.

She blurted out the first thing that came to mind. "No, I'm sorry I don't know what to do to help people when they're sick."

"It's not graduate level work, for God's sake. Do whatever needs doing."

"Nothing is ever right. Nothing is ever enough." Ellis noted the look of utter confusion on Mary's face.

"What does that mean?"

"Just what I said."

"Scoop a litter box. Run a load of laundry. Pick up a few groceries. Sit beside me, hold my hand, and tell me I'll be fine in a day or two. That would be right. That would be enough."

Ellis was quiet a long while. "Not necessarily." The words were nearly inaudible.

"Come on, Ellis. We can sit here and talk in circles all damn day, or you can treat me like an adult and say what's on your mind."

"Kids ruin everything."

"Excuse me? Where did that come from? I thought we were talking about my being mad at you for vanishing for the last three days while Natalie and I battled a stomach virus."

"Never mind. You wouldn't understand." Ellis pushed back from the table and stood.

"Oh, no you don't, VanStantvoordt. Sit down! You can't lob a live grenade into the middle of my imaginary bowl of corn flakes and then waltz off without explaining yourself."

Ellis glared at Mary. "You and your perfect life. You've got the whole freakin' world on a string. Nathan. Your mother. Your sisters. Natalie. You don't even know how good you've got it. Two steps in any direction, and you've got somebody who loves you and cares about what happens to you." Ellis dropped heavily onto her chair.

Mary pounded the tabletop. "You're right. I've got an ex-husband who still loves me, but he thinks I ruined his life. The only reason he still has anything to do with me is because he's the father of my child. My mother? Ha! She loves me, provided I don't dare be who I really am. Most of the time, my sisters are nothing more than a younger version of my mother. Want to wager how long their sisterly love holds up when I tell them I'm a member of Club Lesbian? Let's see, did I leave anybody out? Oh, yeah, my daughter. I can never quite decide which one of us is more intimidated by life.

Natalie because she thinks she's the reason her mommy and daddy don't live together anymore, or me because I'm afraid I'll screw her up so bad she'll spend forty years in therapy. Yep, you're right. I live a perfect existence." Mary squinted at Ellis. "All of which, by the way, has nothing whatsoever to do with your comment about how kids ruin everything."

Ellis rubbed her earlobe between her thumb and forefinger. She knew Mary was waiting for an explanation, but she wasn't sure what she could say that would do justice to all she was feeling. Ellis shoved a statement past her lips. "What I really meant is that I ruined everything."

"For Natalie? For me? For you and me?"

Ellis shook her head. "No, for my parents."

"You've lost me, Ellis. Please, no more riddles. Tell me plain and simple what you're trying to say."

"My mother and father had the life they wanted. He was living out his dream teaching art at the college. Even though she was sick for most of her life, my mother had raised the twins and was happy hanging on my father's every word and wish. Then I came along. It ruined everything."

Ellis doubted that Mary would ever speak. At last, she did.

"Ellis, you didn't ask to be born. Or if you did, like some of the psycho-babble-good-speak folks would have us believe, your parents had to agree to be the vehicles for getting you to the planet." She extended her open hand to Ellis who tentatively hooked her index finger over Mary's pinkie. "Honey, from what you told me, your mom was sick long before you were born. If you hadn't been born, she might have given up on life a lot sooner than she did. The way I see it, chances are real good you didn't ruin anything. You probably saved her life and gave her almost twenty years she wouldn't have had if you hadn't been there to make her want to live."

Ellis wiped a tear from the corner of her eye. "It's my fault she died."

"Why would you say something like that?" Ellis caught the disbelief on Mary's face.

"She died because I convinced her to go to my outdoor graduation ceremony."

"Or she might have died exactly when she did even if she'd never set foot outside the house."

"You can't know that."

"And you can't know that your version is right, either."

Ellis let Mary pull her hand into a warm clasp as she contemplated the possibility Mary had presented.

"Let me give you one other idea to add to the mix, okay?" Mary squeezed Ellis's hand. "Maybe seeing you graduate from high school was the proof she needed that she'd done enough to set you on your way. Maybe her death was her way of giving you both the freedom to explore whatever else you each needed to do next."

"But my father and my brother and sister... I know they blamed me."

"You *think* they blamed you. If you never asked them, you can't know for sure."

"It felt like they thought it was my fault."

"Even if you're right in that supposition, that's their karma. You're only responsible for you."

Ellis used her free hand to caress Mary's fingers interlaced with hers. "I don't know. I don't think I can let myself off the hook that easily."

"News flash. You're the only one who can ever let yourself off the hook. We don't get to control what happens in our lives. We don't get to know why anything happens. All we get to do is decide how we feel about what happens and then pick what we think is the best thing to do next."

"How'd you get so smart?"

"That's a laugh. Look at the mess I've made of my life."

"Are you serious?"

"Well, yeah. Here's a perfect example. I just turned thirty-nine, and even though I've known I liked women for more than thirty of those years, I've got exactly one notch on my headboard to show for it." Mary waited until Ellis looked her in the eye before continuing. "And to this very moment, I don't know if that was a one-to-a-customer deal or if my ticket is still good for another ride."

Without letting go of Mary's hand, Ellis stood. "Come with me, cowgirl. I've heard the rodeo is in town."

"What about getting this house ready to sell and talking about kids and making plans for what we're going to do about us?" Mary let Ellis lead the way through the living room and down the hall.

"Later. Right now, I'm picking the best thing to do next."

* * *

Mary was surprised at Ellis's sudden change in ardor. "What happened between the kitchen and my bedroom? Don't you want to do this?

"Every inch of me wants to do this, but seeing your bed reminded me of the little chat your mother had with me in her kitchen while you were taking Gloria and the kids home the other day." Ellis dropped like a brick onto the seat of the straight-backed chair in the corner of the bedroom.

Mary yanked off her sweatshirt and slammed it into the clothes hamper. "Wonderful. My mother is still ruining my sex life."

"She's got some real strong suspicions about what's going on between us. She quoted the Bible and everything."

"Oh, hell. That's no measure of anything. She quotes the Bible when she changes the TV channel." Mary kicked her shoes off. "You'd better tell me everything she said."

Ellis recounted the conversation, including her lies.

Mary ran a brush through her hair. "I hoped with Kendall puking his guts out and everyone else bolting for the door, Mother hadn't heard Natalie's invitation for you to have a sleepover in her room."

Ellis pressed her back against the chair. "No such luck. I probably shouldn't have lied to your mother."

"Yes, you should have. You don't need to bear the brunt of her wrath. That honor belongs to me."

"So you're going to tell her about us?"

"Of course, but I need to be sure I've done all the groundwork." Mary stepped on the heel of her left sock with her right foot and pulled her foot free, then did the same for the other foot. "But who are we kidding? She already knows. She's merely giving herself a long cruise down 'de Nile' until I fess up and send her to an early grave."

"How do you think she found out?"

"My mother still refers to my birth as the day I ran away from home. She's always known every evil thing I've ever done or even contemplated doing."

Ellis moved to the front edge of the chair. "Aren't you worried that she'll cut you out of her life?"

Mary smiled wistfully. "Some days, that's my fondest wish." She unbuttoned the top button of her shirt. "But she won't. She'll fume loudly and pray unceasingly and say things she'll regret, and eventually, it will fade into oblivion."

"How can you be so sure?"

"It's what happened when Naomi married—gasp—a Methodist. Mother swore she'd never allow the heathen in her house. That lasted about two months, and then Naomi turned up pregnant with her first grandchild, and Barry's horrible deficiency was forgiven, or at least forgotten. Same story with my divorce from Nathan. You'd have thought I'd single-handedly unleashed all the plagues of the Old Testament. She still nags the daylights out of me about that, but she doesn't think I'm the devil's stepdaughter, either."

"So I don't need to worry about her looking in your bedroom window and alerting the DeKalb Police Department?"

"I'm not saying we can be totally free around her, but give me some time to work on her. We might as well hope for the best." Mary undid the next button on her shirt. "And speaking of best, weren't we supposed to be getting on with the best thing to do next?" She crooked a finger at Ellis.

Ellis began undressing as she rose from the chair. "Thanks for reminding me."

* * *

They made love slowly at first, then with an intense abandon that left them both sated, lying in one another's arms. Mary dozed, but Ellis stayed awake, savoring the joy of Mary's long, lean body nestled against her and doubting that anything could ever go wrong between them again. No, they couldn't be together every night, and maybe not even every weekend, but they would journey on together as a team. Yes, there were still misgivings nipping at the edges of her happiness—Natalie being one of the biggest of those—but for those few electric minutes while Mary reposed peacefully beside her, Ellis had the distinct feeling that her life was only going to get better and better.

* * *

Mary stirred awake and spoke. "So you'll help me get ready to move when the time comes, right?"

Before answering, Ellis settled Mary's head in a more comfortable spot on her shoulder and tightened her embrace. "Sure I will. Of course, given the way you made me feel over the last hour, you could ask me to carry every piece of your furniture to Clarkesville one by one on my back, and I'd probably do it. I guess it'll be easier to use my truck, though, huh?"

"I didn't know my body could feel so much pleasure." Mary breathed deeply. "Why is it that everything I want seems to be in direct opposition to something else I want?"

"Such as?"

"I want this house to sell fast so that I don't have to have an endless parade of potential buyers traipsing through it, but at the same time, I don't want it to sell at all, because it'll mean moving away from you."

"Okay, that's one dichotomy. What else?"

"Having you here in my bed, doing what we've been doing is like a dream come true. It was so nice not to have to worry that Nat was going to bang on the door and interrupt us."

"She can be the queen of less-than-perfect timing, can't she?"

"No joke, but even though I'm glad she's not here this very minute, I still miss her. I know she's safe with Nathan, even if he's not making her behave herself, but I feel like there's a giant hole right here in the center of me"—Mary rubbed her chest—"whenever she's gone."

"Understood. Anything else?"

"You bet. There's Nathan. I need him in my life, and I want him to go away and leave me alone. My mom and my sisters make me certifiably insane, but I know they'll always come through for me if I really need them. I'm excited about finding a new house up in Clarkesville, but I'm not sure what it will be like to live there." Mary sighed for dramatic effect. "Do you think I'm on the verge of a nervous breakdown?"

"No, I don't think so. It's more likely a reflection of how complicated your life is."

"I didn't even mention the biggest struggle I'm having."

"Which is what?"

"Now that I know what it means to want somebody, body and soul," Mary said and hugged Ellis extra hard, "all I want to do is lie in your arms."

"That doesn't sound like a conflict of interest to me." Ellis returned the hug and added a kiss for good measure.

"It is when you take all of the other things I mentioned and put them on the opposite side of the scale. Somehow, I need to tell my ex-husband, my daughter, my mother, and my sisters that I'm Gretchen VanStantvoordt's love slave."

"At least that'll keep me out of the crosshairs. They all think I'm Ellis."

"See what I mean? I haven't even told them your real name yet. How will I ever tell them the rest of it?"

"From what I saw of your family the one and only time I've been in their company, they probably won't even hear it until at least the fourth time you say it."

"Yeah, and even then, I'll have to stand in the middle of the table, naked as a jaybird, and shout it through a megaphone."

"Now that paints a picture. Please be sure to videotape the event for me."

"Tape it? No, m'dear. Despite what I said earlier, the more I think about it, the best way to break this to my mother will be for both of us to be there. She won't dare go totally ape-shit if you're right beside me when I drop this little bombshell."

"I don't think your mom's table can support both of us. I'd still vote for your telling her when I'm a safe distance away." Ellis chuckled. "Say, South America, or maybe Australia."

"We'll see." Ellis heard the distress in Mary's voice as she continued. "But first things first, I guess. I need to get this house shined up so that the first people who look at it buy it on the spot." Mary got up to dress.

"I can help," Ellis said as she pulled the comforter into place on the bed. "Where should we start?"

"Nat's room. I think the EPA is considering labeling it a hazardous-waste dump. We should probably wear protective clothing while we're in there."

"I could go out to the truck and get the heavy-duty gloves I use when I'm spraying weed killer."

Mary rounded the end of the bed and wrapped Ellis in her arms. "Good idea. The very last thing I'd want you to damage is those magical fingers of yours."

"Make up your mind, Moss," Ellis said as a new surge of adrenaline hit her. She caressed Mary's lower back as Mary pressed herself tighter against her. "Are we packing up your daughter's room or going back to bed?"

"Let's tackle the brat's room." She kissed Ellis deeply. "And when we've had as much of that as we can stand..." She looked meaningfully at the bed. "I know the perfect reward."

Chapter 9

"Have a good weekend with your dad, sweetie." Mary leaned out the car window to give Natalie a quick kiss on the cheek and waited until she was inside the door to Nathan's apartment before backing out of the parking space. Her ex-husband waved once as he shut the door.

"He knows," Mary said, a hint of hysteria in her voice.

"Knows what?" Ellis asked.

"Knows there's something going on between you and me." Mary pulled onto the street in front of Nathan's apartment complex.

"Do you think he and your mother have been comparing notes?"

"Maybe. Have you ever known him not to chat up a storm when he and I are making the handoff with Nat? He didn't ask us to come in, didn't offer to get Nat's backpack. He just stood in the door and looked at us like we had incurable cooties."

"Maybe he had a rough week at work. Maybe he was watching something on TV he didn't want to miss."

"I've known the man my whole life." Mary turned south on Route 115. "I'll bet he knows."

Ellis tapped Mary's forearm. "So what? We've said all along we need to find a way to tell him and Natalie and the rest of your family. We could maybe make an ally out of him. I bet if he were to come out—pardon the use of the words—on our side when we talk to your mother, it might help in the long run."

"It might, but I wanted to tell everybody in my own way. I worry sometimes now that he's back in the original land of the Bible-thumpers."

"How so?"

"If he didn't want to be my loving and supportive ex-husband, he could get some crazy ideas about having me declared an unfit mother or something."

"Do you really think he'd do that?"

"I hope not, but if his mother joined in the inevitable preaching from my mother and sisters, it's a possibility. It would kill me if I had to become a part-time mother." Her hands shook as she clung to the steering wheel. "What if I could only see Nat once a month?"

It wouldn't be the worst possible situation, Ellis thought to herself. She had the good sense not to say it out loud. The past three months of dealing with Natalie day in and day out (save for the weekends when she was with Nathan) had rekindled her opinion that children were God's demented idea of a poorly executed practical joke.

The downturn in the housing market had slowed house sales to a crippled tortoise's pace. There had only been three lookers at Mary's house, and none of them could make an offer until their own houses sold. Mary and Nathan had agreed that they wouldn't take a contract contingent on the sale of the buyer's house, so things hung in suspended animation.

Nathan had moved to Clarkesville in early January. Every Friday since, except for the weekends Nathan was working, Mary had driven Natalie up so that she could have time with her dad. If Nathan had to come pick her up, he probably couldn't get her until Saturday mornings. Since Mary could flex her schedule, she could have Natalie there when Nathan got home from work Friday afternoon. Mary preferred that arrangement.

Most Fridays, Ellis rode along. The trip back to Atlanta from the foothills—when she was alone with Mary and had the entire weekend to look forward to—almost made the drive up worth the aggravation of Natalie's endless chatter.

"Let's not assume gloom and doom yet, okay?" Ellis suggested. "No point in thinking Nathan is plotting against you."

"You're right, but I can't help but get the feeling the excrement is going to hit the air-circulation device any day now." Mary reached for Ellis's hand and held it briefly. "I love you, you know? But why does being in love have to be such a kick in the pants?"

They drove on past the rolling hills. Mary merged onto the four-lane, weaving along with the heavy Friday-evening traffic. "I swear gas could cost ten dollars a gallon, and all these fools would still be on the road."

"Pot calls kettle black. Film at eleven," Ellis said with a drop or two of sarcasm.

"I know, I know. It costs me about thirty dollars to get Nat to and from her dad's every weekend, but what can I do?"

"I'm not arguing, love, merely making an observation."

"God, I wish my house would sell."

"Yeah, then I could be the one spending thirty dollars to drive up to see you on weekends." Ellis let the sarcasm quotient rise unchecked.

"Sorry. I know there's no such thing as a perfect solution to this mess. I'm starting to feel like I have a split personality." Mary braked sharply to avoid a car that darted into her lane. "Idiot!" She eased up on the accelerator to put a greater distance between her and the car. "I don't want to be away from you, but driving to and from the mountains every weekend is going to be the death of me." She glanced at Ellis. "Are you sure you couldn't move up to the mountains, too? Assuming my house ever sells, that is, and I actually get to relocate."

Ellis silently counted to ten. "We've been through that at least a hundred times. I'm barely able to cover my expenses as it is. Even if I could find enough landscaping jobs up in the hills, which I seriously doubt, the cost of gas to get to them would kill me. It's bad enough now, even though I cluster jobs together so I don't have to drive so much. I don't think my moving to north Georgia would be a smart career move."

"You could do something besides landscaping, couldn't you?" Mary asked quietly.

"Sure, if Wal-Mart is hiring or one of the service stations needs somebody to sell lottery tickets to people who can't even afford to put five gallons of gas in their uninsured pickup truck."

Mary didn't respond right away. "We'll just have to see what happens, huh?"

"Yep."

Mary turned on the headlights. "Another week or two and we'll be able to make this whole drive in the daylight."

"Another week or two and I won't be making the trip with you because I'll still be out on a job at this time of day."

"Then I guess we need to make the most of the rest of this one." Mary reached across the console to touch Ellis's leg. "I love you, El."

"Love you, too." Ellis gripped Mary's hand. And for at least the millionth time, she almost wished she didn't.

* * *

"Thanks for taking the day off to help with the move, Ellis." Mary crammed the vacuum cleaner into the Xterra's rear hatch, already stuffed with Swiffer's litter box, a bag of cat food, several suitcases, and three coolers bearing whatever had been left in Mary's refrigerator. "I can't believe this is really happening."

"I know what you mean." Ellis hoped the growing lump in her throat wasn't evident to Mary. "Sam and I spent more time here in the past five months than we spent at my apartment. She's gonna miss her backyard."

"I'm gonna miss ol' Sammy." Mary leaned against Ellis. "And I'm gonna miss her mama even more."

"I'm still surprised you decided to move when there's only a little more than a month left in the school year."

"Nat's been a mess since Nathan moved up north in January. In her heart, she's already living in the mountains. Because she's spent so many weekends with Nathan, she's gotten to know a lot of kids up there. She'll probably have the easiest adjustment of any of us."

"Good thing she could stay with your mom this week while you finished packing up the house."

"Yes and no. Good to have her gone so she's not underfoot, but it's anybody's guess what Baptist garbage Mom's stuffing into her impressionable little mind."

"I thought you told me you'd already enrolled her in school up there."

"I did, but school only runs six hours a day. My mother has the other eighteen hours to pollute her brain." Mary pantomimed opening the top of her head and pouring liquid into it. "I told you what a battle I had with Mom over putting Nat in public school. She wanted her to go to Christian Academy where my nieces and nephews go."

"Starting tonight, you'll be there to keep the scales balanced."

"Sort of. But there's no such thing as winning an argument with my mother. And you'll have confirmation of that if we ever get around to having that long-overdue discussion with her about our relationship."

"Don't remind me. Today is hard enough already." Ellis offered a sympathetic smile. "What's left in the house?" she asked, hoping to have some last chores that would keep her from acknowledging the hollow ache that was growing bigger with every passing minute.

"My laptop, a briefcase with the notes I've taken for the stories I'm working on, and Swiffer and her carrier." Mary took a shaky breath. "And ten years' worth of memories." She stepped back from Ellis. "The sweetest ones came in the last six months, thanks to you."

Ellis swallowed hard, barely keeping the tears from having their way. "Better get you loaded up and on your way. The truck is already ten minutes ahead of you."

"You're right. Come inside and kiss me one last time." Ellis followed Mary into the house. Swiffer was locked in the cat carrier sitting in the middle of the kitchen floor. She yowled as if she were caught in the rollers of a wringer washer.

"That will be pleasant to listen to all the way to Clarkesville," Ellis said.

"I figure after the next two weeks at my mother's, I'd welcome Swiffer's serenade as a melodic change of pace."

"It's too bad you couldn't get into your new house 'til Memorial Day weekend."

"No kidding. After three months of treading water waiting for an offer on the house, everything happened in a torrent. Lord only knows how much of my stuff will get lost or damaged in storage over the next couple of weeks."

"As long as the guys don't drop those huge crates when they're unloading the truck at the storage facility, it'll be fine."

"I hope you're right." In the living room, Mary took a long look around the barren space. "I brought my baby here when she was two days old. How can she be almost ten already?"

"I remember meeting her right there"—Ellis gestured toward where the sofa used to sit—"the day I fell for you on LaVista Road." Ellis draped her arm around Mary's shoulder. "Quite a detour we've been on since last November, huh?"

"And we're not exactly on the highway to heaven right now, either, with you staying here in the city at your apartment while I'm up in the far reaches of Outer Hooterville." Mary's voice cracked as she spoke.

"Don't start, okay? Neither one of us can afford to think right now about what all this means. You've got to go so you can meet the moving van at the storage place in Clarkesville." Ellis stanched a snuffle. "And I've got to get out of this house before…"

"One last thing, and then we'll go." Mary led the way down the hall to her bedroom. Their footfalls echoed off the walls. Once in the room, Mary cradled Ellis to her bosom. "I'll always remember the way it felt to kiss you for the first time. I never want to know what it might feel like to think we've had our last kiss."

Ellis backed away from Mary's embrace and held both of Mary's hands tightly. She stared into the eyes that had captivated her so thoroughly. "Never the last one. Always only the promise of the next one."

Their final kiss in the house on Wilson Woods Drive tasted of memories and of tears; of love found and of farewell; of pledges understood but unspoken.

* * *

Thank God for springtime in Atlanta. Over the next six weeks, Ellis was nearly overwhelmed with obligations to her customers, and that kept her from missing Mary quite as much as she otherwise would have. Days started early and lasted late. Breakfast was usually a piece or two of fruit and some granola bars. If she got lunch at all, it was a sandwich from a sub shop. Dinner? Like she had energy to fix anything, or eat it, after chasing the lawn mower and hauling mulch around all day.

On June sixth, she spent the morning and early afternoon building rock-ringed gardens and filling them with encore azaleas for a new client in Ormewood, not too far from the zoo and the Atlanta Cyclorama. She stopped to grab a late lunch on her way to another job in Kirkwood, just off Moreland Avenue.

In a rare move, Ellis gave herself the extra few minutes to go inside and eat her lunch at a table instead of pulling through the drive-thru and eating in the cab of her truck. She parked in the lot of a joint she used to know well at the corner of Ponce de Leon and Clifton Road.

As she stood in line at the sandwich shop, she caught the scent of a familiar perfume. She usually steered clear of the stores in the Candler Park vicinity, and if her nose was telling her the truth, she should have stuck to that plan.

"Ellis?"

The voice clinched it. Better she had starved to death than run the risk of stumbling over her past.

She pushed her tray a few inches farther along the rails of the serving line before turning around.

"Hi, Becky." How could two simple words feel like battery acid tumbling on her tongue? She trained her eyes to the left of Becky Blumfeld's face and tried to look a thousand miles beyond Becky's shoulder.

"Gosh, it's been forever since I've seen you." Becky rubbed Ellis's upper arm with her knuckles. "How have you been?"

Any casual observer would have thought it was a perfectly reasonable, social inquiry. From Ellis's perspective, better Becky had run a dagger directly into her heart to spare her the agonizing death of making small talk in a public place.

"Good, thanks. How about you?" She willed herself to look at Becky's face. It was flushed and full, much rounder than Ellis remembered it. She let her gaze drop. "Oh. Oh, wow. I mean. Umm. Good for you."

Becky's distended belly protruded unmistakably.

"Good for us," Becky said, as she pulled the hand of the woman behind her so that she stood by Becky's side. "Ruthann Lockburger, this is Ellis VanStantvoordt."

Ellis and Ruthann mumbled greetings to one another. The clerk behind the counter indicated it was Ellis's turn to order.

"Turkey and swiss on whole wheat. Dress it all the way, extra pickles. Large sweet iced tea. And I've changed my mind about dining in. Make that to go." She turned back to face Becky and Ruthann.

"Why don't you stay and eat with us, Ellis?" Becky asked. "We could catch up on things."

"Thanks, but I can't. I've got another lawn to take care of, and I'm already running late."

"Are you sure?" Ruthann put her hand on Ellis's shoulder. Ellis wanted to swat it away, but controlled the urge. "It would be nice to get to know you," Ruthann said.

Ellis hated the deep, masculine tone of Ruthann's voice. She hated the presumed familiarity Ruthann exuded. She hated the smug possessiveness the woman radiated toward Becky. In fact, Ellis hated every single thing about Ruthann Lockburger and hoped she was very soon diagnosed with a debilitating illness that withered her physically and mentally and in every other way with horrible, painful, indescribable, excruciating agony—but slowly, and for sure without any drugs that eased the suffering.

"No, really, I can't." She fumbled in the side pocket of her cargo shorts for her wallet and traded money for a To Go cup and sandwich bag, then started toward the door.

"Ellis, wait." Becky tugged on the back of Ellis's T-shirt.

"Wait for what? For you to have your baby on one of the tables here so I can applaud your great success?" She gestured wildly toward the seated patrons, spilling some tea from her cup as she did. "Crap." She set the cup on a flat-topped trash can by the door and shook the sticky liquid from her hand.

"Why are you so angry?" Becky said each word as though it tasted of vinegar and lemon juice.

"Who's angry?" Ellis retorted. "What do I have to be angry about? You think it bothers me that you've got yourself a hot new butch sugar mama and that you're well on your way to having the perfect little artificially-inseminated suburban family?" She pointed at Becky's midsection. "Guess again. I forgot about you the day I walked out the door of what was supposedly *our* house eighteen months ago."

"Ellis, don't—"

"Don't what, Rebecca? Don't make a scene in public? Don't tell people your unborn child has a turkey baster for a father? Don't run the risk of telling your cherished girlfriend that she's nothing but a rebound second choice? Just what is it you don't want me to do?"

Ellis and Becky stood toe to toe, glaring at one another.

Ruthann hastened over and pulled Becky away. "Are you all right, sweetheart? Remember what the doctor said about your blood pressure."

Becky took a final look at Ellis, then let Ruthann lead her to a table where their tray of food awaited. Ellis grabbed her iced tea and fled the shop.

Her hand was shaking so badly that she dropped her keys on the pavement beside her truck. As she bent to retrieve them, she hit her shoulder on the door-mounted rearview mirror and dropped the cup, splashing sugary tea all over her work boots. "Damn you, Becky Blumfeld," she screamed. Damn you and your swaggering new partner and your precious baby—the baby that was more important than I was.

* * *

It was almost dark by the time Ellis finished the second job and drove to her apartment. Sam was waiting for her at the door, dancing with joy and with a bladder that urgently needed relief.

"C'mon, kid. Let's take a quick trip to your favorite patch of grass." She grabbed Sam's leash from the hook on the back of the door and snapped it on. Without the benefit of Mary's yard to run in, Sam had put on several pounds over the past month-and-a-half. She fairly waddled as she hurried down the stairs ahead of Ellis. From sunup to sunset, jobs kept Ellis away, so Sam was well on her way to being attention-starved, bored, and overweight. Strenuous physical labor kept Ellis from being overweight, but the other two adjectives applied to owner as well as to dog.

When Sam finished, she tugged on her leash, eager as always to hurry back to the apartment to have her puppy chow. As they climbed the steps, Ellis realized she was as hungry as Sam appeared to be. Her confrontation with Becky and Ruthann at the sandwich shop had left her too riled to choke down the sandwich she'd bought. She debated with herself whether or not it was still safe to eat her turkey and swiss sub, or if the early June heat beating into the cab of her truck for the past couple of hours had soured the mayo. And if she didn't eat that, what else might her meager pantry have as an alternative?

"Hey, neighbor!" Her culinary contemplation was interrupted by the husband of the couple who lived across the outdoor walkway from her unit. Russ came out of his apartment carrying two bags of trash. Sam loped over to him, hoping for some affection and maybe a dog cookie, which Russ often carried in his pocket for Robbie, his Welsh Corgi. Russ set his bags down and obliged with a hearty rubdown of Sam's head and ears, followed by slipping her a crunchy biscuit.

"Hi, yourself," Ellis said. "How are you and Janet?"

"Good. Make that fantastic. Better than fantastic."

"Why's that?"

Russ grinned conspiratorially. "We haven't even told my parents yet, so you're getting the news hot off the press. We found out today that Janet's pregnant. We've been trying for what feels like forever."

"That's great news, Russ." Ellis did her best to sound sincere. "I couldn't be happier for you."

"Thanks." He patted Sam's head again. "We talked about looking into adoption, but there's just something about having your very own kid, you know?"

"Absolutely," Ellis fibbed.

"It's not like we don't know what a mess the world is. The wars in Iraq and Afghanistan and the drought here in the South. The news guys can't shut up about the financial mess the country is in. Then there's global warming and all that, but having a baby is like saying to the world 'Hey, there's hope. We believe in the future.'"

For the effect his words had on her, he might as well have swung his bags of trash into her diaphragm. How many times had she and Becky argued about this? However many times it had been, it always ended with Becky reminding Ellis of how, at their commitment ceremony, she'd promised always to believe in the future. According to Becky, children *are* the future, and Ellis was nothing but a lower-than-a-snake's-belly liar. Now, on what was proving to be one of the most emotionally punishing days of her life, a near-stranger was grinding her face in her biggest character flaw: her disinclination to participate in parenthood.

Ellis felt the sting of tears behind her eyelids. She shifted Sam's leash to her left hand and offered her right one to Russ. "Congratulations, buddy. Give my best to Janet. I hope the next nine months go smoothly for you both."

"Only eight. She's already one month along."

"Like I said, I hope it goes well." Ellis yanked Sam into her apartment and closed the door behind them.

"I can't freakin' believe this. Is the whole world having babies?" As she unclipped Sam's leash and flipped the wall switch to turn on the table lamps on either side of the sofa, the phone rang.

She grabbed a tissue and blew her nose. "I don't care who it is." She unlaced her work boots. "With my luck, it'll be some long-lost friend or relative telling me they want me to be the godmother for their darling infant."

After the fourth ring, the answering machine clicked on. "Hi, Ellis. It's Natalie. Natalie Kimbrough. Mom said I could call you. She said not to use your cell phone number because you might be out working and not to interrupt. And she said you'd be home by now, but I guess you're not. I know tomorrow is your birthday, so Happy Birthday. I hope you get to do something fun. I've only seen you one time since me and Mom moved up to Clarkesville. I'm really lonesome for you. And for Sam. Do you think you could bring Sam up and stay with us for the weekend? Mom said she'd make you a birthday cake. Did you know we're in our own house now and not staying with my gramma any more? My dad has to work all weekend, so I'll be home with Mom. Call us, okay? Tell Sammy I still love her. Bye. Oh, wait…" Ellis heard Mary saying something in the background. "And Ellis, Mom and I think you're really weird." Mother and daughter giggled briefly. They shouted "Happy Birthday" in unison, and the call disconnected.

Ellis kicked off her boots and collapsed on the sofa. Sam nudged her, repeatedly, reminding her that it was past time for an evening meal.

"Have you forgotten that canine children are supposed to be perfectly behaved? You're as big a bother as the human kind." Ellis labored to her feet, went to the kitchen, and tossed a handful of food into Sam's bowl beside the refrigerator.

She knew better than to look at what was hanging on her refrigerator door, but she did so anyway. Shortly after moving to Clarkesville with her mother, Natalie had printed out various pictures she'd taken with the camera Ellis gave her for Christmas. Sam and Swiffer. Mary and Sam. Ellis and Mary. Ellis and Mary with Sam and Swiffer. A shot with Mary, Ellis, Natalie, Sam, and Swiffer taken with the camera's timer delay feature. But the one that got to her was one that Mary had taken of her and Natalie. Ellis was sitting on the sofa in Mary's old living room. Natalie stood behind the sofa with her arms looped around Ellis's neck. She was leaning down so that her face was right next to Ellis's. Natalie had drawn a big red heart around the two of them. Across the bottom she had printed "Me and My Other Mother."

Maybe if it weren't the eve of her thirty-eighth birthday, or maybe if Natalie hadn't ended her phone message with the secret code phrase she and her mother had for "I love you," Ellis could have allowed the photos to have a momentary effect on her feelings and then scurried to squelch those feelings, as she usually did. But the aggregate of seeing Becky, hearing Russ and Janet's news, knowing she'd spend her birthday alone, and having Natalie tell her she missed her and loved her was too much. She needed someone to love her unconditionally, and Sam couldn't fill the bill. She needed that sustaining love, and she needed it now.

She couldn't remember the last time she'd thought about her own mother. What would be the point? She'd been dead for more than half of Ellis's life. Maybe if, as an adult, she'd gotten to know her mother as a person, she'd have a better handle on what prompted this seemingly universal fascination—obsession?—with people wanting and having children.

"I miss you, Mom."

Had she ever spoken those words before? Not that she could recall. "I miss you," she repeated. "Thanks for giving me my original birthday." Suddenly it was imperative that she find a thread, however frayed, back to her mother. She went to the closet in her bedroom and yanked a Foster's Ale box down from the shelf. Using her pocketknife, she slit the four strips of tape holding the cardboard lid shut.

First thing out of the box: her report cards, first through twelfth grades, held together with rubber bands. Next out of the box: her high school year book from Windsor Forest High, Savannah, class of '87. Then a collection of birthday cards, followed by playbills from school productions she'd assisted with behind the scenes, usually as a set builder. Under that was an embroidered dresser scarf that had adorned one of the furniture pieces in her bedroom the entire time she lived in her parents' house. Her mother had done the stitch work on it. She ran her fingertips over the knots on the back side of the cloth. Her imagination played tricks on her. It felt like someone was holding her hand.

On the bottom of the box was a photo album, still encased in its plastic protective sleeve. Ellis lifted it from the box and wiped off the layer of dust. In the oval space on the front was a picture of Ellis, very young and pale, in her Windsor Forest cap and gown. There was a smile on her face, but the look in her eyes didn't match it. Fear? Sorrow? Old beyond her years? A glimpse into the very near future?

Above the photo a side-opening slot permitted insertion of a title or caption. Ellis recognized the handwriting on the piece of cardstock. Her mother had carefully printed, "All Grown Up. Gretchen Alina VanStantvoordt." She pulled the card from the slot. As she had done with the dresser scarf, Ellis let her fingers lightly touch the surface. Almost like a movie being shown against the far wall, she "saw" an image of her mother sitting in the muted light of the living room of the house in Savannah. She was carefully seated on the edge of the chair, her left arm resting on the drop-leaf desk as she wrote a letter to send to Nicolas or Anika. Talking often sent her mother into fits of coughing, so she avoided the telephone and stayed in touch with her twins by letter. But the card in Ellis's hand wasn't written for one of her siblings. It was for her.

"She touched this." The words were whispered, almost like a prayer. "She made this album for me."

Her mother had given her the album when they got home from the graduation exercises that late May afternoon in 1987. She had taken seriously ill that evening and gotten worse by the hour. Ellis's last summer in Savannah was spent at her bedside, watching her die, paper-thin breath by paper-thin breath.

Then there was the funeral, and only a few weeks after that, Ellis left for college. The album, never opened, was packed away with the other scraps of her childhood—a childhood Ellis had always believed was better not reflected on.

Now, some twenty years later, Ellis needed to go home. She opened the cover.

The first picture was of an unidentifiable bundle lying in her mother's arms. Her mother looked drawn and weary. The notation beneath it read, "First picture. September 6, 1969."

"I'm sorry, Mom," Ellis said. "I know I gave you a rough time getting into the world." It had taken three months for her mother to be well enough to get a first photo with her infant. Despite her obvious infirmity, there was no mistaking the complete adoration on Helen VanStantvoordt's face as she cradled her wee one. Ellis blotted up the tear that splashed onto the page.

Next came several pictures of the twins on either side of Ellis. Of course the notes beneath referred to her as Gretchen. No dates or ages were given. Ellis guessed herself to be less than two. She turned the page. Anika held Ellis on her lap, hunched forward so that her face was right next to Ellis's. Ellis read the caption three times. The words didn't make any sense. "Baby Gretchen with her Other Mother, 1971."

Other mother?

The realization hit. Her mother was too ill to care for her when she was first born, or for that matter, for much of her first few years. Someone had to do it. It certainly wouldn't have been her father. It must have been Anika.

She looked through the rest of the album.

Page by page, she studied the pictures and the words her mother had chosen to describe them. Nothing out of the ordinary. Ellis on her third birthday; the three VanStantvoordt children in front of the Christmas tree in 1973; the children on the beach at Tybee Island off the Savannah coast; Ellis with the twins in their caps and gowns on their graduation day in 1974; Ellis waving good-bye from the front steps to Nicolas as he left for Princeton that fall.

She came across another picture of her and Anika. She and her sister stood side by side, but with a foot of space between them. Anika's face looked red and swollen, as if she'd been crying. Neither eighteen-year-old Anika nor five-year-old Ellis was looking at the camera. It was captioned: *Anika leaves for Virginia State, Sept. 1974. How hard for Anika to say good-bye. Gretchen will miss her.*

She continued flipping pages. Ellis's first day of school. Ellis at the fifth grade spelling bee. Ellis with her mother on Mother's Day, 1979. Ellis as a young teen and her father on the front porch, both looking bored and uncomfortable. Ellis holding her first driver's license as she stood beside her father's 1982 Oldsmobile, the car she'd taken her road test in. Assorted Christmases, some birthdays, other snapshots that froze some moment deemed worthy at the time. But none of Ellis with both parents. And no more pictures of her brother and sister.

She strained to remember everything she could about the years after Nicolas and Anika left home for college. She was sure they'd both come home occasionally while they were in college, but those instances were painted in the same blurry impressionistic renderings as much of the rest of her childhood and youth. Her only distinct memories was of them being home for their mother's funeral in early August of 1987 and then for her father's in 2002.

She recalled her sister's wedding. Ellis was nine. Anika graduated from Virginia State with her degree in Visual Communication and Art Design in June of '78, and married in August of the same year. Her mother had been too sick to travel to Richmond for the wedding, so Ellis and her father made the drive without her. Nicolas was one of the groomsmen, and her father walked Anika down the aisle. Ellis remembered wearing a dress that was at least a half size too small and sitting all alone in a pew on the bride's side of the church. She had no memories at all of a reception or photographs, only the long, silent ride back to Savannah after the ceremony, her father driving all night with her sleeping off and on in the backseat of the car.

Ellis thumbed backwards through the album. "No wonder I'm such a weirdo. We sure look like an emotionally constipated bunch."

She was all set to plop the album back in the box but decided to take one more look through it, since tonight would probably be the first and last time she turned the pages. It was no more satisfying on the second pass than it had been on the first. The album wasn't even full; it stopped cold several pages from the back, the clear overlay sheets plastered to the self-stick backing.

She absentmindedly turned the first blank page and then the second one, but when she glanced down, she was surprised to see the page wasn't blank at all. Affixed beneath the overlay was the first page of a letter in her mother's tidy, labored cursive dated May 3, 1987. Her heart fluttered wildly in her chest as she read.

My dear Grettie,

In a few weeks, you'll graduate from high school. We already know you're going away to college in Athens this fall, so I can only call you my baby a little while longer. I will miss you dearly when you go. I wanted to put this album together for you so that you'll have something of home to take with you.

I haven't been a very good mother to you. My sicknesses have kept me from doing so many things I wanted to do with you and for you. I hope you can forgive me for that.

More than just these photographs, though, there are some very important things I need to tell you. Your father and I disagree about this, and he has told me I must not say anything to you on this matter. Although it's not wise to cross him, I have decided that writing it is not the same as saying it, so if he ever finds out I've told you, my excuse is that I used pen and paper and not spoken words. He may be angry with me, but it won't be the first time.

There is no easy way to tell you this, so I will just say it plainly: Nicolas and Anika are your half-brother and half-sister. When I was young and foolish, I fell in love with a man who told me he loved me, too. He only loved me as far as the bedroom, and when he learned I was pregnant, he vanished like a thin fog on a hot summer morning.

I thought my life was ruined forever, but then while the twins were still less than a year old, I took a class at the college and met your father. To my delight, we found love with one another. He agreed not only to be my husband, but also to be a father to Nicolas and Anika. He was nearly forty when we met, so taking on a ready-made family was a big sacrifice for him. He made me promise him one thing, though. He insisted that we not tell the twins that he was not their biological father. Perhaps he thought it was best for them, but I suspect it was more about his wanting to always feel in control. I confess that it also let me bury my shame for my earlier mistake. That's part of the reason I agreed to honor your father's rule not to tell them the truth.

Our life as a family went along well for several years, but then an unexpected blessing came along. We learned that you were on the way. From the second I knew your tiny body was growing inside of me, I promised myself that, if God allowed it, I would give birth to you, even if it was the last thing I ever accomplished. Because my health was already failing, the doctors cautioned us about the risks. Your father wanted me to end the pregnancy in hopes of protecting my health. I refused. The doctor wanted to give me a drug that was supposed to prevent miscarriages. Like most drugs, it had some long name that I don't remember, but its common name was DES. I told the doctor I wouldn't take the drug. Your father was furious with me, first for refusing to end your barely started life and then for not doing what the doctor said I should do.

As you see, I made the right choice. You came to the world whole and healthy, and I have never once regretted my decision.

But your father could be an unpredictable man.

A few days after Nicolas and Anika graduated from high school, he told them the truth about not being their real father. Your brother felt angry and betrayed. Your sister was confused and overwhelmed. They blamed your father for the deceit, and they blamed me for my silence. To this day, they have never forgiven either of us. I believe it's why they almost never come home to see us. They feel that your father regarded them as less important than you. That was never true, but all the years of not being honest with them took their toll. My greatest hope is that by telling you the truth now, you might be able to help heal the wounds that have kept this family apart for the past many years.

A real family is made by love and shared experiences, not by bloodlines. Your sister is the best example of that. I had to stay in the hospital for two months after you were born. Even though Anika was only thirteen, she took care of you that summer. She fed you and rocked you to sleep and tended your every need. She was always ready to do whatever she could to keep you well and happy.

I know your father rarely spent any time with you. He won't admit it, not even to me, but I'm sure he always felt that you were what made me so sick all these years. He's wrong. You were my reason for being alive and my hope for what was to come. You made me want to live through all those times when it would have been so much easier to give up. I don't know how much more life I'll be granted, but living to see you grow into the beautiful young woman you are today has made me the richest woman on earth.

Try not to judge your father too harshly. He did the best he could. Yes, he made mistakes, but we all do. Love can cause people to be blind, but it can also open your eyes in ways you never dreamed of. He did so much for me and for the twins. Always remember that no one is purely all goodness or all evil. We all have a mix of characteristics.

Later this month, you will leave home, and we can never know what tomorrow will bring. Better you have the whole truth than that you spend forever not knowing this.

I pray that you won't be angry with me and your father like Anika and Nicolas were. Please know that I'm only telling you this because I love you more than anything in creation. I have always believed that if you do something for love, even if it at first brings grief, it will ultimately bring joy.

When you find someone special to share your life with, Grettie, whatever they ask of you, if you choose to do it, do it with love. When you were one of God's angels, you asked me to be your mother, and with all the love I could give, I have been. Thank you for being my little girl—and for being who you are now that you're all grown up.

The letter was signed, "Eternal Love, Mother."

Ellis wasn't much of a drinker, but the impact of her mother's letter left her feeling fall-down drunk. If everything she'd ever believed about her family was really a pack of half-truths, how could she believe in anything so intangible as the laws of gravity? She slid off the edge of the bed, where she'd sat for what felt like her entire lifetime as she read her mother's letter, and crashed onto the floor.

Where to start to try to find her way through the multiple quagmires surrounding her? No wonder Anika had looked so shell-shocked in the photograph taken the day she left for college. Her world had been ripped out from under her.

What had her father's insistence about hiding the truth accomplished? Devastation and disillusionment, as best Ellis could tell.

She wished she had at least a tentative bridge to her brother or sister. This wasn't news someone should have to face alone.

Half-brother. Half-sister, Ellis reminded herself. She skimmed the letter for the exact words her mother had penned: *My greatest hope is that by telling you the truth now, you might be able to help heal the wounds that have kept this family apart for the past many years.*

Was there a statute of limitations on heeding a mother's advice? She hoped not, but there was only one way to find out.

Ellis got to her feet, went to the living room to the computer, and connected to the Internet. A people search of Richmond might turn up information on her sister, but she opted for a different approach. Clicking through several submenus on the Smithsonian site, she eventually found a list of primary staff members. She linked to Nicolas VanStantvoordt's email contact page. She got as far as "Dear Nicolas," before her fingers froze over the keyboard.

What's the right thing to say to a man you always thought was your full blood brother, but who you've just learned isn't? A man who possibly hates you—or at least resents you—a man with whom you've never corresponded and whom you last saw at your father's funeral four years ago? For nearly ten years after high school, Nicolas had buried himself at Princeton in pursuit of multiple degrees in Museum Studies. He hadn't married until 1988. Ellis presumed her father had been invited to the wedding, but she hadn't received an invitation. Had one come to her in Athens at UGA, she wouldn't have gone anyway. She wasn't even sure how to spell his wife's name. Sheryl? Cheryl? Sherrill? Or did she go by Cheri? Shari? Sherry?

"This is hopeless." Ellis scribbled down Nicolas's email address from the site and left the computer. "My brains are too scrambled to tackle this right now."

Sam went to the door and woofed. "Guess you want to go out, huh, girl?" Ellis clipped Sam's leash in place and slipped on a pair of worn deck shoes. "Let's make it quick, okay?"

She and Sam headed to the designated doggie area beyond the parking lot. Too late, she realized her newly-pregnant neighbor, Janet, and the Welsh Corgi, Robbie, were already there for the same purpose.

"Hi, Ellis."

"Hi, there, mama-to-be. I hear congratulations are in order."

Janet patted her midsection. "My husband certainly thinks so."

"You don't sound quite as excited as he did when I saw him earlier tonight."

"I'm happy. And even if I weren't, he's so thrilled by it that I'd go through with this just so I could see the way his face lights up every time he tells somebody else that our baby is on the way. He's been on the phone all night calling everyone in his family and all his fraternity brothers. He's like a kid who found an extra-special decoder ring for all the mysteries of the universe at the bottom of his box of cereal."

"And you?" Ellis asked.

"I was an only child. I've only got one cousin, and he's quite a bit older than me." Janet scooped Robbie into her arms. "So I don't have a lot of experience with children. I'm afraid I might turn out to be one of those mothers who duct tapes her kid's mouth shut if he cries too much or locks him in the closet if he doesn't behave."

Ellis laughed appreciatively. "I know what you mean. And I hear they don't come with instruction manuals."

"That won't be a problem for us. Russ's mother and sisters are standing by to give me way more pointers than I could ever use."

Ellis tugged on Sam's leash. "You about done there, kiddo?"

Janet jiggled Robbie's leash. "I wonder if anybody ever used a leash on a kid while they were toilet training him. Who knows? It might be a really effective way to get them to use the potty."

"You could write a book and make a fortune."

"We could use it. Russ has already gone online to see what the average cost of raising a child is now. I think he said it's around nine thousand dollars a year, and that's without saving for college or any of the big expenses."

Ellis gave a low whistle. "Whew. It counts up in a hurry, doesn't it?"

"I'll say. But everyone we've talked to tonight has told us you really can't put a price tag on love." Janet glanced toward the apartment building. "There's Russ." She gestured to his silhouette on the second-floor landing of the garden-style building. "I suppose he's wondering what's taking me so long with Robbie."

"Sam's done here. We can walk back together."

Janet waved to her husband as she and Ellis crossed the parking lot. "Be right there, Daddy." She exaggerated the last word.

Even though they were still several yards from him, Ellis saw sheer joy spread over Russ's face.

"See what I mean?" Janet asked. "That goofy grin is going to be what gets me through morning sickness, swollen ankles, however many hours of labor, and heaven knows what all else. I guess all those people Russ and I talked to today are right. Who cares what this pregnancy costs me? The only payment that could possibly make it worthwhile is seeing the love of my life look like the happiest man in the galaxy."

Back inside the apartment, Sam claimed her usual spot on the sofa while Ellis foraged in the kitchen for something that could pass for dinner. It was nearly nine o'clock, and breakfast had been fourteen hours earlier. Despite all the emotional upheavals of the day, her body was finally ready to cooperate in consuming some food. She decided against risking the sandwich she'd bought during her encounter with Becky. Instead, a slice of pizza left over from three nights ago, a cup of yogurt, and a half a bag of peeled carrots made up the main course. Dessert was two peaches that were just this side of overripe.

She forced herself to sit at the computer and compose an email to Nicolas. It was brief, telling him she had only now learned the truth about the family and asking him if they might begin a correspondence. She hesitated before hitting the send key, but decided it was a case of nothing ventured, nothing gained and turned the message loose.

The blinking light on the answering machine caught her attention, and she remembered Natalie's call from before her trip to her past. She pulled her cell phone from the button-flap front pocket of her work shirt.

"Hi, sweetheart. I was afraid you weren't going to call tonight." Mary's voice washed over Ellis's ears like a healing wave of sound. "I was starting to worry that you'd found someone new to spend your birthday with tomorrow."

"Not a chance, babe. Sam and I are still totally devoted to you." Ellis hunted for a way to explain at least some of the day's events. "It ended up being a really tough day. Sorry to call so late."

"I'm just glad to hear from you. Did you get Nat's message?"

"I did. How's the settling-in process coming along?"

"Only another thirty or forty years, and I'll have all the boxes emptied."

"Sounds like you could use some help."

"What I could really use is someone to explain to me exactly why I thought moving up here was a good idea in the first place. And I could also use a certain female landscaper in my bed and a truckload of tranquilizers."

"Don't ask for much, do you?"

"Only for what I really, truly need."

"How 'bout I take care of one of your requests?"

"Which one?"

"I was never in favor of the move in the first place, so I can't help you out there. If you take a truckload of tranquilizers, there wouldn't be much point in having that landscaper you mentioned climb into bed with you."

"I've checked the weekend forecast, and there's not a drop of rain within a thousand miles of Georgia. You said my only hope of seeing you this weekend was if you couldn't work."

"It may not always show, but I'm a woman, and the last I heard, it was a woman's prerogative to change her mind."

"Don't tease me, VanStantvoordt. It'll break my heart if I think you're coming up for the weekend and then you don't show."

"If I thought I could bail on my jobs for tomorrow and Friday, I'd load Sam up and hit the road tonight."

"You said it was a rough day. It must have been a killer if you're actually blowing off a whole weekend's work. You didn't get hurt, did you? Is your ankle giving you trouble?"

"My work day wasn't what got to me. And my ankle is fine." Ellis cranked her foot and heard the tendons popping. Long days still brought some tenderness and swelling. Maybe two days off would be good for more than just her head and heart.

"If it's not work, what is it?" Ellis heard the anxiety in Mary's reply.

Ellis recounted what she had learned from her mother's letter. She didn't mention running into her now-pregnant ex-partner.

"Wow. Those are some heavy-duty revelations, sweetie."

"No joke."

"How can I help?"

"I'm not sure. Probably just listen to me while I try to sort it all out."

"Can I hold you in my arms?"

Ellis's stomach somersaulted. "Sure. That would be nice."

"So when do you think you'll get here?"

"I need to take care of three yards tomorrow, and I've got four on Friday. I'll call my Saturday and Sunday jobs to push them off 'til next week. Friday night traffic will be a mess, so it'll be at least eight o'clock before Sam and I pull in day after tomorrow."

"Just be careful on the road. I'll wait until late Friday afternoon to tell Nat you're coming up. She can help me decorate your cake."

"Let me talk to her a minute."

"She's already in bed. It's almost eleven."

"Oh, right. I lost track of time. Do something for me, will you?"

"What?"

"When she gets up in the morning, tell her I said she's really weird."

Ellis checked her email inbox before heading to bed. She had one new message. It was from Nicolas. Like hers to him, it was brief.

"Gretchen, I'm glad to hear you know the truth about the family. Anika and I have discussed how it was handled, and we both feel that our parents made serious mistakes in not telling all of us exactly what the circumstances were all along. Anika and I hold no animosity toward you. You weren't responsible for their decisions. We always thought of you as our sister, even though we had different fathers. Perhaps it's not too late for us to move past all this, especially since our parents are gone. If you would like to correspond with Anika, here is her email address and her snail mail, as well. My wife and I have two children now. My job keeps me busy, so I don't have much free time, but I'll try to answer quickly if you decide to write again. I hope you are well and happy. Your brother, Nicolas."

He included their sister's contact information at the end of the message.

Ellis reread the words on the screen. At least he'd left the door open. Yes, it was twenty years late, but she had hope of building bridges to her siblings. Of more immediate concern, though, was getting organized for her trip to Clarkesville for the weekend.

Chapter 10

"I don't care who's at the door. Even if it's Publisher's Clearinghouse with a check for ten million dollars, tell them to go away. Better yet, pretend you don't hear them knocking and stay here with me." Ellis teased the nipple of Mary's breast in an effort to convince her of the urgency of her plea.

Mary gently moved Ellis back so that her lips couldn't reach their target. "I'd rather do exactly that, but it doesn't sound like whoever's out there is going away." She tugged her bathrobe around her and wrapped a towel around her bone-dry hair to add credence to her alibi of being in the shower.

Ellis watched Mary exit the room, then lay back on the pillow and reminisced about the wild, yet tender, reunion she and Mary had enjoyed last night after polishing off most of her birthday cake. That morning, Natalie went with her Aunt Gloria and her three girl cousins to pick blueberries and would spend the night at Gloria and Adam's house. As soon as Gloria's vehicle left the yard, Ellis and Mary hastened back to bed and hoped to spend the rest of the day and all of the coming night there.

They'd already been distracted a half-dozen times or more by the ringing of Mary's cell phone. Then the landline had rung that many times or more. Now someone was pounding on Mary's front door. Ellis gave in to remorseful thoughts about the boatload of annoyances that came with Mary living where she knew everyone and their uncle. Her slide into the gloom was interrupted by Mary racing back into the room.

"Get up! Get dressed! Get out of here! There's been an accident."

Ellis sprang to her feet and threw on her jeans and T-shirt. "Natalie? Gloria? Your mom?"

Mary tossed the robe aside and labored to untangle the knots she'd made of her clothing. "No, Nathan. His brother Mark has been trying to call me for the past hour. He's waiting at the door. He'll take me to the hospital in Demorest to see Nathan."

"I'll go with you." Ellis jammed her feet into her sneakers.

Mary zipped and buttoned her slacks. "Better not. Mark says it's really bad. Nathan's whole family will be there by now. I don't want to have to explain who you are."

Ellis let the bite of the words go without remark. "What about Natalie? Do you want me to try to find Gloria and the kids?"

"You could try her cell phone, but if they're out behind a mountain somewhere picking berries, she won't have a signal."

"Should I stay here and keep calling 'til I reach your sister?"

Mary grabbed her phone, keys, and wallet. "That's a good idea. Don't tell Natalie anything. Whatever this is, I need to be the one to tell her about it. I'll call you on your cell just as soon as I find out what's happened." She bolted through the bedroom door, but was back in a second. She hastily kissed Ellis's cheek. "I'm sorry, babe, but I need to do this."

"I understand." Ellis said the words, even though she didn't mean them. No matter, because Mary hadn't heard them.

* * *

Ellis's phone rang less than a half-hour later. The moment she heard Mary's tear-choked voice, she knew nothing would ever be the same again.

Ellis steadied herself. "Tell me what happened."

Mary sniffed back her tears. "Nathan's dead."

Wracking sobs filled Ellis's ear. She waited for Mary to continue.

"We don't know all the details yet, but Nathan was called out to help with a problem on a power line. The cable company was stringing new wires and messed up somehow. Mark knows the cable installer and called him a possum-eating moron. They told us Nathan was dead before he hit the ground."

"He died from a fall?"

"No, he was electrocuted. Mark says the cable guy's version is pure crap. Nathan was too smart to do any of the stupid things the cable guy says happened." Mary sobbed for several seconds. "Like it matters. He's dead, and no matter whose fault it is, he's gone, and my baby will never see her daddy again."

Ellis listened to the heartbreak on the far end of the connection. When she thought Mary might be able to hear her question, she asked, "Do we know if anyone has located Gloria and Natalie yet?"

"I don't think so. Mark and his dad left here a few minutes ago to go tell Nathan's grandparents. I'm too upset to do anything."

"I'll go to Naomi's and tell her. She and I can tag team on the phone until we find Gloria. One of them should go to your mother's to tell her."

"Okay." More gut-wrenching cries escaped Mary. "But remember, I need to be the one to tell Nat."

"I know. I'll be sure your sisters understand that, too." Ellis waited for a hint more composure from Mary. "As soon as I've talked to Naomi, I'll come and get you. If Mark left, you don't have a way home."

"I forgot all about that. Do you know how to get here?"

"Naomi can tell me. I'll see you as soon as I can get there."

"Hurry, Ellis."

* * *

Less than an hour later, Ellis arrived at the Habersham County Medical Center. The facility was bordering on dilapidated and had none of the bustle that had marked the one Mary had taken her to on that Saturday afternoon seven months earlier. If it hadn't been for the bright red illuminated cross over the emergency entrance, she might have sped right by it on Highway 441.

Once inside, it was a simple matter to find Mary. She was the despondent, crushed, nearly-incoherent woman whimpering in the far corner of the sparse waiting room. Ellis silently cursed every employee in the hospital for not ministering to this creature in such obvious need. She hurried to Mary's side. "I got here as fast as I could."

Mary looked up at Ellis as though the words were gibberish. "What?"

"Let's get you home." She helped Mary to her feet. "Gloria and Naomi are on their way, so we don't want to keep them waiting."

"Nat?"

"She doesn't know what's happened, but she's asking lots of questions about why everyone's trying not to cry."

"What am I going to tell her?"

"The truth, love. The sad, awful, unchangeable truth."

* * *

"I don't believe you!" Natalie screamed. "I don't believe you! You're mean and horrible, and I hate you!" She pounded her fists on her mother's chest. "My daddy is not dead. You're just saying that so we don't have to live here in Clarkesville. You never wanted to come here, and now you're telling lies so that you can take me away from him."

It took all of Saturday afternoon and most of Saturday evening to calm Natalie to the point that she stopped shouting epithets at Mary. Wisely, Gloria asked her pediatrician for a mild sedative they could give the child. Even after she fell into her intermittent, drug-assisted slumber, Natalie alternately clung to her mother's neck and rallied enough to rant and rail and tell her she hated her.

Bad as things were on Saturday, Sunday was worse. Natalie's anger and disbelief were replaced with sullen unresponsiveness. She showed an occasional flicker of interest in Sam and Swiffer, but humans were all beyond worthless, and she'd have none of their succor, pandering, or feeble attempts at compassion.

Mark dropped by late Sunday evening to tell Mary that the Kimbroughs had arranged for Nathan's funeral to be held Tuesday morning at Hill's Crossing Baptist Church.

"We still think of you and Nat as family," Mark said to Mary, tears brimming in his eyes. "We hope you'll sit with us up front for the service."

Ellis watched from the adjoining room as the former in-laws embraced and cried shared tears.

Mary drew back from Mark and managed to choke out a question. "How's your mama holding up?"

"About like you'd expect. Daddy's been a rock for us all." Mark hugged Mary again. "You let me know if you need me for anything, hear?"

"I will. Thanks. And give my love to your mama and daddy." Mary rested her hand on Mark's back as she accompanied him to the door. "I'll see you at the church on Tuesday."

Ellis caught a glimpse of the sun, still sitting above the horizon as Mark stepped outside. Bad things should only happen on ugly, dreary days, Ellis decided. How could any of them ever again feel good on a sunny summer day?

* * *

"Thank God you're here, Ellis. I couldn't have gotten through this weekend without you." Mary, fully-clothed, lay in Ellis's arms, trembling. "I still can't believe he's dead."

"I know what you mean. I only met Nathan a couple of times, but I liked him. He was a great guy." She rubbed Mary's back reassuringly. "A great dad."

Mary started to cry again. "My poor baby. She's going to have to grow up without her father." Sobs shook her body. "It was hard enough trying to raise her with Nathan's help. Now what am I going to do?"

"Let's not think about that right now. We need to focus on getting through the next few days. We can't afford to look further than tomorrow or the next day." Ellis wrapped her arms more tightly around Mary's shivering form. Hard to believe anyone could feel chilled on a night when the thermometer still read eighty-eight degrees at nine o'clock.

Mary struggled to hold back another flood of tears. "I mean it, Ellis. There's no way I could have survived yesterday and today if you hadn't been right here with me. Thanks for agreeing to stay through Tuesday. Nat and I really need you."

"I'm happy to do what I can, but I'm worried my being here will ultimately make things worse for you—because of your family, I mean."

"Screw 'em," Mary said. "The only reason I moved up here was so that Nathan and I would have an easier time sharing custody of Nat. Now that he's gone…" Her voice faded. "Gone, Ellis. Nathan is gone. Gone forever." There was no stopping the tears. "Promise me you'll stay with me, Ellis. Promise."

Ellis stroked Mary's tangled hair. "I'm here, babe. I'll always be here."

* * *

Ellis knocked off at noon on the last Saturday in August and headed north. As she pulled into Mary's yard in the heat of the day, she spied Mary in the garden beside the house. Ellis and Sam ambled across the lawn. Mary was trimming spent blooms off her marigolds. "Want some help?" Ellis asked.

"Thanks, but no. I need to do something I feel competent at. Heaven knows I'm a failure as a mother these days."

Ellis heard the frustration in Mary's voice. "When I was here last weekend, Natalie seemed like her old self."

"That's exactly the problem. One minute she's my happy-go-lucky kid, driving me batty with her endless interruptions, and the next, she's so withdrawn and unreachable I worry that she's never going to talk to me or anyone else again."

"It's been a tough summer for both of you. Maybe she needs a little more time."

"Tough summer is an understatement. Most of my relatives and many of my friends gnaw on me every day about how I need to start bringing Nat to church so that she can get over her father's death." The hitch in Mary's voice prompted Ellis to step into the garden and kneel beside her. "Don't you dare say anything sweet to me, Gretchen VanStantvoordt. I've gone two whole days without crying, and I don't want you ruining that for me by reminding me how patient and supportive you've been."

"I promised I'd always be here for you."

"You did, and you have. You've been up here every weekend since Nathan died. I know you're short-changing your clients to spend time with Nat and me. I don't tell you often enough how much it means to me." Mary took off her glove and touched Ellis's face lightly. "You've been a godsend."

Ellis rubbed a clod of dirt between her fingers. "I wish I could do more." She let the dirt sift through her fingers. "Did you take Natalie to therapy this week?"

Mary rammed her garden shears into the ground. "Yeah, for all the good it's doing. On the drive home, she told me I should stop wasting my money."

"That sounds like your daughter."

"Doesn't it? She said she was tired of having pretend conversations using dolls as her family members."

"Does the therapist ever tell you what she makes of whatever Natalie says in those conversations?"

"Only that she's a typical little girl who misses her dad and wishes that grown-ups would stop telling her how she should feel."

"So will you keep taking her to the therapist?"

"Probably not. School will be back in session next week. I don't want to embarrass her by pulling her out of classes to go see—as she calls her—the lady with all the goofy dolls who always asks the same dumb questions. It looks to me like Nat's having more good days than bad ones, so maybe the worst is over, although you couldn't tell it by her behavior today."

Ellis stood and shook the kinks out of her legs. "What set it off?"

"She wanted to go to Wal-Mart, but I told her I needed to work in the garden this morning and that we'd go this afternoon."

"Why did that upset her?"

"Her comment as she stormed into her room was that she and Daddy always went to Wal-Mart Saturday morning."

Ellis pulled Mary to her feet. "Funny that she went all summer without that being an issue."

"Probably because all the other Saturday mornings, she and I went to Wal-Mart. It was something to do while we waited for you to get here Saturday afternoons."

Ellis stepped back onto the lawn. "Do you think it would help if I talked to her?"

"Feel free to try, but be sure to have your protective shields in place." Mary dusted her hands on her pants as she joined Ellis. "And I really do need to run to Wal-Mart for some mulch and fertilizer. I should have gone this morning, and we could have avoided this whole drama."

"If the horse doesn't stop running, he might win the race. If you'd gone, something else might have triggered a memory for her. There's no way to know." Ellis looked toward the house. "I'll see if I can talk her into going on a Wal-Mart run with me." She crossed her fingers. "Make a list of what you need."

Mary blew Ellis a kiss and went back to her garden.

* * *

"C'mon, Natalie. You know I don't know my way around up here." Ellis poked her gently in the ribs. "I need you to come with me and tell me which roads to turn on."

"Don't want to. I'd rather stay home."

"I tell you what. If you'll come with me so that I can pick up the stuff your mom wants me to get for her garden, I'll buy you the new Taylor Swift CD."

"I've already got the songs on here." Natalie shook her iPod in Ellis's general direction.

"Okay, then you can pick something else. If you stay in your room much longer, you're going to turn into a piece of furniture."

"So?"

"So then I'll have to rub you down with lemon oil and use Swiffer to dust you."

Natalie almost smiled. Ellis pressed on. "And depending on which piece of furniture you turn into, I might have to have parts of you reupholstered or have casters put on your feet."

"Or buy me a headboard," Natalie offered, spreading her arms wide as she sat on her bed, which was pushed up against the wall.

"Yeah, and get you some fitted sheets and a matching bedspread."

Natalie was quiet for a moment. "I guess I could ride along."

Ellis tugged on Natalie's honey blonde hair. "I'd like that, kiddo."

Natalie stood up and gave Ellis a hug. "Can I get the Kellie Pickler CD?"

"Are you sure you don't want Britney Spears?"

"Oh, Ellis, nobody listens to her anymore."

"Whatever you say."

Natalie slipped her hand in Ellis's and held it all the way out to the yard where Mary slaved over her tomatoes and okra. Sam snoozed contentedly in the shade of a nearby tree.

"Got your list ready for me?" Ellis asked.

Mary looked up and smiled. "All I need is six bags of shredded mulch, the biggest bag of Miracle-Gro they've got, and a can of aphid spray." She used her glove to mop her brow. "Let me get you some money."

"Don't bother. I'll just put it on your tab," Ellis said.

Natalie dropped Ellis's hand and scurried over to give Sam a quick rubdown.

"We'll probably run some other errands while we're out," Ellis said. "See you in an hour or two." Ellis opened the passenger door on her truck and waited for Natalie to climb in. Sam lumbered over nearer Mary and flopped on the ground. "Take good care of my dog while we're gone," Ellis said as she walked around the truck.

"I will. And you take good care of my little girl."

Ellis was delighted to hear some animation in Mary's tone, a quality sorely lacking when they'd spoken earlier.

Natalie rolled her eyes. "I'm not a little girl," she said softly as Ellis started the engine. "I'm almost an orphan."

"You're a long way from being an orphan, toots," Ellis said, hoping she sounded convincing. She pulled out of the driveway onto the road. "You've got your mom and your Gramma Anna and your other grandparents. And don't forget your Uncle Mark and your other aunts and uncles."

"Yeah, but I don't have a dad."

Ellis reached across the console and squeezed Natalie's arm. "That sucks. I know how you feel."

"Nobody knows how I feel. Sometimes it's like I'm watching a sad show on TV, but then I remember it's really what's happening to me."

Quite an insight from someone not yet ten, Ellis thought. She tried to recall how she'd felt when her dad died four years earlier. Nothing much changed in Ellis's world. She was long gone from home and hadn't had a meaningful interaction with her father in longer than she could remember. But when Nathan died, every planet in Natalie's galaxy spun out of orbit.

"You're right, kiddo. I don't know how you feel. If you want to tell me, I'd like to know, though."

Natalie looped her finger around several strands of her hair and twisted it into a tight spiral. She drew it across her lips and chewed the ends before answering. "I feel like God is a big meanie and Gramma Anna is a great big liar."

"I guess you think God is mean for letting your dad die, right?"

"Well, yeah."

"Why do you think your grandmother is a liar?"

"Because she says everything God does to us is for our own good and that if I'd pray to Jesus, he'd make me stop missing my dad."

"And have you been praying?"

"I prayed as hard as I could, but it didn't help at all. Gramma always says Jesus is our best friend, but I don't think he likes me very much."

"Because you still miss your dad?"

"Uh-huh." Long pause. "And I prayed for other stuff I didn't get, too."

"Really? What other stuff?"

"I probably shouldn't tell you."

"You can if you want to." Ellis decided against going directly to the Cornelia Wal-Mart and instead headed for a covered bridge Mary had shown her on one of her early visits to Clarkesville, back before the world was wrenched into total chaos by Nathan's death.

Natalie pointed toward the windshield. "Hey, this isn't the way to the store."

"I know. I thought we could sit by the creek and drag our toes through the water for a while. Would that be okay?"

"I guess."

Ellis found her way to the Stovall Mill Bridge on Chickamauga Creek and parked the truck. She and Natalie selected a big, smooth rock to sit on. The summer sun pounded down on them, but a light breeze across the shallow waters cooled the immediate air. Lush greenery enveloped the spot they were in. Squirrels chattered on the branches overhead, and birds made swoops to grab unsuspecting insects midair. Ellis shucked off her sneakers and socks and dangled her feet in the warm water. Natalie kicked out of her Crocs and drew circles on the water's surface with her big toe. She leaned ever so slightly so that she was lightly pressing against Ellis's side.

Ellis savored the moment. "It's pretty out here." She said it more to herself than to Natalie.

"My dad used to say that God made the north Georgia mountains first and that everything else after that was just places he put together from the leftovers."

Ellis put her arm around Natalie's shoulders and drew her nearer. "I'm really sorry your dad died. Tell me some other things you remember about him."

"He liked to eat carrots and peas and tomatoes right out of the garden, even if they had dirt on them. He liked Alan Jackson and Kenny Chesney, but he didn't like Josh Turner or Garth Brooks. His favorite TV show was *Trick My Truck.* He could write his name backwards with his left hand, and when you held it up to a mirror, it looked just like he wrote it for real. He liked fishing better than hunting, and he was teaching me how to put bait on a hook. Wearing dress-up clothes made him feel like he couldn't breathe. That's why they let him get buried in regular clothes, so he didn't have to wear a necktie." Natalie looked at Ellis as if to see if she was paying attention. She was apparently satisfied and went on with her list of what she remembered about her father.

Ellis sat silently by her side, trying very hard not to cry. She doubted that, compared to Natalie, she'd gathered even a small fraction of the memories about her own father, even though she'd had three-and-a-half times as much life in which to do so. Would she have had a larger storehouse at ten than at thirty-four, which was how old she was when her dad died? Probably not. Dedrick VanStantvoordt was far more memorable as an art history buff than as a daddy. Natalie's continuing recitation broke through her own musings.

"And my dad's middle name was Joseph. That was my other grandpa's name, too. I don't really remember him because I was only five when he died. Daddy always said that if he and Mom ever had a baby boy, his name would be Joseph so that both sides of the family would be happy. But I always told him I really wanted a little sister, not a little brother." She stopped and looked at Ellis. "Now I guess I won't ever get either one."

"Probably not, kiddo."

"Couldn't you and Mom get a baby?"

The question knocked Ellis off her pins. "Where did you ever come up with an idea like that?"

"You and Mom love each other. I can tell by the way you act when you're together. People who love each other have babies."

Ellis waited, hoping an appropriate response would come to her. Natalie spoke again before inspiration struck for Ellis.

"That's one of the other things I've been praying for."

"A baby sister?"

"Sort of."

"Sort of?" Ellis had set the boulder rolling down the hill—no point trying to stop it now.

"I've been praying that you'd come up here and live with mom and me. When you leave to go back to Atlanta on Sunday nights, Mom cries and cries. She thinks I don't hear her, but I do."

"I see." Ellis didn't see, figuratively, and was rapidly approaching the point of not being able to see physically, thanks to the number of times Natalie had thumped on her heartstrings, bringing her to the verge of tears.

"And even if you and Mom decide you don't want to get a baby, you and Mom and me could be a family. Like when Daddy still lived with us when I was little."

"Have you talked to your mom about this?"

"Not really."

"Don't you think you should?"

"I already know what she'd say."

"Oh?"

"Uh-huh. She wants whatever will make me happy. She says it all the time." She imitated her mother's voice, "Tell me what you want, Nat. My favorite thing is seeing you smile."

Ellis pulled her feet from the creek and used her socks to dry them. She took her time lacing and tying her sneakers. "Maybe we'd better go so I can get that mulch I promised your mom."

Natalie stood and slipped into her Crocs. "I knew I shouldn't have told you what I've been praying for. It made you mad."

"I'm not mad, Natalie. You surprised me, that's all." Ellis put both hands on Natalie's shoulders and squatted down so that she was face-to-face with her. "I'm glad you told me. It helps me understand how you're feeling."

"I used to do that with my daddy."

"I can't ever be as good at that as your dad was. You know that, right?"

Natalie searched Ellis's face carefully. "I guess. But if you could help Mom stop crying so much, that would help a lot." Natalie's voice dropped to a whisper. "I used to come here sometimes with my daddy."

Ellis stood upright and offered her hand. Natalie grabbed it. Though not a religious woman in the least, she'd have sworn she heard angels' wings rustling in the wind.

* * *

It only took a few conversations—approximately 28,492 of them, by Ellis's estimation—for her and Mary to reach the conclusion that Natalie was right: the best solution for all of them would be for Ellis to leave Atlanta and move to the mountains. One by one, she terminated agreements with her landscaping clients in preparation for relocating. Piece by piece, she hauled most of her furniture to the thrift store to be sold and the proceeds donated to a shelter for battered women. Day after day, she reminded herself of the admonition in her only letter from her mother to use love as her reason for agreeing to honor important requests made of her by the significant people in her life.

So what if everything left of her worldly goods fit in her Tundra? All the issues of how to deal with Mary's family, her uneasiness over helping to raise a child, the tiny little matter of what she would do to make a living, and the showstopper of what to tell anyone and everyone about the relationship between her and Mary still hung out there like nightmare demons under the bed of a sleep-deprived child. But Ellis trusted love to prevail. Both Mary and Natalie made it obvious that they believed they would be better off having Ellis with them full-time. Even if it proved to be the wrong decision, she knew she had made it for the right reason.

Late in the day on the first Friday in October, she stuffed the last of her possessions into the truck, and she and Sam made the now-familiar drive to Mary's house in Clarkesville. Darkness had fallen long before she parked beside Mary's Xterra under the metal carport.

Sam made a quick inspection of the yard, marked a few of her usual places, then she rejoined Ellis on the front stoop. Ellis thought it odd that neither Mary nor Natalie had come out to greet her. She knocked once and let herself in.

"Surprise!" As Ellis entered, Mary and Natalie leaped from either side of the doorway and tooted loudly on noisemakers typically seen on New Year's Eve. The sudden outburst set Sam to barking and running wildly around the living room. Mary and Natalie wore paper party hats that originally said, "Party 'Til the Cows Come Home." The words "the cows" were taped over with white paper, and in their place, "Ellis" had been substituted and an "s" added to make the word "comes."

Swiffer was perched on the back of the sofa, likewise wearing a hat. Hers said, "Are We Having Fun Yet?" The expression on the cat's face, whether from the indignity of wearing a hat or from Sam acting as though she was part of the running of the bulls in Pamplona, left no doubt that she was most assuredly *not* having a good time.

"Hey, what's the occasion?" Ellis asked as she regained her composure. The room was decorated with multicolored streamers and every sort of banner: Happy Birthday, Christmas, Fourth of July, Saint Patrick's Day, Valentine's Day, Thanksgiving, Easter, Halloween, even a blue and silver one that proclaimed "Happy Hanukkah." The one that made her look twice, though, was a homemade one that had a message she'd never in her life seen before. Big block letters shouted, "Welcome Home, Ellis and Sam. We Think You're Weird." The banner was decorated with hand-drawn approximate likenesses of Mary, Natalie, and Swiffer, each holding smaller versions of the Welcome Home message.

Natalie stood grinning, her body seeming to vibrate with happiness. "We wanted to do something to celebrate our first night as a family."

"Right," Mary said. "We haven't gotten to spend any of the last year's holidays together, so we thought we'd do a condensed version of them tonight to make up for lost time and to be sure we always remember the night you came home to stay."

As Mary and Natalie wrapped her in hugs, Ellis let the tears wash down her cheeks. It was thirty-nine years in the coming, but she felt like she was finally where she truly belonged.

Mother and daughter treated Ellis to an eclectic feast with everything from roast turkey breast with cornbread dressing to decorated hard-boiled eggs to watermelon (in honor of

Independence Day) to limeade (as a substitute for green beer) and a heart-shaped cake for dessert. Throughout the meal, they sang songs apropos of various holidays. For what felt like the first time since that awful Saturday in June when word had come of Nathan's death, there was genuine laughter in MaryChris Moss's house.

Ellis dragged her fork over her dessert plate to corner the final bit of frosting. "What a great feast. Thank you both for this wonderful Valen-Patrick-East-Fourth-Birthday-Hallow-Thanks-Mas meal."

"You forgot the most important part, Ellis," Natalie said.

"I did?"

"The welcome home part."

"She's right, you know," Mary said, edging her chair a bit nearer to Ellis. "Every day—holiday or plain old Tuesday—will be better, now that you're here with us."

In a mischievous voice, Natalie said, "You two should kiss or something."

"Natalie! Really..." Mary stopped, obviously not sure what to say next.

Natalie frowned at her mother. "What? It's not like I haven't seen you do it. I'm not a baby, you know."

"Maybe we'd better talk about this," Mary said. "Since you're not a baby, you need to remember that some things aren't mentioned in public."

"But this isn't public." Natalie crossed her arms across her chest. "This is our house."

"Right, but just like we have to practice manners at home so we'll have them when we go out, we need to practice what's okay and what's not okay to say to other people. Understand?"

Natalie shook her head. "Not really."

Mary's eyes pleaded with her new live-in lover. "Feel free to jump in anytime, Ellis. You get to try to keep this leaky little rowboat afloat now, too."

Ellis glanced around the room in hopes of finding an emergency escape hatch. She caught sight of the banner welcoming her home. "Well, you see, toots, it's sort of like the code phrase you and your mom have for saying you love each other without really saying it. Sometimes it might feel a little funny to say 'I love you' in front of other people or whatever, so what do you do instead?"

"We say 'you're weird.'"

"Exactly. That's kind of what your mom and I have to do almost all the time. See, there are a lot of people who don't think it's right for two women to like each other as much as your mom and I do."

"You mean because the Bible says it's a sin?" Natalie said.

Aghast, Mary asked, "Did your grandmother tell you that?"

"No, I saw that preacher on TV. He said gay people will burn in hell because they're a bombed nation in God's eyes."

Ellis overcame the urge to laugh at Natalie's misunderstanding of "abomination."

"I'm glad you understand what it means to be gay, but what you saw on TV is only some people's opinion," Mary said, levelly. "It's really not what the Bible says. But because there's that kind of hatred out there, Ellis and I—and you, too—have to be very careful not to say things that will upset people."

Natalie pondered her mother's explanation. "Sort of like when Tommy Hudgins kept picking on Michael Fitzpatrick because his family goes to the Catholic church instead of to the Baptist church."

"Yep, same kind of thing," Mary said.

"I heard my teacher tell Michael it's okay that he's Catholic, but that he shouldn't keep reminding Tommy about it."

"And that's what your mom and I are saying you should do, too. Don't bring attention to it. You don't need to say anything to anybody about the fact that we're very special friends." She stole a look at Mary. "Don't say anything to Gramma or Aunt Naomi or the kids at school."

"What if they ask?"

Ellis gulped and looked to Mary for guidance.

Mary studied her daughter carefully. "Has anybody said anything to you, Nat?"

"Only Aunt Gloria."

"What did she say?"

"That she thought you and Ellis looked at each other funny."

"When was that?" Mary asked.

"One weekend this summer when Ellis was here with you, and she came to get me so I could play with Amber and Ashley at her house."

"Oh. Anything else?"

"Uh-uh." Natalie shook her head vigorously.

"Here's the deal, Nat." Mary moved around the table to be next to her child. "If anybody ever says anything to you about Ellis and me, you come tell me right away. And remember, you're not supposed to talk about us to other people."

"What if people ask me who she is and why she lives here?"

"You can tell them Ellis is a very good friend of ours."

"But we have other good friends and they don't live with us." Natalie kicked the rungs of her chair, apparently growing weary of the conversation.

Ellis took a shot. "Say that I'm trying to decide what kind of work I want to do next and that while I'm looking, I'm staying here and helping out with things your dad used to do. You know, things like mowing the lawn and taking you fishing."

Natalie lit up like a new candle. "Fishing? Will you take me fishing, Ellis?"

"Sure. Since Georgia lets us fish all year for everything but trout, we can go fishing anytime we want to."

"Sweet! Are we going tomorrow?" Natalie asked.

"Maybe, but I need to get all my stuff put away." Ellis hoped the stall tactic wasn't too blatant.

"No, you don't. We've still got a whole room full of boxes from when we moved in. Mom says they can wait 'til next summer."

"Don't nag, Nat," Mary said. "How about you go to your room and get ready for bed. It's almost ten o'clock."

"I never get to stay up and have fun."

"No grumping." Mary pointed toward the hallway that led to the bedrooms. "Go."

Mary waited until she heard the door to Natalie's bedroom close. "Nice save with the 'you're weird' example." She sat on the chair next to Ellis's. "And excuse me, but fishing?"

"Hey, it worked, didn't it?" Ellis gave Mary a quick kiss. "You and your offspring certainly know how to make a welcome home party memorable. Are you sure I shouldn't grab Sam and make tracks out of here before things get super ugly for you with your family?"

Mary wrapped her arm around Ellis's head in a fake wrestling hold. "Don't even think about it. I'm never letting you go, no matter what sort of crap my family decides to fling. I think I'll have a chat with my little sister first. She seems the most likely not to need resuscitation after hearing the L-word. No point putting it off."

"For real?" Ellis eased Mary's arm from around her neck. "Don't you want to give it some more thought?"

"Nope. What I want to do is get this table cleared off and find out if my first night of forever with you feels as good as I've imagined."

"Let me help." Ellis hurriedly stacked plates and carried them to the kitchen.

Mary followed with an armload of serving bowls. She stashed leftovers in plastic containers. "We'll have a tough decision tomorrow night," she said as she closed the refrigerator door.

"Why's that?"

"We'll have to pick between tonight's remnants and the stringer of fresh fish you and Nat bring back from your first angling expedition."

Ellis scrambled for a smart comeback, but suddenly Mary was in her arms. The urgency of Mary's kiss wiped out every thought—other than the one about getting her to the bedroom as quickly as possible.

But urgent and best-laid plans went awry, and getting to the bedroom wasn't as easy as Ellis hoped. First, Natalie demanded Ellis tuck her in, followed by Natalie's inquiry about where Sam would sleep. That reminded Ellis that Sam hadn't been fed, nor had she been let out for her last visit to the yard. She had no more than tended to Sam's basic needs and deposited the dog in Natalie's room when the child summoned her mother and a glass of water.

"It's my fault she's wound up tighter than a spring-load yo-yo," Mary said as she stumbled back to the master bedroom where Ellis waited. "She had enough sugar at dinner to put her into orbit."

Ellis tried to mask a yawn. "Riling her up with our conversation topics and the prospect of a fishing trip tomorrow probably didn't help the cause, either."

Mary snuggled up to Ellis and kissed her lazily. "We better make sure she's really asleep before we do what I hope you're still wanting to do."

By the time Natalie finally fell asleep, exhaustion had claimed Ellis. She felt like she'd been run over by a whole pack of children in soccer cleats. She helped Mary ease out of her clothes and then dragged her weary self out of her jeans and sweatshirt.

She lay in Mary's arms, skin against skin, too tired to do anything more than think about making love.

She yawned loudly. "If I said you had a great body, would you hold it against me?"

"I already am," Mary said. "And I plan to do so every night for the rest of my life."

"Perfect. And if I told you I'm probably too tired to do anything more than lie here like this with you tonight, would you hold that against me?"

"Not for a minute. To tell the truth, all that hash-slinging and banner-making wore me out." Mary brushed her fingertips lightly over Ellis's back. "We've got from now until forever, so I can give you a rain check for one night."

"Here we are, together at last, an old boring couple."

Mary leaned down to reach Ellis's lips and kissed her soulfully. "Too many words. The only ones that count are here, together, and couple."

* * *

For the tenth time in as many minutes, Ellis got up from her chair in the living room and looked out the front window. Yes, Sam would woof to announce Mary's return from her conversation with Gloria, but dang, what was taking so blasted long? What if Gloria went ape shit and smacked Mary with a frying pan? Worse, what if she'd called Anna and Anna had shown up to give Mary the worst tongue-lashing of her life?

I never should have let her talk me out of going with her, Ellis thought. If we're a team, we should do this sort of thing together.

At long last, Ellis heard Mary's Xterra. Ellis met Mary on the front steps and fired her questions one after the next. "What happened? How did it go? Are you all right? Should I pack my stuff, move away, and leave no forwarding address?"

Mary's smile helped erase Ellis's worst fears. "Walk in the park. As we suspected, Gloria had almost all of the puzzle pieces in place."

"She's okay with it? With us, I mean?"

"For the most part, yes." Mary kissed Ellis after they stepped inside and closed the door. "Turns out that Adam has an uncle on his mother's side who's—to use my sister's words—a pretty boy. Once she reminded me about him, I remembered seeing him at Gloria's wedding. To tell the truth, I think she was a little jealous of him." Mary stifled a laugh. "He was almost prettier than she was."

"Does he live around here?"

"No, he moved to Atlanta right after high school, and unlike me, had the good sense to stay there."

"Does he have a partner?"

"Does it matter?"

"No, I was just curious."

"Gloria didn't mention a partner, but that doesn't mean he doesn't have one. From what she said, I got the impression that Adam is one of the few people in his family who hasn't written the uncle off as a lost cause."

"Does Adam see him or talk to him?"

"Some, but it sounds like the uncle isn't any more interested in spending time with the family than the family is in having him around."

"How loving and supportive."

"At least Adam left the door open. Gloria told me that the uncle was a lot younger than the rest of the kids in the family. He and Adam were more like siblings than separate generations."

"I guess it can't hurt to have at least one more family member playing for our team."

"The uncle?"

"I meant Adam, but sure, I'll count old Uncle What's His Name, too."

"Isn't that funny? Now that you mention it, Gloria never once called him by name."

"Shadow people don't get names, babe. We're merely the poor, misguided unfortunates—those lesser beings who populate the lower rungs of nearly every group."

"There are worse things than going through life unnoticed." Mary kicked her shoes off and curled in a corner of the sofa.

"No doubt." Ellis plopped beside her. "Would it be all right, though, if I noticed how good it feels to be next to you?"

"If I can notice the same thing about you." She welcomed Ellis's kiss.

"Thanks for telling your sister about us."

"Thanks for giving me a reason to need to tell her by moving in with Nat and me and making this house our home." Mary held Ellis tight. "And it was lots easier knowing you'd be here to hold me when I got back today."

"Today and every day, love. I promise."

* * *

Over the next couple of weeks, Mary made room in closets and drawers and Ellis stowed her clothing and other personal items. Mary found a great deal on a small second-hand desk for Ellis. It fit nicely in the corner of the third bedroom where Mary wrote her articles for *Georgia Life.*

Once Ellis had her computer hooked up, while Mary labored on her assignments, Ellis spent time scouring the Internet for job leads around Clarkesville. To say that she found slim pickings would be to overstate her success.

One morning after another fruitless search, she skimmed through her emails and came across the message she'd saved from her brother. Wow, she thought, it was more than four months ago that I found that letter from Mom and wrote to Nicolas. I still haven't gotten in touch with Anika. With all that's happened since Nathan died, I haven't had time to even think about what I might say to my sister.

She looked across the room and saw Mary typing furiously on this month's magazine stories. As always, the sight of her beloved Mary made her heart seize with joy. *My heart and soul. My family.*

Ellis opened the bottom desk drawer and pulled out the photo album she'd looked at for the first time in early June. She hurried past the pictures to get to the page where her mother's letter began. She read quickly until she found the line she wanted to be sure she remembered exactly: A real family is made by love and shared experiences, not by bloodlines.

She drank in another lingering eyeful of the beauty known as Mary Moss.

Family.

It was time to connect with her sister and brother, time to let the healing start. It was time to forgive Becky Blumfeld and embrace the wonder that only a family can provide.

* * *

Ellis snapped her cell phone shut and clutched it to her chest. A tear wedged its way out of the corner of her eye. She meandered outside to look for Mary, who had told her she'd be pruning the butterfly bushes.

"How did it go?" Mary laid her long-handled loppers on the ground.

"The last time I talked to my sister was at my dad's funeral in 2002. And we didn't really talk much then. She and Nicolas came to Savannah together, and neither one of them brought their spouses or their kids. All any of us wanted to do was get the service over with and get out of there."

"When was the last time you'd seen her before that?"

"She came home a few times while she was in college, but I really don't remember much about her."

"But you told me your mom's letter said she took care of you when you were a baby."

"Uh-huh. And now that I've talked with her—really talked with her—for the first time in my life, I can't believe I ever had a bad thought about her. And she's already a grandmother. I've never even met my nieces, and now I've got a grand nephew and there's another baby on the way."

"Congratulations, Auntie Ellis."

"That would be Aunt Gretchen to them."

Mary chuckled. "Oh, right. I forgot. Let's go inside, Gretchen, and you can tell me everything your sister said."

Ellis grabbed Mary's outstretched hand and they ambled across the yard. "I should have recorded the call. We covered so much I'm not sure how I'll be able to tell you all of it."

"Try," Mary said as they stepped inside the front door.

"Anika said she and Nicolas were convinced that Dad told them he wasn't their real father right before they left for college because he wanted Mother and him and me to be the *perfect* family. They thought it was his way of saying, 'Have a nice life; stay the hell away.'"

Mary and Ellis dropped side by side onto the sofa. "Do you think that was his intention?"

"Who knows? My dad sure wasn't Mister Warmth and Personality, but I never thought he was intentionally cruel. Maybe he figured since they were adults, they deserved to know some bastard had abandoned them."

"One time you told me you always felt like it was your parents and the twins who were the real family and you were the afterthought."

"Yeah, I figured she and Nicolas hated me for coming along and messing up their happiness."

"Turns out they thought the same of you."

Ellis twisted her index finger in front of her ear and made a goofy face. "God, this world is a screwed up place. It's a miracle we're not all permanently institutionalized."

Mary kissed Ellis's cheek. "Forgive me for saying so, but hearing all this about your family gives me comfort."

"Why? Because misery loves company?"

"Kind of. But it's more like we can look at ourselves and say, 'Look, despite all the crap we went through with our families, we've made it this far, and we're still functioning adults. We are what we are in spite of our past, not strictly because of it.'"

Ellis considered for a moment. "Sort of like hope triumphing over doubt."

"Exactly." Mary lifted Ellis's arm so that she could cuddle against her. "How else would anyone ever decide to bring a child into this loony bin known as planet earth?"

"Sometimes I wonder if this thing we call life is really remedial play for retarded third-graders in a distant galaxy."

"Could be. We can't know for sure, so we might as well try to enjoy the ride." Mary pulled Ellis's other arm around so that Ellis was hugging her. "Now, I want to hear the rest of what your sister had to say."

Ellis filled her in on the details she'd gathered from her hour-long call with Anika. It boiled down to some major misconceptions between Ellis and her half-siblings due to a glaring lack of information; a bond of love that, although neglected, was still in existence; and promises to find ways to be part of one another's lives.

"I can't wait for you and Anika to have your first fight," Mary said.

Ellis pushed Mary away so that she could see her face. "What an awful thing to say."

"Not at all. It'll be nice to have the spotlight on *your* sister's annoying behavior for a change." Mary poked her finger on Ellis's chest as she spoke "your."

Ellis grinned. "That's one of Natalie's favorite ploys—whining about not having a sibling to blame and to boss around."

"Can you blame her?"

Ellis grew pensive. "Maybe for the first time ever, no I can't. Every kid should have a brother or sister to help them navigate life's highways."

"And detours," Mary added. "Don't forget the detours."

* * *

Ellis reread the letter she'd written to Becky. She'd spent much of the next morning striving for the right mix of gratitude and appreciation for their years together, conciliation for her strident behavior when she had run into her and Ruthann in June, and congratulations on finally fulfilling her dream of being a mother. Satisfied that she'd found acceptable words, she opened the small lockbox that held her important papers and took out the promissory note Becky had given her when they dissolved their union. In bold letters, she printed PAID IN FULL across the Terms of Payment section of the note. In her regular cursive, she added a line at the bottom of the page: *Use this for your child's college education, music lessons, or soccer equipment. Best wishes to all three of you. Love, Ellis.*

Chapter 11

"I really think it would be better if I stayed home." Ellis ran her finger around the edge of the pie plate sitting on the kitchen table. "You could leave me a slice of this apple pie, though."

"Honestly, Ellis, you're worse than Natalie." Mary swatted Ellis's hand to keep her from picking at the pie crust. "Thanksgiving is for families, and you're part of this family now. We're going to Mother's, and that's the end of the discussion."

Ellis had managed to avoid any serious confrontations with Mary's family in her first two months in Clarkesville. Of course, avoiding confrontations meant pretty much avoiding the Moss family altogether. She had spent a strained afternoon with them two weeks earlier to help celebrate Natalie's tenth birthday. Thanks to the general confusion generated by six children clamoring for more ice cream and squabbling over who got the next turn with Nat's sing-along karaoke mike, the seven adults in attendance hadn't talked about anything more pressing than getting the candle wax out of baby Erin's hair. But now the holidays were upon them, and Ellis's dodge-and-weave tactics weren't going to work as well.

"Is everybody going to be there?"

"If by everybody, you mean my sisters and their families and my mom, then yes, everybody will be there." Mary crimped a sheet of aluminum foil over the pie. "And if we don't get going, we'll be late. You do not want to give my mother a reason to declare Thanksgiving a disaster due to a delay in serving her turkey."

"All right. Message received. What else do we need to take?"

"A large dose of patience and good humor and our adorable ten-year-old."

"Ten going on twenty-eight, as her dad might have said." Ellis regretted the words as soon as they'd left her lips.

Ellis watched as Mary distracted herself with checking that the stove burners were turned off and looking out the window over the sink. "Our first Thanksgiving without Nathan. Some days, I still expect him to come through the door calling for Natalie to hurry up."

Ellis stepped over behind Mary. "I'm sorry. I should have thought before I spoke." She kissed the back of Mary's neck. "I'll try to be smarter from now on."

"No, I think it's good we talk about him, especially in front of Natalie. She needs to remember her dad and know that it's okay to miss him."

"Do you miss him, Mary?"

"Of course I do. He was a part of my life forever. He was one of my best friends, and don't forget, without him, I wouldn't have Natalie. I suspect I'll miss him every day for as long as I live."

A tiny wave of jealousy washed over Ellis. Would she always have to compete against Nathan's ghost?

Mary turned and wrapped her arms around Ellis's midsection. "But I'm at least a thousand percent happier with you than I ever was with him. My love for you is so real. With him, I was always forcing myself to pretend I felt things I knew I'd never feel."

"I'm happy to hear you say that. I worry sometimes that you'll regret asking me to move up here to live with you."

Mary took a step away from Ellis. "Why? Why would I possibly regret having you with me every single day?"

"Because of what it's doing to your relationship with your family. I don't intentionally eavesdrop on your phone calls, but sometimes I can't help but overhear what you say to your mom and sisters."

"Sister," Mary corrected. "Gloria's come a long way since that day she and I talked about us and Adam's uncle. She can see how happy I am and how much better Nat is doing now that you're here."

"Okay, so Gloria's come around, but I'm not sure your mother hasn't convinced Barry to meet me at the door with a shotgun if I show up for dinner today."

"Barry's an asshole sometimes, but he's a harmless asshole."

"Harmless if you discount the half-dozen hunting rifles he owns."

"He can't have you stuffed and hang your head on the wall over the fireplace. I think you're safe." Mary glanced at the clock on the microwave. "Honey, I know you've got some worries about Naomi and Barry and my mom, and I swear I'm willing to talk to you about anything that's bothering you, but we've got to pull Nat away from whatever she's messing with in her room and get to Mother's."

"All right. I'll put the pie in your Xterra and make sure Sam's settled in for the afternoon. You get the rug rat, and we'll do our version of the Plymouth Rock thing at Anna Moss's house."

* * *

Seven hours later, Mary, Ellis, and Natalie returned home. Among them, they lugged enough leftovers to last until next Thanksgiving. As they entered through the kitchen door, Sam bolted out past them for the yard.

"Nat, I want you to go to your room and get ready for bed. If you're going shopping with Aunt Gloria and Amber and Ashley tomorrow, you need to be in bed with lights out by eight-thirty tonight." Mary crammed containers into the refrigerator.

"We're not walking to the Mall of Georgia, Mom. I don't need to go to bed early."

Mary leaned against the closed refrigerator door. "I'm not in the mood for a debate. Please, for once in your life, just do as you're told, okay?" She hugged Natalie and gave her a push toward the hallway.

"'Night, kiddo," Ellis said. "See you in the morning."

Natalie trudged out of the room.

"Who pooped in your pumpkin pie?" Ellis nudged Mary with her hip. "They're not leaving for the mall until ten o'clock, so Nat will be up in plenty of time to be ready."

"I know." Mary pulled a chair away from the kitchen table and sat down. "I guess since I can't send the rest of my family to their rooms, I'm taking it out on my kid."

"I take it something happened between you and your sisters while I adroitly avoided helping clean up after dinner." Ellis dropped into the chair across from Mary.

"More like didn't happen." Mary twisted her face into a snarl. "I'd try to say something about how great you and Nat are getting along, and my mother or Naomi would act like they were deaf."

"And this surprises you why?"

"Not a surprise, but sure as hell an annoyance."

Ellis held her hand out for Mary to take. "Let me see if I can balance the ledger."

"I suppose you're going to tell me you and Barry and Adam bonded over your touch football game with the kids." Mary accepted Ellis's outstretched hand.

"Well, I don't know about Barry, but Adam and I had a very interesting conversation."

"Do tell."

Ellis heard the sarcasm in Mary's voice. She cleared her throat before replying. "Good afternoon, Miss. Welcome to Moss Motors. I see you're looking at our newest dual-fuel hybrid. Would you like to take a test drive?"

"Did someone slip a hallucinogenic into your mashed potatoes?"

"Not so far as I know, but your brother-in-law did ask me if I thought I'd like to try my hand at selling cars at your dad's old dealership."

Mary reeled in mock astonishment. "Adam asked you to come to work for him?"

"Uh-huh. We agreed it would be on a trial basis for a few months to see if I'm any good at it and if he wants to keep me on."

"Call me Cliff and do drop over."

"I'd rather call you sweetheart and ask if you'd let me take you to bed."

"In a minute," Mary said as she brushed the back of Ellis's knuckles. "Maybe my family isn't a total waste after all."

"I admit, your mother and Naomi could still double as side-by-side cold storage lockers, but Gloria was really nice to me today, and laugh if you want to, but that touch football game gave me a chance to get to know Barry on his own turf. I can't imagine he'll ever be one of my favorite people, nor will I make his top ten, but we talked about the pros and cons of reinstituting the two-point conversion option and the merits of challenging a call and using instant replay to decide. At least we found some common turf."

"My little jock."

Ellis saw the light in Mary's eyes as she spoke.

"It was more than that. I saw how he treated his sons. It was clear he's absolutely devoted to them. And he was good with his nieces, too, in a clumsy, manly sort of way." Ellis paused. "And both he and Adam talked about how fantastic Nathan was."

"That's nice. I always liked how the sons-in-law got along so well. As big a screw-up as this family is, picture what it would have been like if those in-laws had hated each other's guts."

"Yeah, and they said something else that really made me think."

"What's that?"

"They said they really wished he'd lived long enough to get that son he always dreamed about having."

Ellis noticed Mary swallow hard. "It would have meant the world to him," Mary said. "Not that he didn't love Nat, but there's something about men and their sons."

"It probably would have meant a lot to you, too, huh? And we dare not forget the girl in the back bedroom who claims she's incomplete without a sibling of her very own."

"Gretchen Alina VanStantvoordt! Someone *did* lace your green bean casserole with LSD. More than once in recent weeks, I've heard you waxing eloquent about the merits of having children."

"I'm not waxing anything. I'm merely reporting what was discussed on your mother's front lawn after too much turkey and dressing."

Mary got to her feet. "Come on. We need to get you into bed before you tell me you've got baby names picked out. I wouldn't necessarily object, you understand, but I want to be sure you're not trying to cast me in a supporting role in a grade B remake of *Invasion of the Body Snatchers.*"

Ellis went to the door. "Let me get my dog in, and then we can do some mutual body invading in the bedroom."

*　*　*

"You can invade me like that as often as you want to." Mary exhaled contentedly, savoring the afterglow.

"You make it sound like I'm a hostile nation." Ellis dragged her fingers through Mary's tousled hair.

"Not at all. But maybe the prospect of paid employment has boosted your confidence levels in more than one arena."

Ellis sat up a bit straighter. "Now that you mention it..."

"I was joking." Mary tugged on Ellis's close-cropped hair.

"I know, but after the way things went with Naomi and your mother today, we can't keep putting off talking to the rest of your family about us. If everything is going to blow sky high, I'd rather know it once and for all and get it behind us. It would be stupid for me to go to work at the dealership if your mother is going to make Adam kick me out a week later. It's still her dealership, after all."

"You sound like your mind's made up."

"It is. When I emailed Anika and Nicolas to wish them happy Thanksgiving, I told them I was thankful that they were back in my life, and I told them about you and Natalie—the whole truth about us—and how much the two of you mean to me. I even used the line from my mom's letter."

"What line?"

"That a real family isn't determined by bloodlines, but by love and shared experiences. It's true for them and me, and it's really true for you and me."

Mary wrapped Ellis in a hug. "All right. We'll talk to my family." Her voice dropped an octave. "But first, show me again how you've perfected your invasion strategies."

* * *

Despite how poorly the auto market was doing, in her first week as a sales trainee, Ellis sold two cars. That was a good sign. In the course of the same week, she and Mary survived their obligatory, cursory, staring-daggers-through-them conversations with Mary's mother and Naomi to confirm their suspicions about the relationship between Mary and Ellis. No one had ruptured a blood vessel or summoned the National Guard. Another good sign.

It was Friday night, so the showroom stayed open late. Ellis stopped for a burger and a milkshake on the drive home. By the time she got there, the only light in the house shone through the master bedroom window. Ellis slipped out of her Moss Motors blazer as she entered the room. "Hi, love. What are you reading?"

Mary, sitting on their bed, tucked the book against her, her finger marking her page. "It's Nat's baby book. I found it when I was sorting through some of the last boxes from the move."

Ellis kicked off her loafers and undid her belt. "Mind if I join you?" She draped her dress slacks over a chair.

Mary slid over to make room. "You'd better."

Ellis took the book from Mary. "Can we start over from the beginning?"

"I already have. Twice. I'd forgotten just how beautiful she was." Mary pointed to the photo of Natalie wearing her pink knit beanie in the hospital bassinet. "Amazing. The most gorgeous child in all of creation, and I gave birth to her."

"Not a surprise to me. Take a look in the mirror." Ellis edged in for the kiss she'd been craving.

Mary stared at the picture a moment, then closed the book and set it aside. "I need to ask you something really, really important, Ellis. And I don't want you to tell me what you think I want to hear. You have to tell me the truth."

"I always do." Ellis raised her hand as though taking an oath. "I swear."

Mary hitched herself up on her knees and straddled Ellis's legs. "Lately, I've been thinking—"

"That it's time Natalie stopped being an only child."

Mary's eyes about popped out of her head. "How did you know?"

"How could I not?" Ellis cupped Mary's chin in her hands. "I've seen you with little Erin, watched you puddle up over the baby shampoo commercials on TV, and heard all your remarks about how Natalie has grown so fast and isn't your baby anymore."

Mary bounced up and down on the mattress. "What do you think?"

"Ask me a year from now when I'm changing yet another dirty baby diaper."

"You mean it? We can try?"

If it meant she could bask in Mary's radiance for even one more moment, Ellis would have promised her anything. She was reminded of how her neighbor at the apartment in Tucker had said all the difficulties of being pregnant were worth it just to see her husband's joy every time he told someone that their baby was on the way. "Sure. You have to do the hard part, though. I draw the line at morning sickness."

"Oh, Ellis. You're the best. The absolute best." Mary jumped from the bed and danced around the room. "I hope I'm not too old."

Ellis opened her arms, inviting Mary back to bed. "Don't be silly. A bigger question is who you'll get to be the sperm donor."

Mary claimed her spot next to Ellis. "I've thought about that. Let's make it simple. If we use the sperm that Nathan and I froze when we thought he might have cancer, the baby will be Nat's full brother or sister."

Ellis pursed her lips. "Do you think they're still good? Well, active, I mean?"

"They should be, and I've thought about something else, too."

"Sounds like you've done a lot of thinking, missy." Ellis stroked Mary's thigh. "Tell me what else."

"If we try with Nathan's sperm and it doesn't work, then that will be the end of it."

"Isn't that limiting your options?"

"I suppose, but it's what feels like the right boundaries to put on it. It if takes, it was meant to be, and if it doesn't, well…"

"If it doesn't, we listen to Natalie moan about your ineptitude as a mother for the rest of our natural lives."

"Oh, good. You understand."

Mary's kiss triggered an undeniable response from Ellis. "Want to pretend we could make a baby ourselves?"

Mary rocked suggestively against Ellis's upper leg. "What a great idea. Hurry up, will you? That sound you hear in the background is the last few hopeful minutes ticking off my biological clock."

* * *

Gloria grabbed the pitcher from the trivet on the table in her living room. "More iced tea, Ellis?" She stood beside Ellis's chair, pitcher poised.

"No, thanks. This is plenty."

"Stop playing hostess, Gloria," Mary said. "The kids will be home from school soon, and Ellis and I really want to talk to you about what we're planning to do without three nosey girls interrupting us every five seconds." She bounced baby Erin on her lap. "At least this one is young enough that we won't have to worry about her blabbing everything she knows to Mother."

"Or to Naomi." Gloria set the pitcher down.

"Right. So, what do you think of the idea?" Mary shifted Erin to the floor where she could play in the stack of toys there.

"It'll probably kill Mother."

"Don't hold back, little sister. Come on and tell us how you really feel."

"You asked what I thought, and quite honestly, I can't imagine how Mother will survive the horror of it all. She's barely had time to adjust to the news of you two being a couple."

"What horror? I just want to have another baby before my eggs are too old to hatch."

"A baby by artificial insemination. And don't forget, you're not married. By Mother's standards, it will be a freak baby born in sin and destined for eternal hell."

"But it will be conceived from my husband's sperm."

"Your ex-husband. Your deceased ex-husband, to be more precise. And conceived while you're living with a woman who Mother regards as leading you directly to the devil's front door." She glanced at Ellis. "Sorry, no offense meant."

Ellis watched as the conversation ball was lobbed back and forth between Mary and Gloria. They left her no time to answer.

"Don't you dare blame Ellis for this. I was a lesbian long before I met her. Besides, you said yourself that I'm happier than you've ever seen me."

"Easy, Mary. I wasn't blaming Ellis. I was simply reminding you of what you already know. Much as Mother loves playing Gramma, she's not going to hang banners in the church sanctuary proclaiming the impending birth of her seventh grandchild. Not if it's procured the way you're talking about getting it."

"Procured? We're not going to Babyland General Hospital and picking a Cabbage Patch Kid off the shelf. We're going to use a tried-and-true method of making a baby. Well, without the usual inaugural act, but you know what I mean."

For the next twenty minutes, Mary and Gloria bickered over the imagined consequences of Mary being impregnated with the sperm she and Nathan had put in frozen storage. Ellis might as well have been a picture on the wall for all she contributed to the discussion.

Ellis heard gravel crunching in the driveway. She looked out the window and saw Adam pull up out front after collecting Amber and Ashley from the Christian Academy and Natalie from the elementary school. The children thundered into the house, and Adam honked twice, his usual signal before heading back to the car dealership. Ellis seized the opportunity of the girls' arrival to excuse herself to the kitchen to make after-school snacks. She'd heard all she needed to of the exchange between Mary and Gloria, anyway. Based on what had been said, when the furor faded—*eventually* faded, that is—Gloria would be supportive, as she'd been all along. No bets on the rest of the Moss family, though.

Half an hour later, she and Mary were on their way back to their house. Natalie stayed behind to play with her cousins. The remaining daylight in the early February sky was already heading toward dusk.

"So, did you and your sister reach any conclusions?" Ellis asked as she pulled onto the road in front of Gloria's house.

Mary's tone was derisive. "Yeah, that the world is only meant for heterosexual Baptists, and that the rest of us are taking up valuable space intended for God's chosen people."

"I think you're being too hard on Gloria. She only wants you to be sure you understand the consequences."

"You're right. Gloria isn't the ringleader in the fight against us infidels. My mother is the immovable object."

"I guess that means you've changed your mind about making a trip to Atlanta to visit the sperm bank."

"Oh hell no, it doesn't. This is right for you and me and Natalie. I'd be happy to have my family's support, but if I don't get it, what difference will it make? I've never really had it anyway, so it won't be much of a change."

"Not even from Gloria?"

"She'll do her best to stand in our corner, but Mother still occupies the rest of the house. I can't expect my little sister to wreck her life by alienating herself and her kids from the family matriarch."

Ellis waited a minute before posing a familiar question. "I'll ask this one more time. Would it be any easier if we were to move back to Atlanta where we could be in a more gay-friendly environment?"

"I'll give you the same answer I gave you every other time you asked me that. Who needs the smog and the crowds and the noise and the traffic? It's so quiet and pretty up here. Nat loves school. She's got a pile of friends, and she gets to hang out with her cousins. You're doing great selling cars at the dealership. I like our house. With the insurance proceeds we got when Nathan died, it's all but paid for. It surprises me to hear myself say it, but this is home, Ellis. I want to live here with you—with you and our kids."

Our kids. Ellis wasn't sure if the surge she felt was excitement or terror, or both. Thoughts of parenthood crowded her mind.

"Uh, honey?" Mary said.

"What?"

"You just drove right past the turn to our house."

Chapter 12

After Natalie left for school on April first, Mary and Ellis lingered over coffee in the kitchen. Mary pulled a thin, rectangular package wrapped in paper decorated with pink, blue, and yellow baby booties from one of the cabinets and handed it to Ellis.

"What's this? A Mary Moss April Fool's joke?" Ellis shook the box.

"Not exactly. In fact, it's something that should be fairly useful for us in about two-hundred-and-sixty-six days."

Ellis did a quick calculation. "That's about nine months." She tossed the box aside, leaped to her feet, and pulled Mary to her. "Does this mean what I think it does?" Happy tears trickled down her cheeks. She moved back so that she could see Mary's face.

Mary brushed Ellis's tears away. "Uh-huh. I've peed on a stick every day for the past week, and it looks like Nathan's boys were still up to the task. I saw the doctor yesterday, and she confirmed it. We're going to be parents."

Locked in one another's arms, they clung together and swayed to the ancient rhythm Mother Earth imparts to women ripe with new life.

"Who else knows," Ellis asked.

"Only you, me, and Doctor Jenkins."

"Can you wait until I get home from work tonight to tell Natalie?"

Mary recoiled in mock horror. "Tonight? I wouldn't dream of telling Nat tonight."

"Why not?"

"Have you met my daughter? Need I remind you of her ability to pester the life out of absolutely everyone? I want at least a few functioning brain cells when the baby gets here in December. If we tell her now, by the time school's out, she'll have made lunatics of us both. By the time I deliver, we'd have to be fitted with drool cups and be tied to our wheelchairs."

"Point taken. But this feels like news that should be shared."

"And share we will, but let's wait a while. My sisters can be almost as annoying as Nat. I'm thinking we'll break the news in late May or early June."

Ellis smiled at Mary's comment. "Right again. Can I tell Anika and Nicolas?"

"Sure. Your siblings, we can trust. And they've been so good about writing and calling since you and Anika talked last fall." Mary retrieved the unopened package from the table. "Don't you want to see what I got you?"

Ellis undid the paper and opened the box. Inside was a baby book, much like the one Mary had kept for Natalie. "I can't believe you found one with rainbows on the cover."

"The Internet is a marvelous tool. I had to send all the way to Washington state for this, though." Mary turned to the family tree pages. "See? This lets us list both the biological parents and the nurturing parents. Isn't that a cool way to label us?"

"As I've said so many times, I don't know how good I'm going to be at this parenting thing. I might not be much of a nurturer." She eased onto one of the kitchen chairs. "What if I stink at it?"

Mary caressed her shoulders. "Not a chance. You'll be a natural. Besides, Nat will be monitoring our every move. How far wrong can we go with our own live-in baby police?"

Ellis laughed. "Yeah, she'll keep us in line."

* * *

"I'm gonna get a baby! I'm gonna get a baby!" Natalie careened around the living room like she was riding an electric pogo stick. "Finally I'm gonna get my baby sister." Natalie hugged her mother, hugged Ellis, hugged Sam, hugged Swiffer, then hugged her mother again.

As Natalie clung to her mother's stomach, ear pressed tight to the abdomen wall, Mary looked over her daughter's head at Ellis. "Now you know why I insisted we wait until school let out for the summer to tell her. If we'd told her back in April, she would have been the death of us. As it is, the next six months will feel like a century."

Natalie relaxed her grip, patting her mother's tummy as she drew away. "When's my sister going to get here?"

"The baby is due on Christmas Eve," Mary said, "but maybe it'll wait a day and come on my birthday."

"Or maybe she'll come early and get here for my birthday."

"Let's hope not, Nat. We don't want the baby coming in early November. It needs time to grow and develop." Mary flexed her biceps. "We want heap strong baby."

"All right. I'll wait for her 'til Christmas Eve."

"You know, Nat, it could be a boy," Ellis said.

"I hope it's a girl."

"So you've mentioned a time or two," Mary said, "but either way, we're all going to love this baby and do our part to help out around here, right?"

"Right." Natalie started for her room.

"Where are you going?" Mary asked.

"I need to call Ruthie and Jordan and MacKenzie to tell them about our baby."

"Maybe you should wait a while on that," Mary suggested.

"Why? We're not ashamed of the baby, are we?"

A look passed between Mary and Ellis. "Of course not." Mary waved Natalie on her way. "Go call your friends."

Once Natalie was safely out of hearing range, Ellis asked, "Should I be hauling out the hoses to douse the flames when the locals plant the burning crosses in our front yard?"

"I don't think there'll be much reaction to the news of our expanding family." Mary rubbed her belly. "If anything, the worst of the Bible-thumpers will cast dirty looks my way when they see me at the grocery store or hustle their children away from my evil presence, but most people are so wrapped up in their own lives, they won't pay much attention to ours."

"I hope you're right, little Mama."

"I've told you I hate that name. Why do you keep calling me that?"

"Because you're so darn cute. And you are a little mama."

"I'll be a big mama in a couple more months. And I sure as heck hope that now that I'm past the first trimester, I'll feel better."

"Me too, sweetie. Not the big mama part so much as the feel better part."

"This isn't at all how it was when I was pregnant with Nat. I remember feeling energized and excited. This time, I feel punk. I'm not sick, really, just drained and blah."

Ellis pulled Mary into a warm embrace. "At the risk of getting my face slapped, remember, you're ten years older for this pregnancy than you were for the first one. And you've had a heck of a time over the past year-and-a-half, what with selling the house in

Decatur, moving up here, Nathan's accident, and all the other changes you've been through."

Mary led her to the sofa. "Thank goodness some of those changes have been good ones—like picking you up off the side of LaVista Road and dragging you and your dog home so I could nurse you back to health."

"Ah, yes, the first of our many detours."

"Would you rather have traveled a different road?"

"And missed all this gorgeous scenery?" Ellis kissed Mary deeply. "Not a chance. Best trip I've ever taken."

* * *

"Ellis. Wake up, wake up right now." Mary shook Ellis by the shoulder.

Ellis squinted at the clock. "It's only five o'clock. What's wrong?"

"I'm having contractions."

"The baby's not due for another three months. It's got to be something else."

Mary spoke through gritted teeth. "I've done this before. I know what this is. We need to get to the hospital."

Ellis jumped from the bed. "What about Nat? Should I get her up?"

"No, let her sleep. Call Naomi and ask her if she can come over and stay with her."

"Don't you mean Gloria?"

"I want Gloria to come with us. It'll have to be Naomi." Mary clenched her fists around a handful of blanket. "Oh, God. Here comes another one. Hurry, Ellis. These are coming five minutes apart."

Ellis snatched up her cell phone from the nightstand and called Mary's doctor's answering service. Then she called Mary's sisters. While waiting for them, she raced to the bathroom, splashed some water on her face, ran a brush through her hair, and yanked on some clothes. Within fifteen minutes, both sisters were standing in the bedroom. Naomi looked like she'd rather be in at least the fifth circle of Dante's hell.

With quick instructions to Naomi about what to say—and not to say—to Natalie, Ellis and Gloria guided Mary out of the house and helped her lie down on the backseat of the Xterra. Gloria hastened into the passenger seat, and Ellis peeled out for Gainesville, a very long thirty-five miles away.

Out on Highway 365, a road crew was setting up for some repaving work. Ellis slowed down long enough to make sure there were no cars in her way, then darted around the dump trucks and graders. "No more damn detours," she shouted. "Gloria, call the hospital and tell them we'll be there in about ten minutes. Tell them to be sure Doctor Jenkins is on her way and that she'll meet us there. She knows Mary is only twenty-six weeks along. She's got to do something."

"Honey, she's only a doctor," Mary said quietly. "There might not be anything she can do."

Even though Ellis made the drive in record time, she felt as though it had taken hours. At Lanier Park Hospital, she swung under the canopy at the emergency entrance.

Ellis sprinted around the Xterra and helped Mary from the backseat. An emergency room nurse with a wheelchair hastened to meet them.

"Is this Mary Moss?"

"Yes," Ellis said. "Is Doctor Jenkins here?" She watched as Mary gingerly eased herself into the wheelchair.

"She's not answering her page, but one of her partners is on his way. Doctor Grizzard should be here any minute."

"I feel a contraction starting." Mary gasped in pain. "This can't be happening."

"We'll take you to the OB ward and get you set up in a room," the nurse said as she pushed the wheelchair into the ER. "One of you needs to get her checked in."

"You probably should be the one to do that, Ellis," Gloria said. "You've got all her insurance information and everything."

"Okay. Will you park the car while I do that?"

"But one of us should stay with Mary."

"I'll be all right." Mary said. She wrapped her arms around her midsection. "Just hurry, though."

"I'm taking her to the third floor," the nurse said. "Someone from Admitting will meet us there. Check-in will be quick. Both of you can meet her in her room in a few minutes."

Ellis stood beside the admissions person and her computer on a rolling cart and answered what had to be about six hundred questions. She carried a copy of Mary's insurance card in her wallet, so that helped speed the process a bit. By Ellis's estimate, two weeks later, she was at last free to rejoin Mary.

"Hi, how're you doing?" She sat on the edge of the bed, pushed a lock of Mary's hair back from her face, and tucked it behind her ear.

"Awful. They gave me a shot that's supposed to delay labor. I think it's mostly a sedative, though. It's all I can do to stay awake. I keep having contractions, so I don't think it's working."

"Don't fight it. Sleep. It's probably the best thing for you. I'll be right here when you wake up."

Mary swallowed twice, then slipped into fitful slumber.

Ellis stole a quick kiss and went in search of Gloria. She found her in the waiting room, cell phone in hand.

"What's the big idea?" Ellis demanded. "After you parked the car, you were supposed to stay with Mary while I got her checked in."

"I went straight to her room from the parking lot, but she insisted I call Natalie to tell her not to worry. The nurses wouldn't let me use my phone in there, so I had to come out here."

"Oh, okay. Sorry to snap at you."

"We're all on edge, Ellis. It's all right. Besides, that drug the doctor gave her really knocked her flat."

"I know. She could barely talk when I was in there a minute ago. I think she's sleeping now."

"This is all so different from when I had my babies. Everybody seems so tense, so bossy. When I had Erin year before last, it was like a big party in my room. I've got a bad feeling about this."

"Don't even say that. I mean it, Gloria. She's going to be all right."

"Sorry. I'm a little worried, I guess." She momentarily gripped Ellis's hand.

"I don't have anything to compare it to," Ellis said. "Promise me you'll help me get through this."

"I will," Gloria said. "Maybe there won't be anything to get through, and we can all go home in an hour or two."

"Maybe." Ellis smiled weakly. "Did you talk to Natalie?"

"No, but I reached Naomi. Natalie's already awake and hopping mad that we didn't bring her to the hospital with us. She said you promised she could cut the umbilical cord."

"Let's hope there's no cord to cut. It's way too early for that baby to come. Maybe this is just false labor. What do they call that—Braxton Hicks or something?"

"Maybe." Gloria glanced up the hall. "That's Doctor Grizzard. He's the one who gave Mary the shot. Looks like he's going into her room."

Ellis jumped up. "I need to talk to him." She raced up the hallway and caught him before he went inside.

"Doctor, what can you tell me about Mary's situation?"

"She's already dilating. The contractions are long and strong and coming close together. Anything closer than twelve minutes apart before thirty-seven weeks means she might be in for some bad news."

Ellis fought the nausea that assailed her. "What about the baby?"

"It's too soon to know." He pushed the door open and they both stepped inside. "Let's hope the drug works and that we don't have anything more serious to deal with than keeping Mary in bed for the rest of the pregnancy." He did a quick exam and asked the nurse for Mary's vitals. Mary barely roused from her stupor. He paused in the doorway. "Sit tight for now. She's in no immediate danger. The drugs are doing what they can. The rest is up to God."

Ellis lingered by Mary's bedside. The nurse spoke to her. "You're welcome to stay in here with her if you want to, but she's pretty well out of it. It might get to be a long day for you and your sister." She straightened the sheet on Mary's bed. "Maybe you should get something to eat and try to get a little rest yourself out in the waiting room. We'll come get you if there's any change."

"She's not my sister," Ellis said matter-of-factly, "and I have no intention of leaving her, not even for a minute."

* * *

Ellis flew down the hall to where Gloria was sitting, cell phone pressed to her ear. "Mary's awake, and it looks like the baby is coming. Hurry. She needs us."

Gloria jammed her phone in her purse and raced along beside Ellis. "The baby is coming so early."

"Gloria, what if... if..."

"Don't even think that way, Ellis. This is a good hospital. Doctor Grizzard knows what he's doing. Like you said before, Mary and the baby will be just fine."

Gloria put her hand on the doorknob. "Ready?"

"No, but I don't think I have a choice."

The delivery suite was stuffed to overflowing, complete with an incubator. "Who are all these people?" Gloria asked.

"We've brought in a team of neonatal specialists to help," Doctor Grizzard said. "Given the degree of prematurity, every second immediately after birth will be crucial."

Mary was still half-doped from the drug that had failed to delay the delivery. The doctor went on with his preparations for delivery and peppered them with questions: Had there been any bright red bloody discharge from Mary's vagina? Had they noticed any swelling or puffiness of the face or hands? Had she complained of pain during urination, or had they seen any other signs of urinary tract, bladder, or kidney infections? Any sharp or prolonged stomach pain? Acute or prolonged vomiting? A sudden gush of clear, watery fluid from the vagina? Low, dull backache? Intense pelvic pressure?

Ellis answered each question with a no. Mary groaned her concurrence.

The doctor pressed on. "I saw from the records that the mother is nearly forty-two and that Doctor Jenkins referred you to a geneticist."

"Yes, she did. We saw him right after we knew for sure Mary was pregnant," Ellis said.

"We?"

"Mary and I are life partners, Doctor." She clutched Mary's hand. "I guess Doctor Jenkins didn't fill you in on that."

"I see. Well." He flapped the sheet draped over Mary's lower body. "Not my place to judge your choices."

Ellis wasn't sure his tone or the expression on his face (what she could see of it around the mask) matched his words.

"Since I can't look at the data right now," he said, "tell me what the genetic tests showed."

Ellis answered for them. "Mary was impregnated with her ex-husband's sperm for this baby. Since that same pairing produced a healthy girl almost eleven years ago, there didn't seem to be any cause for concern."

"Did you do amniocentesis?"

"No," Mary and Ellis answered together, but Mary's voice was thick and low, nearly unintelligible.

"Why not?"

"Because I knew I was going through with this pregnancy regardless of what the fluid showed." Mary struggled to form each word. "Why waste our time and the insurance company's money?"

"All right, then." The doctor examined the birth canal. "Looks like it's about show time here. Since you've done this before, Mary, you know that you'll have to keep your feet in the stirrups and do some pushing." He gestured to Gloria. "You might want to take her other hand so she'll have something to hold onto. Let's get to it."

* * *

Mary felt as though she were watching herself from someplace far away. The drug's effects left her limbs like lead and her brain locked in impenetrable fog. If only she could wake up in their bed in Clarkesville and feel Ellis safe and protective beside her.

She heard the doctor give orders to the three nurses and other strangers in white in the room, who went about each task in a very business-like manner. No happy banter, no speculation of baby's gender, no questions about possible baby names or potential colleges. Mary thought back to Natalie's birth. The nurses then had done their best to give nervous Nathan something else to think about, plying him with questions about everything from his favorite sports teams to how many toes was he hoping to see. The excitement in the room had been tangible, thrilling. A baby was being born, and angelic choirs were tuning up to herald the jubilant event.

Not this time. She'd seen happier funerals. *Oh, dear God, please don't let my baby die.* The doctor brought her back to the moment.

"Push." Pause, pause, pause. "Okay, push again."

Mary did as she was told.

A few more pushes, and in a matter of minutes, the baby was out.

The silence was horrifying. Why wasn't the baby crying? Why wasn't someone telling her if it was a boy or a girl? Why weren't Ellis and Gloria saying something—anything?

In a flash, one of the nurses grabbed the tiny form from between her legs, clipped the cord, wrapped a blanket around the baby, put it in the incubator, and whisked it away. All of the others who had been hovering in the room scurried out, leaving only an ominous feeling of dread.

"Is my baby dead?" Mary's voice seemed to come from every corner of the room.

"No," Doctor Grizzard said, "but we need to do a brain scan, set up a breathing monitor, get IVs running, and establish a sterile incubator environment as quickly as possible."

"How bad is it?" Mary asked.

"I don't know yet." The doctor pulled off his latex gloves and rested his hand on Mary's knee, still elevated from having her foot in the stirrup. "I don't want to alarm you, but I don't want to give you false hope, either. This is a very early birth. We'll know better in a few hours." He tossed his gloves into the waste receptacle. "Try to get some rest. We'll see you sometime this afternoon."

* * *

Minutes fell off the clock face so slowly that Ellis was sure the red oaks she saw from Mary's hospital room window had grown another ring. Gloria had offered to leave Mary and Ellis alone, but they told her they needed her to be there to hear whatever it was the doctor would have to say.

And so they waited. No one could come up with a safe topic of conversation. Somehow, everything led back to the frighteningly small bit of humanity that had left Mary's body on the forenoon of September thirtieth. The silence gnawed at their ears. Ellis and Gloria had long since turned their cell phones off. How many more times could they tell Naomi that they didn't know anything yet and that they'd call as soon as they did?

Chapter 13

"Mary, honey, can you wake up?" Ellis patted her gently on the cheek. "The nurse says we can go see the baby."

Mary sat bolt upright in bed. "Why don't they bring the baby in here?"

"The nurse told me it's too risky."

"Because I delivered so early?"

"Right. Fourteen weeks makes a big difference."

Mary shook her head as though dislodging cobwebs. "I guess I dozed off."

"You did, and that's a good thing. We all could use some rest." Ellis held Mary's elbow as she jammed her feet into her slip-on shoes.

"What time is it?" Mary asked.

"Almost three. You slept a couple of hours."

"Are you sure I delivered a baby this morning? After Nat was born, I felt like someone had ripped most of my innards out." She rubbed her stomach lightly. "I know the baby's not inside me anymore, but I feel so hollow, so empty. It's not at all like it was the day Nat arrived."

The nurse took them through the hospital corridors to the neonatal intensive care unit, NICU—which she pronounced "nee-cue."

"Why is the NICU so far from the maternity ward?" Gloria asked.

"When the hospital was first built, it wasn't equipped to handle premature births. The NICU area was added later." The nurse paused outside the entry doors. "And it's closer to the OR. Preemies sometimes need surgery quickly, and having the NICU close can save precious minutes."

Gloria, Ellis, Mary, and the nurse all scrubbed up thoroughly before slipping into disposable sterile paper gowns and paper shoe covers. Then they stepped into the heart of the NICU. The dim, iridescent light in the room reminded Mary of the hue cast by the special growing lights her mother used for her violets. The whoosh and hiss of various apparatuses blended in with the hushed voices of everyone in the room.

Six incubators held the smallest human beings Ellis, Mary, and Gloria had ever seen. Nurses reached through special openings to administer care to babies so small and so fragile they looked like the merest of miscues would crush them.

"He's over here," the nurse said.

"So it's a boy?" Ellis asked, clutching Mary's hand. Gloria stood on Mary's other side, dabbing at her eyes with a tissue. "I've been so worried about Mary, I didn't even think to ask."

Mary peered into the incubator and burst into tears. "He's barely even there. There's nothing but skin and bones. He looks like a shrunken old man."

Tongue-tied and overwhelmed, Ellis and Gloria each wrapped an arm around Mary. They wept until Ellis was sure every possible tear had been shed, and then they wept anew.

* * *

An eternity later, Doctor Jenkins joined them at the incubator.

"Hello, Mary. Nice to see you, Ellis. Congratulations on your new son. I'm sorry he got here so soon, though."

"Hello, Doctor. This is my sister, Gloria. What a relief that you're here. Where's the other doctor—the one who delivered the baby? Did he get a chance to update you?"

"He did. And I've talked with others who were part of your NICU team, as well." Doctor Jenkins gestured toward the door. "Let's go to one of the consult rooms where we can talk."

"You'll make sure my baby's okay, won't you?"

"Everyone in the NICU will give him the very best of care, but a neonatal specialist will be handling your case from here on."

"Why?" Even Mary noted the shrillness of her voice and softened her tone. "I mean, why can't you be our doctor?"

"Your son is going to need a lot of care. You want to have a doctor who's had experience with extremely premature babies. I've phoned Anthony Hill and asked him to come to the hospital as soon as he can. He's the best in the area."

Doctor Jenkins ushered the three women into a small room down the hall from the entrance to the NICU. As they took seats, she opened the file folder she'd been carrying.

"I'm sure you have a number of questions, but perhaps the way for us to begin is for me to tell you what we've learned about his condition so far." The doctor looked from Mary to Ellis to Gloria and back to Mary. "I've got several pages of notes here, and I'm afraid it will feel rather overwhelming. Stop me if you need me to repeat something, okay?"

Mary nodded mutely.

Doctor Jenkins said, "He weighs a fraction of an ounce more than two pounds, and both his one-minute and five-minute APGAR results were very poor. We repeated the test in ten minute intervals for the first hour, and he never scored above a three."

Gloria interrupted. "Isn't seven to ten considered normal or healthy?"

"That's correct, but APGAR doesn't always indicate long-term outcome. We've got several monitors on him, and as you saw, the staff in the NICU is watching everything very carefully."

"What are they watching for?" Ellis asked as she edged nearer to Mary so she could take her hand.

"For one thing," Doctor Jenkins said, "they're monitoring body temperature. His thin skin makes it impossible for him to maintain any warmth. The incubator keeps him at a constant, viable temperature." The doctor went through a long list. With each item, she gave a description of the symptoms, complications, and risks, but it was all Mary could do to hear each additional cause for concern, let alone absorb its full meaning. Jaundice, apnea, inability to breast- or bottle-feed, extremely low blood pressure and heart rate, underdeveloped digestive system, and probable incomplete nervous system, including possible brain damage.

Mary interrupted. "He has brain damage?"

"Not necessarily," Doctor Jenkins said, "but because of the situation with his lungs, I felt I needed to mention it as a possibility."

"I don't understand. Are we talking about his brain or his lungs?" Mary chewed on her lower lip.

"Both. As I'm sure you know, to keep the brain—and the rest of a human's organs—healthy, the blood has to be well-oxygenated. In your son's case, this is especially worrisome. The most critical area of development in any premature newborn is the lungs. The alveoli—tiny air sacs—have to fill with air and remain open. They're how oxygen gets into the blood. In the last stages of pregnancy, from thirty-four to thirty-seven weeks, the cells in the alveoli normally produce a substance called surfactant.

"Surfactant reduces the surface tension of fluids that coat the lungs so the air sacs can expand at birth and the infant can breathe normally. If there's no air in his lungs, they can collapse and cause respiratory distress syndrome. Because your baby arrived at twenty-six weeks, he didn't have enough surfactant. His lungs were so stiff that he couldn't breathe on his own. We've administered surfactant to try to help the situation. Without sufficient air, he can't keep oxygen in his blood, and without that, all his organs—especially his brain—are at risk."

"Is he breathing on his own now?" Mary asked softly.

"Yes, but his incubator is oxygenated. And I need to tell you that the treatments we've done to help him breathe carry the risk of causing inflammation of the lungs, but again, we're watching him very, very closely."

"So that's what he's up against," Ellis said.

Doctor Jenkins paused before replying. "I wish I could say that was the complete list, but I want to at least mention some other possibilities." She glanced at the notes on the chart in her hands. "As I've told you, he may suffer from episodes of apnea, which means forgetting to breathe. If the blood supply is interrupted to his brain, that will increase the danger of bleeding or injury to the brain. Also, because his brain isn't mature, he very likely won't have the usual sucking or swallowing reflexes needed for normal feeding."

No one else in the room spoke, so the doctor continued. "His immune system isn't fully developed, which creates a risk of serious infections, including a generalized infection of the bloodstream, called sepsis. Some premature infants also develop an inflammatory disease of the intestines called necrotizing enterocolitis. That happens when feedings don't properly pass through the intestine. We'll know this is happening if we see blood in his bowel movements. He's also at risk for a condition called retinopathy of prematurity, or ROP. His eyes are so sensitive that they might react to oxygen and light by growing extra blood vessels. Those blood vessels can pull on the retina and cause it to separate from the back of the eye. Obviously, this can cause vision problems for him."

Mary looked frantically from the doctor to Ellis to her sister and back to the doctor. This couldn't be her baby boy the doctor was talking about. Not her precious, newborn son. Not Natalie's baby brother. No, they had the wrong infant.

"You're not going to give us one shred of good news, are you?" Mary asked.

"I'm sorry," Doctor Jenkins said. "I could have given you this information in smaller doses, but I wanted to brief you as fully as possible before you meet with Doctor Hill."

"How much more do you need to tell us?" Ellis leaned wearily against the chair back, still holding Mary's hand.

"Not much. Only one or two other possibilities."

"I'd just as soon hear it all and be done with it." Ellis looked at Mary. "What about you, babe?"

"Might as well. How much worse can it get?"

The doctor offered a thin smile. "He'll probably be anemic for at least the first two months because he can't produce new blood yet, and we'll have a hard time keeping his blood sugar levels under control. We're fairly certain his kidney and liver functions are compromised. You probably noticed his skin is already looking yellowish because of the excess bilirubin in his bloodstream. We'll need to be on the lookout for kernicterus if his bilirubin levels get too high."

"What's kerni—whatever you said?" Gloria asked.

"A form of brain damage, but let's not borrow trouble." Doctor Jenkins closed the folder she'd been holding.

"Like what you've just described isn't trouble enough," Ellis said.

"I know this is disheartening. I'm sure Doctor Hill will suggest that you speak with one of the hospital's counselors as soon as you can. You'll be dealing with a lot of stressful experiences in the days to come, and the more support you get, the better you'll be able to handle them." Doctor Jenkins looked from face to face. "Can I answer any immediate questions for you?"

"Is he going to live?" Mary's even tone belied the gravity of the question.

The doctor put her hand on Mary's forearm. "We'll do everything we can for him medically. Beyond that—"

Tears rimmed Mary's eyes. "I want to be with him now."

"Sure, sis," Gloria said. "We'll all go."

"No, just me." Mary rose and left the room.

"I've dealt with a number of premature births," Doctor Jenkins said. "In almost every instance, the mother believes she's somehow to blame."

"Is she?" Ellis asked.

"No, certainly not. Spontaneous early birth is still, in large measure, a mystery." She stood and offered her hand to Ellis. "I wish you and Mary all the best, Ellis. Later today I'm going to examine her carefully, and if everything checks out, I'll sign discharge papers for her to go home in the morning. No need for her to spend more than tonight here. If you need anything, please don't hesitate to call me."

After Doctor Jenkins left the room, Gloria and Ellis stared blankly at one another. At length, Gloria spoke. "What should we do?"

"Damned if I know. I guess we should at least check on Mary."

They made their way back to the NICU. Through the glass panels on the entrance door, they saw Mary standing beside the baby's incubator, watching her half-day-old infant son.

"Do you think we should go in?" Gloria asked.

"Uh-uh. Whatever is going on right now is strictly between her and the baby." Ellis gazed at her devastated partner. "Maybe we should grab something for us to eat and bring a sandwich back for Mary. I don't think any of us has had a bite all day. Some of the nurses offered her some snacks after the baby came, but she wouldn't touch a bite."

"We've all been too upset to eat, but I think I could eat something now," Gloria said.

"I'm not sure I can gag anything down, but we ought to try. And it would feel good to step out of this hospital, even if only for a little while."

Ellis tapped on the window to get Mary's attention. She pantomimed walking away with fingers of one hand on the palm of the other and then feigned eating. Mary indicated she understood.

On their way out, Ellis and Gloria passed through the waiting room. Clusters of Hispanics talked rapidly in their native tongue.

"I think I know how they feel," Gloria said, gesturing toward a group that seemed especially distraught.

"What do you mean?"

"Ninety-five percent of what's been said to them today has been in a language they barely understand. For all I got out of what Doctor Jenkins told us, she might just as well have been speaking Swahili."

"Yeah, I know what you mean. And from what I did grasp, we're all going to have to learn a lot of foreign languages to get through what's ahead of us."

Chapter 14

Ellis returned to the NICU and stood quietly beside Mary, who was still only inches from the incubator. "Hi, sweetie. You doing all right?"

"How can I be doing all right? It's three months too early. Everything's all wrong."

Ellis saw a mixture of fatigue, disbelief, and confusion on Mary's face. She tried again. "I know things aren't right. I wondered if you might want to sit down for a while and have a chicken salad sandwich." She lifted the brown paper bag a little higher so that Mary could see it. "Gloria and I found a nice deli a couple of blocks from here."

"Where is she?"

"I sent her home. She was worried about how Barry would handle the three girls on his own. Besides, she was exhausted."

"I should call Nat."

"I talked to Naomi a little while ago. Natalie will spend the night at her house. You could call her right before bedtime, maybe." Ellis willed herself to look into the incubator. "He sure is little, huh?"

"Almost not there at all," Mary said. "I really messed up this time."

Ellis wrapped her arm around Mary's shoulder. "This isn't your fault, love. Doctor Jenkins even said so. These things just happen."

Mary slumped against Ellis. "But it was my body he was supposed to grow inside of. I must have done something wrong to make him need to come out so early."

"Let's not drag ourselves through that briar patch tonight, okay?" Ellis drew Mary a few steps from the incubator. "Take a break and come sit with me for a while."

Ellis took Mary from the NICU back to the small room where they'd met with Doctor Jenkins.

"I got you some coleslaw and a cookie, too," Ellis said as she pulled the contents from the bag. "And some tea."

"Thanks, babe. I guess I should try to eat a little."

Mary ate three bites of her sandwich and picked at the cup of slaw. She broke off a piece of cookie and handed the rest to Ellis. "Not much of an appetite. You can finish this."

Ellis put everything back in the bag and set it aside. "We said we wanted to see the baby before we decided on a name. We promised we'd wait until Halloween to even start discussing possibilities—"

"Why name him? He probably won't make it through the night." Mary's chin dropped to her chest.

Ellis left her chair and knelt in front of Mary. She grasped Mary's shoulders, then lifted Mary's head with the palm of her hand. "Don't talk like that about our son. I know you're tired, and for sure this is *not* what we expected, but we're not giving up on him. Not tonight, not ever."

"Ellis, he's half the size of any of the babies in the NICU. You heard what Doctor Jenkins said about all the problems he has."

"Problems he *might* have. All we know right now is that he's premature, he's had trouble breathing, and he has some jaundice."

Mary let her head fall back. She stared at the ceiling a long time. She finally looked at Ellis, still kneeling in front of her. "If Gloria took the car, how are you getting home?"

"I'm not going home. I'm staying here with you and our little boy tonight." Ellis took Mary's face between her hands. "We're a family, remember?"

"You never really wanted kids, Ellis. I know that. You just did this because you felt sorry for Nat… and for me."

Ellis looked Mary in the eye. "You're right, I didn't think I wanted kids, but then I got to know you and your daughter. It took me a while, but I finally figured out that what makes me happiest is doing what makes you happy. Maybe I didn't know what I was signing on for, but one thing I'm sure of—my life isn't worth a damn without you, and you not only want kids, you need them. So, since I need you, that pretty much looks like a complete circle to me."

"But this nightmare isn't the way I wanted you to learn about being a parent. How can I ask you to be a parent to that tiny lump of a person in there? I don't even know how to be a parent to him."

"Then I guess we'll learn together." Ellis dragged her plastic chair close to Mary's. "He needs a name, though. I want to call him by name."

"We were so careful not to let the sonogram techs tell us the baby's gender. Even though I didn't say so, I've thought all along the baby would be another girl, so I didn't think much about boys' names. And we promised Natalie she could be in the delivery room. You *know* she'd have had a dozen suggestions." A half-smile played on Mary's drawn and pale face. "She's gonna be pissed that she got a brother instead of a sister."

"She'll adjust." Ellis patted Mary's upper leg. "Besides, Nat and I already discussed this situation, so I've got the perfect suggestion for what to call him."

"Oh, yeah?"

"Uh-huh. Let's call him Joseph."

Mary's lower lip trembled. "That was my dad's name."

"I know, and it was Nathan's middle name. Technically, he's the baby's father, so Joseph seems like the perfect name."

Without leaving her chair, Mary fell clumsily into Ellis's arms. "Joseph Moss. I think my dad would be proud. Well, maybe not exactly proud, since I'm now a divorced woman with a baby by way of artificial insemination, but at least his name will live on."

"We need to pick a middle name," Ellis said. "Any ideas?"

Mary righted herself in her chair. "Yep, I do have a suggestion. Let's name him Joseph Ellis Moss."

Ellis blinked back tears. "That's sweet, but won't it upset your mother and the rest of your family?"

"Maybe, but I don't care. You said it best just a little while ago. He's our baby boy. It'll be up to you and me to take care of him."

Ellis stole a quick kiss. She offered Mary her hand as she stood. "Let's go see Joey."

* * *

"But he was doing so well." Mary's lament pierced the usually quiet NICU. "It's like every tiny bit of ground he gained over the past week has been lost again."

"Preemies rarely progress on a straight line," Doctor Hill said. "His heart rate fell to a dangerously low level, so we had to put him back on the ventilator. His jaundice worsened, so we gave him another transfusion." He offered a sympathetic pat to the back of

Mary's hand, resting on an oxygen tank. "I know this is very frustrating for you."

Mary jerked her hand away. "Frustrating? Dammit, Doctor Hill, frustrating is when you can't find your car keys or you get caught in traffic. This is well past frustrating."

Mary had been at the hospital nearly around the clock for the first week of Joey's life. Two of the babies in the NICU when he was born had been released to go home. None of the other babies in the unit looked a fraction as feeble as her son. Doctor Hill might have great credentials as a neonatologist, but as best Mary could tell, he didn't have a clue about how it felt to be a parent with a baby in an incubator.

"Well, his condition is stable at the moment. The nurses know to alert me if anything changes."

Mary scowled at the doctor's back as he left the unit. She felt the front of her T-shirt moisten. "Wonderful. Time to pump again." She slipped behind a draw curtain, yanked the breast pump from her tote bag, and affixed it. Every three hours or so, she used the pump, then carefully saved the milk to be fed to Joey through his gastric tube. His tummy was so tiny, though, he couldn't accommodate all that she was producing, so the milk from every third pumping was thrown away. Pump and dump was one of the hardest things she'd faced. All that wonderful nutrition going to waste while her son had gained only two ounces since birth.

She checked the clock on the wall. She needed to pull herself together. Ellis was bringing Natalie to the NICU for her first visit that afternoon. Thanks to a teacher's in-service day, Nat had the day off from school. Mary and Ellis had done what they could to describe for Nat the challenges facing her baby brother, but Mary knew all the explaining in the world couldn't fully prepare an almost-eleven-year-old for the shrunken, tube-laden, translucent-skinned being lying all but motionless in his two-by-two glass prison.

* * *

"That ugly thing is not my baby brother." Natalie flopped onto a chair in the waiting room. Ellis and Mary each claimed a chair on either side of her.

Mary reached to stroke her daughter's head, but Natalie jerked away. Mary said, "We told you he didn't look much like the other babies you've seen. He's only a week old, and because he was born too early, it's going to take him awhile to catch up."

"I don't care. I just want to go home." Natalie squinted her eyes at Ellis. "None of this would have happened if you hadn't shown up and wrecked everything."

"Nat, that's not true, and you know it." Mary looked at Ellis as she spoke.

"It's okay to be mad at me," Ellis said, leaning nearer to Natalie. "I'm mad, too, but I don't know who to be mad at."

"What've you got to be mad about? You don't have a freaky monster for a brother."

"You're right. I don't." Behind Natalie's back, Ellis motioned for Mary to leave. "Tell me why that makes you mad."

"Hey, I need to go take care of some things," Mary said. "How about I meet you two in half an hour?"

Ellis waved as Mary exited the waiting room. Natalie remained mute. "Tell you what, kiddo, let's go to the Dairy Queen and get an ice cream cone."

"Okay. I sure don't want to stay in this stinky, creepy place."

Out in her truck, Ellis picked up the thread of the conversation. "You were going to tell me why having Joey as a brother makes you mad." She poked Natalie playfully on the arm. "And you might as well tell me why you're mad at me, too."

"I'm not as mad at you as I am at him."

"Can you tell me why?"

"I wanted a pretty little sister who'd play with me and be my friend. All I got was that wrinkly, ugly boy who can't do anything."

"Like your mom said, we need to give him some extra time to grow. It's not even Halloween yet, and he's already here. He wasn't supposed to get here 'til Christmas. Think how hard it would be for you to already be picking out what to wear to the Christmas pageant at school when you don't even know for sure what you'll wear for trick-or-treat."

"I do so know. I'm going to be Gabriella from *High School Musical*. I want to get my hair done and everything."

"Okay, but my point is that you can't expect Joey to be ready for Christmas when he hasn't even done Halloween yet."

"But it's not fair. He's not cute. He's not anything I ever want to look at again."

"How about we make a deal?"

"What kind of deal?"

"You don't have to go back to the hospital. The next time you see him will be when we bring him home to stay."

"Which I hope is never."

Ellis fought off the urge to snarl a reply. She drove a few blocks, jaw clamped shut. What could she say to a child who somehow sensed her whole world was about to unravel? Ellis couldn't wrap her adult mind around the boggling circumstances Joey's birth had wrought. How could she expect Natalie to fare any better?

"Is he a sign from God?"

"What?" Ellis jerked the steering wheel reflexively.

"Gramma Anna says it's God's way of saying you and Mom shouldn't have done what you did."

Ellis choked down the bile in her throat. "Look, Nat, your grandmother and I don't agree on a lot of things, and this is one of them. But let me ask you a question. Was Joey the only baby in the room?"

"Nuh-uh. There were other babies in those little glass boxes."

"They're called incubators. And, right, there have been lots of other babies who were born early, just like Joey, or who were born with something not quite right about them. As far as I know, Joey is the only baby in there who came from a home like your mom and you and I have. To me, that says a baby born too early is just that— a baby born too early. It's not a sign from God or a sign of anything else, either. It happens sometimes, and it's the family's job to love that new baby as best they can regardless of how little he is."

"Jordan told me her mom says he'll always be a retard."

"Jordan's mom doesn't know everything." Ellis turned into the parking lot at the Dairy Queen. "Even the doctors don't know what's going to happen to Joey, so there's no way Jordan's mom can know that. He might grow up to be a rocket scientist or a rock star." She shut off the engine. "Just like you might."

"Uh-uh. I'm gonna be president, like Hillary Clinton."

Who the hell knew what that child had picked up from the news? "Hillary lost to Barack Obama."

"Good. Then *I'll* be the first woman president."

Chapter 15

Ellis kept her promise to Natalie about not having to return to the hospital to see Joey. She left Nat in the truck while she dashed into the NICU to tell Mary she was taking Natalie back to Clarkesville.

"She hates me, doesn't she?" Mary asked.

"Like the rest of us, she's been knocked on her butt. Give her some time to adjust, babe. In the past eight days, we haven't been able to make sense of any of this, so how can we expect our daughter to handle it?"

Mary's eyes misted over. "You've never called her that before."

"Called her what?"

"Our daughter."

"Well, she is, isn't she?" Ellis gave Mary a quick hug.

"Will you be back this evening?"

"Of course. I'm going to pawn Natalie off on one of your sisters again, catch a quick shower, make sure the dog and cat are fed and tended, and then I'll be here to sit with you. I'd better go before Natalie figures out how to hotwire my truck."

"Do something for me, okay?"

"What's that?"

"When you leave Nat with Gloria or Naomi, tell her her mom says she's weird."

"I'll go you one better. I'll tell her we both think so."

* * *

"He's gained a couple of ounces since yesterday." The NICU nurse pointed to the entry she'd just made on Joey's chart. "Looks like that last transfusion helped." She studied Mary's expressionless face. "Would you like to touch him?"

Mary's eyes flew open wide. "Could I?"

188

"Sure, but you need to scrub up first. Lather all the way to your elbows and use one of the sealed, sterile brushes on your fingernails. When you're ready, I'll help you slip your hand inside the sleeve of his incubator."

Mary did as the nurse instructed, nearly rubbing her hands and forearms raw in the effort. She stood by Joey's incubator, and the nurse demonstrated how to insert her hand into the enclosure.

Tentatively, she brushed her fingertips across the biggest part of his thighs, barely as wide as two of her fingers held side by side. Tears sprang from her eyes. *I love you, little man. I'm sorry I couldn't keep you inside of me as long as you should have been there.* She looked through the glass, seeing her hand hovering above him. She wanted to touch him everywhere, cradle him, explore every finger and toe, every wrinkle, but he was too delicate, too easily bruised. She wrestled with her fear of hurting him, holding those two fingers lightly on his leg. *Fight, Joey. Fight for all you're worth. It might not seem like it right now, but life is worth fighting for. Ellis and Nat and I will be beside you every inch of the way.*

"Ms. Moss." The nurse spoke softly. "I wish I could let you have longer with him, but we need to be so careful about keeping germs away from him."

"Okay." Mary pulled her hand back, stealing one more feather-light touch against his cheek as she extracted her hand from the incubator. She looked the nurse in the eye. "Thank you. I needed that."

The nurse patted Mary's shoulder. "So did he, Ms. Moss. So did he."

* * *

The next three weeks were a seesaw ride of progress and setbacks. Joey would gain another few ounces, only to have to be put back on the ventilator because of more breathing problems. Or his heart rate would drop dangerously low, and more drugs had to be pumped into him.

At the end of his first month, he weighed two-and-a-half pounds, enough so that for the very first time, Mary and Ellis were permitted to hold him.

"We call this kangaroo care," the nurse said to them. "He'll be wearing just his diaper, and we'll put him against your bare chest, between your breasts, with a blanket over him to help keep him warm and for modesty's sake."

Mary went first. She sat in the rocking chair, and the nurse carefully placed him on her chest. "This will be so good for him. Try not to be nervous. Yes, he's very small, but you won't hurt him. He needs to know your scent, your touch, and the rhythms of your speech and breathing. All our NICU babies love kangaroo care."

Ellis watched in awe as baby Joey nestled on Mary's bosom. Warm tears tracked down her face, and Ellis didn't even care.

"If you want his other mother to have some time with him today, we'll have to keep your session short. We don't want him out of the incubator too long." The nurse looked from mother to co-parent.

"No, today is all for Mary," Ellis said. "I'll wait until tomorrow."

"Whatever you say," the nurse said. "We'll try to do a few minutes of this every day. It helps maintain his body warmth, and it's good for regulating his heart and breathing rates. We usually find that as soon as we start kangarooing our babies, they gain weight and sleep better because they cry less."

"This may help *him* cry less, but it's not doing that for me," Ellis said as she swabbed the moisture from her cheeks. "How does he feel, Mary?"

"Like I'm holding a kitten. I'm afraid if I sneeze, I'll blow him right off me."

Mary stroked the sole of Joey's foot. Ellis rubbed Mary's back. "Then I'd better let you be the only one who does this. I'd probably do something stupid and set him back a week."

"You'll do fine," the nurse assured her. "After a time or two, it'll feel perfectly natural."

"Maybe for someone who's had practice with other babies. I'm not so sure I'll ever get it right."

"Enjoy your little Joey," the nurse said as she stepped away to check on the baby in another incubator.

"How about that?" Mary asked. "We must be the smartest parents on the planet."

"Why?"

"They call this kangaroo care, and a baby kangaroo is a joey." She stroked the top of her baby's head. "We knew exactly what to name this little guy."

* * *

For Natalie's eleventh birthday on November tenth, Mary and Ellis took time away from the NICU and hosted an all-out blowout. Natalie and every kid from her class, plus all her cousins, had a huge celebration at the combination roller rink and bowling alley in Cleveland. Ellis hauled in three decorated cakes and six half-gallons of ice cream for the kids to eat after an afternoon of skating and bowling.

Ellis noted the wistful look on Mary's face as the last child straggled out of the facility with his parents. "A glob of icing for your thoughts, babe." She held up a spatula of creamy icing.

"I can't help but wonder what Joey's eleventh birthday will be like," Mary said.

"No doubt every bit as chaotic as this one, but he'll probably only want boys at his party."

"I hope that's the worst of what we'll have to contend with."

Ellis pretended not to hear and went on with the task of wiping down the tables in the party room.

*　*　*

It took two full months, but right before Thanksgiving, Joey passed the four-pound mark and was permitted to move out of the enclosed incubator into an open baby bed in the NICU. He had to use a nasal cannula when he ate and had to have two more transfusions, but at least he wasn't gaining ground only to lose it a few days later.

Mary permitted herself another rare absence from the NICU to have Thanksgiving dinner with her family. Ellis seized the reprieve from Anna's impersonation of the Arctic and instead opted out of joining Mary in deference to spending the day with Joey.

As had been the tradition since her husband had died seven years earlier, Anna Moss offered the prayer before the meal.

"Heavenly Father, we are so grateful for all the gifts you have given us this year. We have the blessings of health and home and divine salvation through your son, Jesus Christ. Most of all we are thankful for our family, for Naomi and Barry and Matthew and Kendall. For Gloria and Adam and their three beautiful daughters. For Mary, and for Natalie. Thank you for this table full of delicious food and for—"

"Mother, you forgot to mention some of our family." Mary did her best to speak civilly.

"MaryChris Moss, you will not interrupt me while I am praying to our Heavenly Father."

"I will if you leave out two of the most important people in my life when you're praying." Mary stole a look at her younger sister. Gloria smiled almost imperceptibly.

"I don't think it would be appropriate to mention Nathan, dear. It might upset Natalie," Anna said.

"You know perfectly well that's not who I meant."

"Well, I cannot imagine who else there might be."

"How about your newest grandson, Mom?" Gloria said. "And the woman who's been right beside your daughter every day while their son struggles to get out of the hospital?"

Anna gasped in unmistakable horror. "I can't believe the two of you would ruin our family gathering with that sort of filthy talk. Your father and I raised you girls to have respect for us and for God's holy laws." Anna could have committed homicide with the daggers flying from her eyes. She thumped her fists on the table. "Either apologize or leave my table."

Mary toyed with the idea of relenting, but before she could speak, Adam rose from his chair. "I don't think Mary needs to apologize, Anna. As far as I'm concerned, Ellis is part of this family, and she and Mary need all the support we can give them."

Gloria beamed at her husband, but catching the glower on her mother's face, dropped her head. Adam remained standing, and Barry joined him.

"And are the rest of you turning against me, too?" Anna asked.

"Mom, it's not turning against you as much as it is *not* turning against Mary." Naomi's voice was faint, hesitant. "Adam's right. Mary and Ellis have been through a lot these past couple of months. Their little boy really needs a lot of help. We either love them, or we don't." She pulled in a deep breath. "As for me, I've decided to love them."

Anna fled from the table. Adam and Barry resumed their seats.

Mary looked around at the familiar strangers seated around the table. "I... I don't know what to say..."

"What's to say, sis?" Gloria picked up the bowl of peas in front of her. "Let's eat before everything gets cold."

"What about Mother?" Mary asked.

"She'll stomp and huff for the rest of the day, but by the time we're making turkey sandwiches out of the leftovers tonight, she'll act as though it's been a typical Thanksgiving."

"How can you be so sure?" Mary asked.

"I'm not, but can you picture her not being involved in our lives?" Gloria dished peas onto Amber's plate and passed the bowl to Naomi. "We need to present a united front, like when we were kids and wanted to get bigger allowances or later bedtimes."

"This is way bigger than bedtime or an extra fifty cents." Mary picked up the basket of rolls and helped herself before handing it to Barry.

"Bigger issue, same tactic. She lives and breathes for her kids and grandkids. We'll keep chipping away at her until she comes around." Gloria offered a lopsided grin. "As the baby of the family, I've elevated this tactic into an art form. Now, will someone please pass the white meat and get that sweet potato casserole down here, too?"

* * *

Four hours later, Mary was ready to head back to Gainesville to spend a little time with Ellis and their son. Anna came into the kitchen as Mary was saying her good-byes to her sisters and brothers-in-law.

"Mom, I'm—"

Anna cut Mary off before she could go further.

"I've prayed about this all afternoon. I can't change it, so I'll have to ask God to help me find ways to accept it. I don't know if that can happen, but I do know this. I don't want to talk about it, so I'll ask all of you to never bring up your... your... your situation at home with Ellis. If we can have that as an understanding, I'm willing to try to keep peace."

Mary opened her arms to invite her mother's embrace. Anna hugged her, but it was stiff and awkward. "We'll all try, Mom. I promise." She looked to the others for support.

"Fine." Anna pulled away. "Now, have you taken some food to bring to Ellis? She'll be hungry after a long day alone at the hospital. Be sure to take her some pie. I think she likes apple better than pumpkin." She pulled a pie off the counter. "Maybe you should take her a slice of each."

* * *

At the hospital, Mary scrubbed up and joined Ellis in the NICU. "What kind of day did he have?" Mary asked.

"Pretty good. I held him twice for about ten minutes each time." Ellis's voice caught. "He held on to my finger for a little while the second time he was on my chest."

"That's great, honey. He knows you and he trusts you."

"I guess." Ellis smiled in spite of herself. "So how was Thanksgiving?"

"You won't believe it." Mary quickly recounted what had transpired at her mother's house.

"Adam stood up for me?"

"Literally and figuratively. I've never been prouder of my brother-in-law. Your working at the dealership has let him see how terrific you are. And Barry even grew a pair and showed some backbone, too."

"That's great. We need to look up Adam's uncle sometime and tell him what a great person his nephew turned out to be."

"You're right. We should."

"I'm glad your family is finally starting to understand what we're up against with this little guy." Ellis gazed down at sleeping Joey.

"I stopped by the house and put a bunch of leftovers in the fridge. I brought you a sandwich and some pie in case you're hungry now." Mary handed her a zip-top bag.

"Starved. Thanks."

They left the NICU and sat in a nearby waiting room. Ellis polished off her meal and dug in her pocket for a tissue to wipe her hands. "Oh, I almost forgot." She pulled a folded sheet of paper from her pocket. "A reporter and a photographer from the *Gainesville Gazette* were here this afternoon. They're doing a human interest story for tomorrow's paper about special things to be thankful for, and they're featuring the preemies here in the NICU. Here's a copy of the release form I signed saying it's okay to use Joey's picture in the article."

Mary skimmed the page. "We'll have to be sure to pick up a couple copies of the paper so we can put the story in his baby book."

"Yeah, barely two months old and already a newsmaker." Ellis smiled warmly at Mary. "Are you going to spend the night here again?"

"You know, I think it might be nice to sleep in my own bed tonight. I've only done that a few times in the past two months."

"Where's Nat?" Ellis asked.

"She went home with Barry and Naomi. My sisters were talking about taking the older girls with them on a major shopping blitz tomorrow."

"Then the two of us could have our house all to ourselves for a few hours."

"Maybe even have some you-and-me time without fear of interlopers."

"If you don't count a moderately-demented feline and an attention-starved dog."

"It's been hell for every member of our family since Joey got here." Weariness laced Mary's words.

"It's been a big change, that's for sure." Ellis lifted her arm and cradled Mary's shoulder.

"Let's say good night to our son and make tracks for home."

*   *   *

After work the next day, Ellis made her usual drive to Gainesville to visit Joey in the NICU and catch a quick evening meal with Mary. To her surprise, Mary wasn't in the NICU. She searched the usual places—waiting rooms, snack bars, restrooms, consult rooms near the unit—no Mary. She finally asked one of the NICU nurses if they knew where she might be.

"Try the courtyard down on the first floor. I saw her out there on one of the benches when I came in for my shift."

Dusk had settled, but Ellis went to the open-air courtyard accessible from the main lobby. In the twilight, she made out Mary's lone form.

"Hey, babe," she said as she sat next to Mary on the bench. "Kind of chilly and dark to be out here, isn't it?"

"So? I might as well get used to it. I suspect it's how the rest of my life will be."

"What are you talking about?"

"Here." Mary forced a crumpled newspaper into Ellis's hands.

"It's too dark for me to read this."

"Nothing in it you'd want to see." Mary choked back a sob.

Ellis moved nearer. "What's going on?"

"The paper has a picture of every baby in the NICU except Joey."

"But I signed the release form saying it was okay to use his picture and tell his story."

"I know, so I picked up the paper while I was out at lunchtime, and I flipped through it to find the story. Two pages all about the hospital's wonderful neonatal care facility and the miracles they work with premature babies. Pictures of the other five babies. Not word one about Joseph Ellis Moss and all he's been through."

"Somebody at the *Gazette* must have screwed up." Ellis laid the paper aside.

"No, it's no screw up. I called and asked why my baby was left out of the article."

"Is it because we're gay?"

"You know, it almost would have been easier to take if that was why they did it."

"It's not?"

"No. When I asked the reporter why Joey hadn't been included, she told me it's because he looks so sick. They only wanted to feature babies that look like they're going to get better. She said her editor made her delete Joey's picture because he didn't think it was appropriate post-Thanksgiving reading material."

Mary's palpable distress hung in the crisp, early evening air. Ellis sat mutely beside her. Several minutes passed.

"Fuck the *Gainesville Gazette,*" Ellis said at last. "Fuck them and everyone else who's ready to give up on our son." She got to her feet. "Come on, Mama, we need to go see our baby."

Chapter 16

"I didn't think this day would ever come." Mary dabbed a tissue at the tears seeping from the corners of her eyes. "Joey's going home today." She looked at Ellis with a mix of relief, disbelief, and terror. "It feels like he's been in the hospital for years."

"I'm taking it as a good omen. He was in NICU for seventy-seven days. Double sevens. That's good luck, don't you think?"

"Might as well call it that." Mary laughed nervously. "We'll probably need all the luck we can get." She clutched the accordion folder full of instruction sheets for Joey's medications, doctors' phone numbers, preemie care briefing documents, emergency procedures for everything from apnea to zero weight gain, operating booklets for his breathing and heart monitor apparatus, and a host of other information. "At least I won't need a conditioning program. I can just do some bent arm curls with this folder to build myself back up." Another nervous laugh.

Ellis and Mary exchanged tearful good-byes with the NICU staff and the parents of other preemies still in the unit. Joey was wrapped in extra layers of blankets to ward off the chilly mid-December air. He weighed just over four pounds, like the new smaller-sized bags of sugar in the grocery store, and he was about as big, but not nearly as well-rounded, thanks to head and arms and legs.

Ellis held him in the crook of her elbow as they made their way to the Xterra. She'd purchased the smallest car carrier on the market and secured it in the backseat, but when she placed Joey in it, he was swallowed up whole. They strapped him in as snugly as possible and tucked extra diapers around the edges in hopes of keeping him in place.

"Ready?" Ellis asked Mary as she slipped the key in the ignition.

"Big choice. We're on our own now." Mary looked at Joey beside her in his car seat. "How can something this little need so much attention?"

"Law of inverse proportions, maybe," Ellis said as she backed out of her parking space.

Joey whimpered, and Mary stroked him reassuringly.

Ellis caught Mary's eye in the rearview mirror. "Should I stop so we can see what he wants?"

"No, let's hope he's like Nat and once we get out on the road, he'll fall sound asleep until we get home."

But he didn't. Whimpers turned to cries and cries to screams. Joey bellowed at the top of his miniscule lungs all the way from the hospital to the house in Clarkesville.

"Do we need to call a doctor?" Ellis grabbed the accordion folder as she exited the Xterra, leaving Joey for Mary to deal with.

"And tell him what?" Mary snapped. "That he's crying and won't stop?"

"I'm worried about his lungs."

"If he's crying, his lungs are fine. It's when he stops and turns blue, we need to worry."

"How would I know that? I've never been responsible for a baby before."

"I've never been responsible for a three-month premature baby before. I don't know what the hell's the matter with him." Mary lifted him from his carrier. The screams abated slightly. "Maybe he's scared. The only place he's ever been is the incubator and the NICU."

"Yeah, maybe that's it." Ellis shifted the folder to her other hand so she could close the doors of the vehicle. "Let's get him inside. Maybe he's hungry or needs a diaper change."

*　*　*

Joey didn't want to eat, and his diaper was dry. Mary tried every trick she knew, but Joey was having none of it. The only tool in his box was crying, and he wielded it like a master for the first five hours he was home.

Mary sat in the wooden rocker, gingerly tipping the chair to and fro while Joey dozed on her chest. "Thank God Nat's at Gloria's. As unhappy as she is about Joey showing up at all, if she'd been here for this performance, I don't know what she'd have done."

"Let's hope he's gotten it out of his system. Gloria's bringing Natalie home in a little while, and tomorrow's a school day, so she'll need her sleep. Me too, if I'm going to sell any cars at the showroom in the morning."

"Like I don't need a good night's rest." Mary paused in her rocking.

"I didn't say that, and you know it."

"We need to get something clear right now, Ellis. I'm not going to be the only one who deals with him when he cries."

Ellis moved nearer the rocking chair. "Never said you would, sweetie." She reached to touch Mary's face, but Mary pulled away. "Want to tell me what's bugging you?"

Huge tears splashed down on the baby in her arms. "Oh, Ellis. This is going to be so hard. Any baby is a lot of work, but Joey is so fragile that it'll take ten times as much effort for him. I'm too old to be doing this, even for an average baby. How can I possibly take care of Nat and do my job at the magazine and be a decent partner for you while I'm spending every waking moment worrying about what Joey needs?"

"It'll work out, babe. We'll find a way. I'll learn what I need to know to do my part, and Natalie will pitch in, too. We can ask Gloria and Naomi to help out on the days when it feels like too much to do alone. It'll all look better tomorrow. You're just tired and overwhelmed right now."

Mary wiped her nose on her sleeve. "And don't forget hormones. My hormones are in hyperwarp."

"Okay, and hormones." Ellis smiled reassuringly. "Want me to take him and put him in his crib?"

"I'll do it. You fix us something to eat. The last thing I had was that stale sweet roll from the vending machine at the hospital this morning."

"How about some spaghetti and a salad?"

"Sounds good." Mary eased up from the chair. As she did, Joey squawked, and soon he was in full wail again.

They ate dinner in shifts, Mary eating while Ellis paced the floor with Joey howling, then Ellis wolfing down a plate of pasta as Mary tried unsuccessfully to quiet her son. He was still crying when Gloria arrived with Natalie at seven-thirty. At nine p.m., Ellis convinced Natalie to get ready for bed and went to her room with her. They talked about what Natalie hoped to get for Christmas and what was going on at school—everything and anything except the crying baby in the other room with Mary. Natalie's bedroom was far enough from Joey's crib in Mary's office that, after she'd exhausted her stall tactics, with the door closed, the noise was muffled enough that she could slip off to sleep.

Around 10:30, Joey fell asleep and Mary and Ellis hastened off to bed. Less than two hours later, he was up and crying. Not just crying—yowling and screeching, nonstop.

"Do you think I should call the doctor now?" Ellis braced for Mary's response.

"It's the middle of the night. I don't think this is an emergency, so no, don't call the doctor."

"What should I do?"

"Let's do what every other parent does. We'll search the Internet."

They took turns holding Joey and scanning article after article about premature infants. Nothing they found qualified as good news, and most of it was downright terrifying. They learned that every stimulant in a typical home (lights, noises, smells, textures) is exaggerated for a hypersensitive preemie. Very probably, Joey was in total sensory overload, and his still-underdeveloped nervous system couldn't cope with the bombardment of incoming information.

"Now what?" Ellis asked in exasperation.

"In the morning, we'll take everything out of this room except his crib and a comfortable chair. We'll get the right kind of light bulbs that won't hurt his eyes and some all-natural fiber rugs to put on the floor. We're going to check the label on every blanket and piece of clothing, and if it's not one-hundred-percent cotton, we're giving it away. By this time tomorrow night, this nursery will be as free of conflicting sensory input as we can make it. And Joey won't leave this room until we're sure he's ready to handle something new."

They searched on, combing site after site, hoping for at least a glimmer of good news or a reason to be optimistic, but every source they consulted underscored the strong likelihood that, given his extremely premature arrival, Joey would face multiple difficulties. Some even advocated considering the possibility of institutionalizing a severely challenged child.

Mary looked at the baby in her arms and gave voice to the fears that assailed her. "Doctor Jenkins warned us that he might have brain damage because of lack of oxygen due to his lung problems. What if that's what's making him cry so much?"

"Let's not assume the worst possible situation, babe."

"I'm not assuming anything. You heard what the doctor said, and you've read the same things I've read tonight. We may as well face it, Ellis. The odds are he won't be a normal child." Mary drew a shaky breath. "I know what I'm about to say might make you leave me, but I've got to say it."

Ellis put her finger across Mary's lips. "There's nothing you can ever say that will make me leave you. Now, what is it you wanted to say?"

Mary let the tears roll. "He's my little boy."

"He's *our* little boy."

"Right, our little boy, and no matter what happens or what anyone might say, I'm never going to put him in an institution. I can't lock him away someplace and pretend he doesn't exist."

"No argument from me, love. His home is here with us. It's where he'll always belong." Ellis took dozing Joey from Mary's arms and gently kissed his forehead.

Mary smiled through her tears, then opened yet one more Internet site about premature infants. They passed the night in fits and starts. If Joey slept, they slept. When he was awake, one held him while the other pulled up even more disheartening information on the computer.

Shortly before dawn, they came across an article by Emily Perl Kingsley entitled "Welcome to Holland."

In fewer than a dozen paragraphs, she used an analogy to describe what it felt like to be the parent of a child with a disability. She spoke of anticipating a trip to a long-dreamed of destination, only to find that instead of going there, the plane took you somewhere totally different. It wasn't an ugly or unpleasant place, just not the location you had in mind and had planned for. She talked of how you might need to learn a new language and how you'd meet people you wouldn't otherwise have in your life. She also spoke of how hard it was to hear others speak of their wonderful experiences in that place you had imagined yourself going.

But then she said if you're open to it, you'll notice all the marvelous opportunities that exist in this surprise locale. You might never get to leave this unexpected new land, and yes, you may always grieve missing out on the original destination, but nonetheless, this new place is, indeed, special and you might as well enjoy the trip.

202

Ellis handed Joey to Mary and clicked the mouse to close the site. "Tell me what you're thinking, love." She cupped her hand around the back of Joey's head as he rested in Mary's arms.

"I'm wondering how, more than twenty years ago, that woman knew to write exactly what I needed to read tonight."

"Amazing, isn't it?"

"Uh-huh." Mary fixed her gaze on Ellis. "I'm going to ask you something, and I'll only give you this one chance to change your mind, so you'd better think it through before you answer me." Her voice faltered, but she continued to speak. "Do you want to cancel out, Ellis? Surrender your passport and not take the scary trip that's probably ahead for Joey—for all of us?"

Ellis didn't hesitate. "Of course not. We packed swimsuits and flippers, but if it looks like we might need parkas and snowshoes, so what? We'll make the trip together."

"You don't mind that we could be traveling on some poorly-marked roads?"

"Not for a minute. The very best part of my life has been the detours I've made with you."

* * *

If the first night was bamboo shoots under fingernails, the first week was a combination of sleep deprivation, water boarding, hanging in the stocks, sessions stretched on the rack, and being draped in the pillory. Sleep in anything more than two-hour increments was a rare occurrence in the Moss-VanStantvoordt household for anyone other than Natalie and Sam and Swiffer.

When school recessed for winter holiday break, Natalie went to stay with her aunts and grandmother. For Anna's part, she had yet to even lay eyes on her new grandson, despite Mary's repeated invitations for her to come to the house and meet him, now that he was out of the hospital. Everyone was keeping their promise to Anna about not discussing Mary and Ellis's relationship in her presence, which also meant that Anna was getting precious little information about her late husband's namesake.

Naomi and Gloria came by daily to check on Joey's progress. They'd even convinced their husbands to visit their new nephew, but Joey's endless crying ensured that Adam's and Barry's stays were brief. Like Gramma Anna, none of Joey's cousins had seen him, either. In truth, his own big sister was cutting a wide swath around him, too. Natalie had twice stepped into his nursery and peeked at him while he slept, but she refused to hold him or sit in the same room with him when he was awake.

For the first time in her life, Mary didn't spend Christmas day with her family. She and Ellis stayed home with Joey. As had been the case every day, he slept fitfully and cried most of the time he was awake.

Late in the day while Mary was in the nursery feeding Joey, Ellis heard a vehicle pull in out front. She opened the door and saw Gloria's van. To her amazement, Anna, Amber, Ashley, and Natalie climbed out of the passenger doors. Gloria lifted the hatch and everyone grabbed an armload of containers.

"We thought y'all would like some Christmas dinner," Anna said as she lumbered up the steps. "It won't be as good as when it first came off the stove, but it'll hold body and soul together until breakfast."

"That's very thoughtful, Mrs. Moss." Ellis held the door open wide and stepped aside so Anna could enter. "Mary is giving Joey his Christmas dinner right now. She should be out in a few minutes."

"Naomi stayed with the boys and little Erin. She'll make sure Barry and Adam get some supper, too." Anna swept the room with a glance and then took the foodstuffs to the kitchen.

Gloria and the girls trooped into the living room. "How was Joey's first Christmas?" Gloria asked.

"About like every day, sorry to say." Ellis accepted Gloria's hug. "Thanks for bringing dinner for us. We're so tired, neither of us felt much like cooking."

"It was Mother's idea," Gloria said as Anna reentered the room.

"No point letting all this food sit at my house," Anna said. "It's Christmas. Families belong together."

"Girls, take those things out to the kitchen and put them on the counter." Gloria pointed the way. "And remember what I said about being quiet."

Natalie and her cousins deposited their bundles as directed. As they returned to the living room, Ellis tugged on Natalie's hair. "Hey, kiddo. I've missed you. Merry Christmas. I didn't get to talk to you when your mom called you this morning."

Natalie hesitated, then wrapped her arms around Ellis. "You're weird, Ellis."

"You, too, toots." Ellis tickled Natalie's ribs before releasing her from the hug.

Mary emerged from the rear of the house. "I thought I heard voices. Hi, Mom. Merry Christmas."

Anna rushed to accept Mary's embrace. "It just wasn't Christmas without you, MaryChris. Happy Birthday, sweetheart."

"Now, Mom," Mary said sternly as she stepped back, "you know I only accept birthday wishes on June twenty-fifth."

"Oh, I... well... it's just that..."

"I'm teasing, Mom, but today hasn't felt much like Christmas or my birthday."

"I'm sorry to hear that, honey. We brought you and Ellis some dinner. Maybe that will help." Anna took two steps toward the kitchen. "I'll fix you a plate."

Amber, Ashley, and Natalie sat in a row on the sofa. Mary smiled warmly at the trio. "Merry Christmas, kids. Who do you think you are, the Three Wise Guys?"

"Mom said we had to be quiet," Amber said, "because of the baby."

"Quiet is good, but you don't have to be statues." Mary scrunched in beside Natalie. "Don't I know you from someplace? Oh wait, you live here, don't you?"

"You're so weird, Mom." Natalie strained for aloofness, but it was evident she ached for her mother's attention.

"You're weird, too, Nat. And I've missed you." Mary squeezed her daughter hard.

Gloria perched on the arm of the sofa. "Ellis said Joey's had another rough day."

"Lots of tears, not much sleep for him or us." Mary's voice was laced with exhaustion.

"Maybe he'll outgrow that soon," Gloria said.

"Your lips to God's ears," Mary replied, then remembering her mother's presence, added, "Sorry, Mom. No offense."

"Why would that offend me? From what I hear, you could use some help from God with your son." Anna stood in the doorway with a heaping plate of food in each hand.

Before Mary could comment, Joey's keening cry erupted from his room.

"I'll get him," Ellis said.

"No, you and MaryChris need to eat," Anna said. She handed a plate to each of them. "It's time I met the new Joseph Moss."

A moment later, Anna came back with Joey in her arms. "He certainly is tiny," she said as she paused in front of the rocker.

"Natalie, you come take him from me so I can get settled in this chair."

Natalie didn't budge.

"Gramma needs your help, Nat," Mary said. "Go on." She nudged her daughter.

Reluctantly, Natalie inched over to her grandmother. "I'm only going to hold him one minute."

"That's all I'll need you to do." Anna carefully put the baby in Natalie's arms. To everyone's surprise, Joey's wails subsided.

"Hey, he likes me!" Natalie's smile beamed around the room.

Mary set her plate on the end table and joined Natalie and Joey. "Of course he does. You're his big sister."

Forgetting that she was holding the baby to allow her grandmother to get seated, Natalie scooted into the rocker, baby Joey still in her arms. Amber and Ashley crowded around and peered at the little boy. Gloria moved nearer, too.

"You said he was ugly, Natalie, but he's not." Ashley pointed at Joey. "His face is kinda smooshy, and his skin looks funny, but I think he's cute."

"He used to be ugly when he was in the hospital," Natalie said. "He got born too early, and he needs some time to catch up, that's all."

Anna leaned in close and studied him intently. "I see a lot of your father in him, MaryChris. I think he's going to be very handsome."

Ellis set her untouched plate of food on the table. She stood apart, surveying the group surrounding young, and blessedly quiet, Joey. For several minutes, he was just another newborn, basking in the devotion of his extended family. There were no fears about potential illnesses or daunting problems or special needs. He was a precious gift, loved and welcomed and cared for.

Ellis reflected on the chance encounter of a blocked roadway that had brought her and Mary together. She recalled all of the detours and backtracks they'd had to make over the past two years when life's events—most notably their son arriving three months early—refused to conform to their plans.

Because of Mary, she'd found a way home to her brother and sister, and by the looks of things, now Ellis had a whole new family, too. Her eyes misted over as her gaze lingered on her precious Mary, who had one hand on Natalie's shoulder and was tenderly tracing the outline of Joey's fingertips with the other. Everyone—

Anna, Gloria, Natalie and the girls, and Mary herself—was lost in rapt adoration of the newest member of the clan.

Mary looked up at Ellis. "Come over here, Other Mother. You need to be part of this happy family moment."

Ellis touched Joey lightly on his cheek, then squeezed into the circle beside Anna. As she did so, Anna tucked her arm around Ellis's waist. Ellis savored the sheer joy of the peace and unity surrounding her and Mary and their children. How 'bout that, she thought. It's another MaryChris Moss miracle.

Jane and her good friend Joey, the inspiration for *Detours*.

About the Author

Jane seems to have misunderstood the definition of retirement. In late 2004, she left Federal civil service after more than 30 years with the same agency, but instead of spending her days sipping lemonade in the shade of the North Georgia pines, she's writing her own books, editing books by other authors, and helping with the administrative tasks at Blue Feather Books, Ltd.

And then there are the cats—*lots* of cats—and the four dogs that fill her <cough cough> free time. She'll readily tell you, though, she's never been happier. If you don't find her at her desk or in the backyard, look for her at the local animal rescue shelter where she frequently volunteers (and from which she far too frequently brings home "the last one—I promise.")

Jane was born and raised in a farming community in northwestern Minnesota, where she received her elementary education in a one-room country schoolhouse. She holds a Bachelors' degree from St. Cloud (Minnesota) State University. Ask her politely and she'll show you her diploma, chiseled on a stone tablet.

In addition to spending time at the computer writing and editing books and taking care of Blue Feather Books business, Jane enjoys tending her gardens, feeding the wildlife on her property, and playing the piano.

Coming soon from Blue Feather Books:

Lesser Prophets, by Kelly Sinclair

We were the despised, the unloved, the fitfully tolerated, the novelty acts, and in some fortunate places, the embraced and even cherished.

In those safe harbors, we celebrated each stage of our growing emancipation even though others of our tribe were faced with hangman's gallows or less deadly alternatives and dared not show their true faces. We passed as "normal" when possible, and we were penalized when we could not pass. We only had freedom when they said we could be free. That was our world. We knew none other.

But then God, or Fate, or the Omniscient Divine—or merely happenstance—negated all the rules, and our status was forever changed.

This is how the new world began. We were the *Lesser Prophets*, and this is our story.

Coming soon, only from

Make sure to check out these other exciting
Blue Feather Books titles:

Tempus Fugit	Mavis Applewater	978-0-9794120-0-4
In the Works	Val Brown	978-0-9822858-4-8
Addison Black and the Eye of Bastet	M.J. Walker	978-0-9794120-2-8
Diminuendo	Emily Reed	978-0-9822858-0-0
Merker's Outpost	I. Christie	978-0-9794120-1-1
Whispering Pines	Mavis Applewater	978-0-9794120-6-6
Greek Shadows	Welsh and West	978-0-9794120-8-0
From Hell to Breakfast	Joan Opyr	978-0-9794120-7-3
Journeys	Anne Azel	978-0-9794120-9-7
Accidental Rebels	Kelly Sinclair	978-0-9794120-5-9
Playing for First	Chris Paynter	978-0-9822858-3-1

www.bluefeatherbooks.com

Praise for Jane's Previous Novels

Second Verse ISBN 978-1-932300-94-9

Jane Vollbrecht is renowned for creating genuine characters whose only super powers are the inner and outer strength of ordinary people as they cope with real life issues. In *Second Verse,* Vollbrecht asks her readers to examine relationships in life and death situations, questions the wisdom of commitments in sickness and in health, and demonstrates how the strength of love outweighs interference from outside forces... Vollbrecht captures readers with conviction, honesty, and humor in this character-driven plot... The ultimate message of *Second Verse* is that, in truth, we all might be well advised to hear the music of life that's playing all around us and then to dance—dance like it's what we were born to do and like there's no one watching.

—Lambda Book Report

In Broad Daylight 978-1-932300-76-5

In Broad Daylight is a great story and so much deeper than the "run-of-the-mill" stuff that is out there. Older women lead vital lives with fascinating stories; I'm glad to see that sort of character in this book.

—Brenda Adcock, author of *Pipeline, Reiko's Garden, Redress of Grievances, The Seahawk,* and *Tunnel Vision.*

Close Enough 978-1-932300-85-7

If Jane Vollbrecht were a baseball player, her batting average would be close to 1000. *Close Enough* is another home run for readers. This book is as close to real life as it can get and still be fiction.

—K. C. West, co-author of the Shadows series.

Breinigsville, PA USA
22 November 2009
228001BV00001B/67/P